## The Two-Faced Lord

The first time Felicia saw Lord Cleary, he was holding a pistol. And when he fired a shot that ripped through her shoulder, he thwarted her plan to steal a valuable necklace from him to save her fiancé from ruin.

But soon after that violent introduction, it was not the menace of his marksmanship but the passion of his kisses that she encountered, as she fought against the impulse to totally surrender to this masterful man's seductive skill.

Felicia had seen both sides of Lord Cleary now—but she still did not know which one was the more dangerous. . . .

# LORD CLEARY'S REVENGE

# SIGNET Regency Romances You'll Enjoy

# LORD CLEARY'S REVENGE

## MIRANDA CAMERON

A SIGNET BOOK

**NEW AMERICAN LIBRARY**

Copyright © 1985 by Mary Kahn

SIGNET, SIGNET CLASSIC, MENTOR, PLUME, MERIDIAN AND NAL BOOKS
are published by New American Library,
1633 Broadway, New York, New York 10019

First Printing, August, 1985

1  2  3  4  5  6  7  8  9

PRINTED IN THE UNITED STATES OF AMERICA

TO

**Larry** and **Helene,**
**Margaret** and **Ruth,**

and
especially to

**Adam Hall,**

who, without knowing it, helped me
to do the "impossible."

# One

"Stand and deliver!"

The hoarse shout came from the masked rider who appeared suddenly from behind a clump of bushes at the foot of the hill. It shattered the quiet of the night, charging the fresh clean air of the rain-washed Heath with tension.

Though it was spring, Hampstead Heath at this time of night was deserted, the faint moonlight showing the tall gentleman in the curricle that he could count on no one to come to his aid. But Richard Nicholas Allandale, the sixth Earl of Cleary, seemed not a whit discomposed. He was obliged to bring his horses to a plunging standstill, for the highwayman had barred his way, but not a muscle moved on his handsome tanned countenance, and his steely gray eyes remained impassive.

"Turn out your pockets," shouted the robber, his voice muffled by the large black scarf hiding most of his face. A battered hat covered his head, a nondescript greatcoat his body. He moved closer, his horse prancing nervously, the pistol in his hand wavering slightly. It flashed through Lord Cleary's mind that he must be just a beginner.

"Careful now, no tricks, or I'll shoot," ordered the highwayman.

Pulling back his caped greatcoat, Lord Cleary reached slowly into his coat pocket, his hand emerging with a fat purse, which he tossed into the robber's outstretched hand. "Are you satisfied?" he said with a sneer.

But the highwayman only shook his head. "This ain't everything." He motioned with the gun. "Out with the gewgaws."

The earl's eyes narrowed in a hard stare. Nobody knew beforehand that he would be carrying jewels on his person tonight. And only three persons knew now, those three who had played cards with him this evening. But while two of them were constantly in need of the ready, he could hardly think they would stoop to a robbery. On the other hand, it could be one of Sir Edward's servants, who had overheard his conversation. It was highly probable that Sir Edward was quite behind in paying their wages, and their needs could have overcome their scruples.

He reached into his pocket once more and withdrew a hard object wrapped in a handkerchief. He unwrapped it, and the object burst into scintillating light. On the white handkerchief nestled a magnificent necklace of bright rubies and glittering diamonds, red-and-white fire in the pale light of the moon.

The robber's hand trembled as he grasped the necklace. He stared at it as if mesmerized, his gaze averted from his lordship for a split second. In that instant the earl acted. His silver-mounted pistol was out in a flash and pointing at the robber. "Drop your gun," he commanded in a cold imperious voice.

The highwayman started, and the pistol wavered in his hand, but he thrust the necklace into his pocket while setting his horse in motion. The earl, however, had no intention of letting him escape. He pulled the trigger. A loud report reverberated through the night, the robber cried out and swayed in the saddle, and his startled horse reared, throwing him to the ground, and bolted. The "gentleman of the road" lay where he had fallen—motionless.

For the next few moments the earl had his hands full

controlling his spirited horses, which had been startled by the shot. But soon he had steadied them, and jumping down, he ran up to the robber.

A red stain was fast forming on the upper arm of the highwayman. The earl tore away the black scarf, and a deathly-pale young face stared at him in the moonlight. The eyes were closed, and the full lips, almost feminine in their shape, were bloodless. Just a lad, a mere stripling, thought the earl, pity and anger stirring in his heart. So young to start on a life of crime. He had to be one of Sir Edward's servants. The earl glanced at his fidgeting horses, wishing now he had taken his groom along. But he usually dispensed with him when calling on Hermione.

The battered hat of the lad had fallen off, but the red hair was tightly bound with a scarf. The earl unbuttoned the much too large greatcoat and removed it. The coat underneath was of good blue cloth, but again much too large and too long. The earl fashioned a pad out of his own snowy handkerchief and bound it fast around the bleeding arm with the black scarf of the robber.

The boy stirred and groaned as the earl performed his ministrations, and tried to get up. "Lie still," the earl commanded.

His work was soon done, but the lad had to be properly attended to by a doctor. Lord Cleary gazed into the large green eyes, enormous in their fright and pain. The bloodless lips opened. "Save your breath—don't talk," said the earl.

"Will you . . . call . . . the constable?" whispered those bloodless lips. Terror seemed to have gripped the young robber.

"That depends. I should like to talk to you first. I fancy this is your first attempt at high-toby."

The boy nodded weakly, then his head lolled and he lost consciousness once more.

"Damnation," swore the earl. He was not in the habit of shooting children.

He carried the boy to the curricle, placed him on the

box, sprang up himself, and, supporting the boy with one hand, expertly guided his spirited pair with the other back to London and to his town house in Grosvenor Square.

Rawlins, the butler, nodding in the hall, awaiting his master's late arrival, was startled out of his habitual impassiveness at the sight of his master with a bloodied lad in his arms. But he recovered quickly and hurried off to fetch water, linen, and restoratives, while the earl carried the youthful robber to the Green Saloon and deposited him on the sofa.

Having divested himself of his greatcoat and coat—he preferred his coats made so that he could shrug himself into them and remove them without any assistance— the earl rolled up his shirtsleeves and set about to bring the stripling out of his swoon.

As he removed the scarf from the lad's head the better to bathe his brow, a riot of auburn curls tumbled down. An incredulous look sprang to Lord Cleary's eyes. Swiftly he undid some buttons of the overlarge coat and slid his hand inside.

"Hell and the devil confound it," he swore as his hand encountered the soft rounded mounds. "It's a girl." He had been held up by a girl. And not just a common girl, by the looks of it. Behind him he heard a gasp and turned around to see his butler with his mouth hanging open, his eyes starting from their sockets.

"Keep your mouth shut about this, Rawlins," the earl snapped.

His brow furrowed. In the bright light of the wall sconces he could see that the girl was uncommonly pretty, even beautiful, the long dark lashes contrasting with the paleness of her face.

Abruptly she groaned, and her eyelids fluttered open. The large green eyes stared frightened and confused into his face. The girl moved and winced with pain.

"Pray lie still. Who is your doctor, and can you trust him to be discreet?" he asked.

"Dr. . . . Dr. Bennet. And—yes, he . . . he can be discreet," she whispered.

"Have Dr. Bennet fetched on the instant," the earl commanded the butler, then picked up the glass of brandy which the butler had poured and held it to the girl's lips, while Rawlins hurried off, shaking his head.

The girl protested feebly, but swallowed a little, sputtering and coughing, and the color returned slowly to those deathly-pale cheeks.

"What the devil possessed you to hold me up? Surely things are not in such a desperate state. And who the devil are you?" His lordship's none too amiable temper threatened to slip its leash. The girl was obviously Quality. He could see it now by her hands and her countenance. But that she could bring herself to such an act! Improper and shocking though it was, it must have required an inordinate amount of courage and resolution.

"Who are you?" he repeated.

"Felicia. Felicia Mannering," answered the girl in a quavering voice, dreading his reaction to this intelligence.

A loud oath escaped the earl's lips. His countenance darkened, and a deep scowl settled on his brow. "Vellacort's betrothed? I might have known. What else can one expect from the fiancée of the man who murdered my brother!"

"That isn't fair," the girl protested, indignation flashing in her eyes. "You don't scorn or cut my uncle . . . or my cousin . . . yet they are on good terms with Darcy."

"They did not choose to be related to him."

"And Darcy did not murder your twin," she continued. "He killed him in a duel, a fair fight. I am very sorry for it, but those things do occur—unfortunately— when gentlemen fall out and decide to settle their disagreement in this fashion."

"Disagreement? Yes, disagreement over a damned—" He broke off, recollecting himself, as she, overcome by her weakness and pain, closed her eyes. "That's to no purpose now," he said shortly. "Pray be still and don't talk until I have attended to your wound."

He was a trifle at a loss. He wished to bathe the wound properly, yet felt constrained to strip her, and contented himself with just stanching the flow of blood and bathing her face. And gazing at that beautiful countenance he wondered that his cousin Beatrice, jealously guarding Lester, her only son, from designing females, had agreed to house this beauty under her roof. Her husband, Lord Palmer, had probably insisted she do it. "How is it that I have never met you until now?" he could not help asking.

Felicia's eyes remained closed, but she said in a low voice, "I spent most of my life in the country, with my ailing aunt. I collect . . . you were fighting Boney . . . when I had my Season. And I but just now came out of black gloves . . . so I did not go out much."

The earl frowned. He was not surprised. Felicia Mannering was just as poor as her uncle, Sir Edward, and probably possessed few fashionable clothes. And he knew that his cheeseparing cousin Beatrice would grudge the least groat spent on the child.

"But I have called on Lady Palmer many times, yet I have never met you," he wondered aloud.

Felicia's eyes flew open. She bit her lip. "She . . . she deemed it advisable for us not to meet . . . because of the circumstances."

Ah yes, the circumstances. The earl's lips pressed into a tight harsh line. The circumstances of his brother's murder. Almost a year had passed since that fateful day, but his wound was still as fresh as ever. Anger and grief, never far from the surface, stirred within him again. Darcy Vellacort had murdered his brother, for all that Jerome Banister had sworn that it was a fair fight. Fair fight indeed. But of course Banister would cover up for him. Now he recalled hearing somewhere that Banister had once been trying to fix his interest with his cousin Felicia. That would explain his keeping his mouth shut about the murder. He was doing it for her.

Felicia stared at the earl's stern profile. How grim he looked, yet so extremely handsome. She could not help observing it, in spite of her pain and fear. He had the same patrician nose as his brother, Marcus, but the features of his face were sharper, more resolute, and by far more handsome. But perhaps because of his forbidding mien he appeared a trifle older than his age of six-and-thirty.

In build he was rather like Marcus, large and powerful, with broad shoulders and muscular but shapely legs, yet whereas Marcus was a dandy, the earl apparently eschewed the adornments of an exquisite. And his breeches and topboots, the Bedford crop of his black hair, and his spotted Belcher handkerchief proclaimed him a sportsman. Yet they were both great sportsmen. . . .

That notion to hold a curricle race had started it all. And then that stupid quarrel. Killing Marcus in the duel had almost ruined Darcy. If it hadn't been for Felicia's intercession with Lord Palmer, a diplomat and a friend of the Prince Regent, Darcy would have been obliged to flee the country. But another scandal would not be forgiven so easily. As it was, he had to prove himself, his conduct, before being allowed to take up a post as Lord Palmer's secretary.

Felicia stirred restlessly. Oh, if only her shocking, foolhardy act hadn't jeopardized Darcy's career and his future. She almost hadn't gone through with it, she had been so scared. If only her will had not overcome her fear. If she brought disgrace and shame upon Darcy now, and as a result he did not get the post . . .

That thought was not to be borne. Far rather would she release him from his pledge (though her heart would break) than hurt him by dragging him into a scandal of her making. Darcy, himself under a cloud, could not afford a wife ostracized by the *ton.*

She stirred again. "What—what will you do now?" she asked in a tremulous voice, her countenance expressing her apprehension. "I . . . I own that what I did was dreadfully shocking and unpardonable, but I was desperate, you see. And I didn't find holding you up easy, either. I was terrified. I scarcely knew how I contrived to force the words out . . . and I thought I'd drop Lester's pistol."

Lord Cleary scowled. She had made a very poor choice in Vellacort, he thought. Perhaps she *was* of the same cut as he. Why did she wish to steal the necklace? "Wait until that sawbones has attended to your wound, and then we shall talk." He paused. "I deeply regret to have been obliged to hurt you, but you brought it on yourself. What foolhardy lark was this?" he suddenly exploded. He took another breath. He wished she weren't so lovely, even in those ridiculous clothes. And she looked so absurdly young, though he knew she must be about two-and-twenty. Her chest was heaving. Apparently she was suffering great agitation as well as pain, yet how full of pluck she was. He sighed. He should carry her to the guest bedchamber, it suddenly occurred to him. Or should he wait for the doctor?

An apologetic cough at his elbow startled him. Rawlins, coming in on silent feet, announced the arrival of the doctor. "I apprehended you wished him here with all speed, and I sent a carriage for him."

The earl nodded.

The next moment a short roly-poly man tripped into the room. Upon seeing Felicia Mannering, he stopped. His eyes bulged. Then he rushed forward. "My dear Miss Mannering, what has occurred?" He turned fiercely on the earl. "This is your doing, my lord. You have lured her into your abode and she has been forced to defend her honor."

"I am not in the habit of seducing respectable females," said the earl through his teeth. "I can assure you her virtue is quite intact."

The doctor still looked skeptical. "Then what . . . Miss Mannering . . . this attire!" he cried, shocked, as he now became aware of her garb.

"I hope Miss Mannering can count on your discretion, doctor," said the earl. "I can assure you that your conjectures, whatever they may be, must fall wide off the mark. Miss Mannering was on an errand of mercy when she was—was attacked by a footpad. I had no notion who she was until I brought her to my house. I trust this tale will not reach Lady Palmer's ears."

The doctor shook his head. "Of course not. She would turn the poor child out. That's all she is waiting for, a good excuse to give her husband for washing her hands of Miss Mannering. And where would the child go to live then? To her uncle's bachelor lodgings? Or to Banister? Her only other relation is a distant male cousin in Jamaica, who hasn't been heard of in years."

"Then as you agree on the need for discretion, doctor, why waste time on idle chatter? I suggest you apply yourself now to your task," the earl chided him in a stern voice.

Whereupon the doctor, affronted at this rebuke, instantly became businesslike and began to issue orders.

In a short time Miss Mannering, carried up by the earl himself, was ensconced with the doctor in the guest bedchamber, while the earl kept pacing the saloon with impatient steps, wishing Dr. Bennet would hasten with his examination, and trying hard to suppress an unwelcome anxiety for Miss Mannering's welfare. After all, there was no need for alarm. As far as he had been able to ascertain, the wound was not serious. Yet for all that, it seemed to him an exceedingly long time before the doctor joined him in the saloon and assured him that indeed the injury was not serious and would heal soon. "We must expect a fever to develop," he added, "but in a man this injury would be considered the veriest scratch, not enough to prevent him from going abroad—with his arm in a sling, of course."

The earl could not help feeling a relief out of all proportion to the incident. "Can she be moved? She should be taken home. I suggest that you call on her tomorrow morning, pretending her maid had sent for you. Miss Mannering could have fallen and hurt herself. No one need know the exact nature of her injury, except her personal maid."

The doctor nodded. "You are being quite considerate, my lord, taking into account how much you hate her fiancé."

The earl shrugged. "She is not responsible for his action. You don't see me cut Banister or Sir Edward. In fact, I was playing cards with them tonight."

The doctor gave a relieved sigh. He wished to question the earl as to Miss Mannering's strange errand, but Lord Cleary firmly shepherded him out of the saloon and the house. Then he ran up to the guest chamber and lightly knocked.

# Two

After being bade to enter, the earl opened the door to behold Miss Mannering propped up on the pillows, still a trifle pale, but much more composed, and dressed in one of his shirts, her arm interestingly in a sling, her bright auburn curls put in order, a hesitant half-fearful, half-hopeful smile on her lips.

"I am much obliged to you, my lord, for your forbearance," she said. "I—I know I don't deserve it, but . . . the situation was desperate indeed."

"Yes, now we come to this mad lark of yours," said the earl grimly, sitting down on a chair beside the bed, wishing he would not have to stare into those large beseeching green eyes. "I trust it has nothing to do with Vellacort. The doctor assures me you are well enough to talk for a few moments. And I feel you *do* owe me an explanation."

The girl nodded unhappily. "I don't know if you would consider it satisfactory, but perhaps if you are not at odds with my uncle, you might not be too overset at my disclosures. Oh, and I assure you I would not have kept your purse. I was going to drop it—"

She broke off and closed her eyes for a moment.

The earl leaned forward, his countenance expressing his concern. "Pray do not talk if you feel too weak. I shall understand perfectly. We can discuss this at some later time."

Felicia opened her eyes and said resolutely, "No, we can't, for I must get that necklace back. And I am quite able to talk."

"Are you in much pain?" he asked with contrition.

"No, no, not now. Well, not enough to signify." She made an impatient gesture and winced. "It is so difficult to explain, for you see, it doesn't reflect well upon my uncle."

"Nothing that Sir Edward could have done could compare with murder in cold blood," said the earl in a harsh voice.

"Darcy did *not* murder your brother! It was a duel," repeated Felicia stubbornly, two red spots burning on her pale cheeks. "He had no intention of killing him."

"Then how is it that he did? All the world knows how poor a shot Vellacort is."

"Not anymore."

Lord Cleary's brows snapped together. "You mean there is some truth to the tale that his aim has improved?"

"Of course there is. It's *because* Darcy was such a poor shot and was teased about it that he decided to improve. So he practiced—in secret, on his estate near Barnet. He meant to surprise everybody. Nobody knew about it except me. *That's* why he killed your brother. And if what Jerome says is true, they were both foxed. It was just bad luck—for you—that your brother was killed. It could well have been Darcy. They were evenly matched."

"Then he learned to shoot well in order to make sure he would kill my brother," said the earl inexorably, his concern for her forgotten as his rage and grief revived.

"He wouldn't, he couldn't have," protested Felicia. "He would never stoop to anything as underhanded and wicked as that."

"Naturally you would think so. You're in love with the fellow and cannot do otherwise. But *I* know different. I know that what happened that night in Barnet was a foul and deliberate murder, and I shall not stop until the whole truth is out in the open and the death of Marcus is avenged as it should be. And I intend to make haste to bring this about, for if Vellacort gets his post and leaves England with Lord Palmer, he might never come back, and would escape his just deserts altogether."

The expression on the earl's face was alarmingly severe. Felicia's heart hammered with fright. Up until this day she had never realized the extent of Lord Cleary's hatred for her betrothed. Oh, she knew they had become enemies and hated each other, but she never dreamed the earl would thirst so much for revenge, or plan to bring it about. She shuddered.

He looked so implacable, so fierce. And those large gray eyes of his were staring at her with the hard look of a judge pronouncing sentence. She shuddered again. If only she could make him believe it was a fair fight. But he would not believe Jerome's words. "There was another witness to the duel," she abruptly recalled. "Jerome said there was an ostler or a groom who acted as a second for your brother, or anyhow, he was a witness. Why don't you ask him precisely what occurred?"

The earl gave a scornful laugh. "You think I haven't tried? I fancy that other witness is nonexistent."

"But he must exist. Jerome has said so. That man was working at that inn in Barnet, where the duel took place. You must—"

Felicia hadn't realized that in her excitement she had raised herself from her reclining position, her cheeks flushed, her green eyes burning with fear and despair. Now as she made a sharp impatient movement, the pain seared through her arm, and she felt her senses reel. She fell back on the pillows, closing her eyes.

"Damnation!" swore the earl, conscience-stricken again as he now perceived beads of perspiration and the lines of pain on her countenance. He waved a bottle of smelling salts under her nose, then poured a glass of water from the carafe on the nightstand and pressed it to her lips. "Pray drink this and forgive my hot-tempered, insensible nature. It is absolutely of no use my arguing with you on that head, for neither of us will be won over, and it'll only make your fever worse. I beg your pardon. Pray forgive me."

Those magnificent eyes opened once more, and as the earl was quite close to her, holding the glass to her lips, he found himself staring into them, and he fancied he was drowning in those deep green pools.

"I forgive you, for I feel for you in your grief. And it must be particularly deep, since you were twins," said Felicia. "But I wish I could make you understand—"

"No. Pray let us leave the topic of Vellacort for some future date, when you are fully restored to health and I am in the mood to listen."

Felicia sighed and moved her head restlessly. "Very well. I am rather tired. And I must explain to you about the necklace."

"Ah yes. That I *should* like to know." He cast at her a worried glance. "If you are able to—"

"Yes, yes. I must. I knew you had bought the necklace, and—"

"How could you possibly have known about it? I did not know myself I would be buying it. I did not even know of its existence until I mentioned at your uncle's card party this evening that I had need of a trinket tonight and I had forgotten to buy it."

"It—it was Lester who told me."

"That blabbermouth!" swore the earl. "Couldn't keep his mouth shut, as usual. But why would he blab to *you* about it?"

"The necklace would have come to me in the course of time, and he knew it. I had even worn it upon several occasions. He also knew that I had urged Uncle to sell it, to pay his shocking debts. But Uncle wouldn't do it. He must have been rather more in his cups than usual to have agreed to sell it and to forget—" She broke off, biting her lip.

"He forgot that he had willed it to you. Well, he is an older absentminded gentleman, and he forgets things, I agree." He frowned. "There was no need to hold me up. Merely to explain to me the situation. I collect you knew where I was taking it."

She nodded.

The earl frowned again. "That impossible gabster. This goes beyond all bounds—to speak to a lady upon such a subject."

"He—he didn't. I guessed that part, that it was for—for your *chère-amie;* but I contrived to make him tell me that you would be going to Hampstead tonight, and I hit upon this notion of getting the necklace back."

"I can appreciate the urgency. You did not wish me to dispose of it tonight, when you wanted it for yourself—"

"No, no! Oh, how can I tell it to you," cried Felicia despairingly. "It was *not* because I want the necklace for myself that I was desperate to get it. I knew Uncle must have forgotten that he had sold it already. I don't know when. What you have bought, my lord, is paste. A very good replica, but not worth even a tenth of what you must have paid for it, I'm sure. I did not wish you to know of it."

The earl's countenance hardened.

But Felicia continued. "I was quite distracted when I learned of it. I don't know how I contrived to conceal my agitation from Lester. Fortunately Lady Palmer came in, and he excused himself at once and left the saloon. So now you know why I wished to get it back. Uncle—he did not do it deliberately. He just forgot. And he must have been foxed. But I couldn't allow you to give this necklace to your lady friend. Think of the scandal if she or you had discovered it was paste. I fancy you would have been quite angry and—and not kept quiet about it, and poor Uncle by then would have spent the money already."

"Ah yes, the money. How did you propose to give *that* back to me? Or did you?"

"Well, I couldn't give it back to you tonight, could I? And I couldn't go to Uncle and ask him to give you the money back, for he doesn't know I know the necklace is paste. I—I fancied you wouldn't feel the loss of the money much, and I would contrive somehow to see to it that it was restored to you later. And," she added with spirit, "were I just to stop you and beg you to return the necklace because it is paste, I was persuaded you would have made a dreadful fuss about it and accused Uncle of cheating you, and it would have become known, and—and I didn't wish it for him, for he is not in good health and this sort of scandal might prove fatal to his constitution."

"Very touching," Lord Cleary said with a sneer.

Felicia disregarded his comment. She was feeling quite worn out, but carried on gamely. "And even had I accosted you at this late hour and begged you to return the necklace because it had been promised to me, do you think you would have been inclined to do a favor for Darcy's fiancée? After all, *I* was only to inherit the necklace, and it is still Uncle Edward's and *he* can do with it as he pleases. I did not think—I was afraid you would not listen if I tried that purely selfish approach."

Lord Cleary sighed, passing his hand across his face. "You are right. I would hardly have wished to oblige *you*, Vellacort's betrothed. I doubt if I would even have listened, not when I myself—" He broke off.

Felicia cocked her head at him, glancing at him quizzically. "Not when you yourself were a trifle foxed too. Yes, I had taken *that* into consideration also. It is absolutely of no use trying to persuade a gentleman to one's own thinking when he is in his cups. But now— are you willing to listen to me *now* about Uncle?"

"Aye, I'm willing. Your prank has quite sobered me up. Now, don't be in a taking over this whole matter. I have a fondness for your uncle, so I'll tell him that I have changed my mind about the necklace, but I'll let him keep the money as a loan or in case I change my mind again and wish to buy it from him after all."

"It is quite generous of you, my lord, and I am exceedingly grateful; but you are not obliged not to ask for your money back, unless—" She bit her lip. "Unless he has lost some of it already."

"Don't let that worry you. And especially not now. I

shall order a carriage to take you home immediately."
He hesitated. "Pray enlighten me upon one more thing.
How did you know that the necklace was paste?"

"I—I told Uncle I wished to wear it to a party, but
instead I took it for appraisal. I knew Aunt had had it
appraised and that it was very valuable. I thought telling Uncle the exact large sum he could get for it now
might persuade him to sell it."

"I see. Well . . . pray accept my deepest apologies for
having hurt you. That I could have—"

"Oh no, no. You are not to blame. You did not know
you were shooting at a female. And I am very much
obliged to you for—for showing such understanding
and being willing to keep quiet about everything. And
for your help."

The earl waved her thanks away with a wry grimace.
"After what I did to you, what else could I do but make
amends? I'll send my groom to find your pistol, and
make sure your horse is back at the stables."

He bowed and left the chamber, only to return a few
moments later to gather her up in a blanket and carry
her to his chaise. Over Felicia's protests he insisted on
driving her home himself, saying that the fewer servants knew what had occurred the better, a sentiment
with which she heartily concurred.

Relaxing against the sumptuous squabs of his carriage, with the earl on the box handling the ribbons,
Felicia felt greatly relieved that poor Uncle Edward
would be spared a scandal or worse, but she was quite
perturbed by the earl's fierce hatred of her fiancé and
his desire for revenge. And she was determined to
clear Darcy of murder in his eyes. But she was too tired
and too ill to think much on it now. The doctor's
draught was taking its effect, and she found herself
nodding to the gentle rocking of the chaise.

In no time at all the carriage had stopped in front of
Lady Palmer's town house in Berkeley Square. The earl
took her down and carried her to the side door, where
her faithful maid was anxiously awaiting her return.
Upon seeing her mistress carried in, she almost screamed,

but clapped a hand to her mouth in time. The earl explained briefly what had occurred and carried Felicia to her bedchamber, the maid preceding him through the dark and silent house.

Having deposited Felicia on her bed, he stood staring at her for a moment, a strange unfathomable expression in his hard gray eyes. Then he said gruffly, "Pray do not distress yourself with depressing thoughts. Pretend that the whole incident has not occurred. I'll wager as soon as your wound has healed, you will contrive to forget it." He turned to the maid. "Look after your mistress well," he said. Then he bowed and allowed himself to be led out of the house.

# Three

Felicia shifted restlessly on the bed. The afternoon sun slanting in through the windows brightened the somber decor of her small bedchamber. The dark oak paneling appeared less gloomy in the radiant light, and the sun's rays shining through a lattice of leaves on a tree branch outside made a pleasing pattern on her white sprigged bedcover. And Felicia's robe of apple-green silk and the many flowers in vases all about the room added cheerful splashes of color.

Bertha, her aunt's and now her maid, was observing a chambermaid remove wilted flowers, and through the partially open door Felicia could hear Lester Winwood's voice on the landing.

Several days had passed since her rash act, and though she had developed a fever, her strong constitution and youth prevailed and today she was feeling much better.

To her relief and gratification, Lord Cleary had kept his promise about the necklace and had also kept quiet about her escapade. Lady Palmer had been vexed at her accident, and surprised and suspicious at his calling to inquire about Felicia's health. Felicia fobbed her off by telling her she had met Lord Cleary through Uncle Edward, letting her infer that it must have been during one of the infrequent times when he took her out driving.

But though Felicia felt grateful to the earl and much relieved that she had contrived to save her uncle from disaster, she could not forget the earl's thirst for revenge. Well she remembered his harsh words and the fierce expression on his face, so at variance with the concern and understanding he had shown to her. She sighed as she recalled—with some feelings of guilt and disloyalty to Darcy—the sensation of being carried in his lordship's strong arms. Even in her pain-befuddled state she had found the experience exceedingly agreeable. And she could sympathize with him, having herself known much bereavement. First her mother had died, then her father—in the war with Napoleon—and now but a short year ago her aunt. Yet her sympathy for and her reluctant liking of Lord Cleary could not still her fear, and she wished very much to consult with someone on the subject.

The deep fragrance of roses intruded cheerily on her grim thoughts. She looked up.

Bertha had placed a vase with rearranged red roses on the nightstand. "There now, don't these roses from Lord Cleary look pretty. Don't you be so blue-deviled, miss. You'll be well enough to go to Vauxhall. I declare I was that surprised when I heard her ladyship offering to take you along."

So had been Felicia. That sort of offer would not likely be repeated soon, so she should take advantage of it.

"I'll wager 'twas his lordship, Lord Palmer, as made her do it." Bertha snorted, her pink-cheeked homely face twisted in indignation. Felicia wanted to say that it hadn't been his influence this time that had brought about the invitation, but Bertha continued, "It's not my place to say it, but it's a pity, it is, that his lordship is away from home so much. It ain't right for a young miss to be shut up in the house all the time, yet alone carry out"—she glanced around, but the chambermaid had stepped out—"silly orders her ladyship fancies to give. 'Do this, do that—and keep out of the way.' Unpaid companion, that's what you are. It ain't fair."

Felicia grimaced. "After all, she gives me room and board."

"And uses you shamelessly, besides constantly reminding you of her 'generosity,' the great favor she has done for you. Favor, ha! If it weren't for Lord Palmer, her ladyship would never have taken you under her roof, and it's a fact."

Felicia silently agreed. While she appreciated Lady Palmer's tolerating her presence in Berkeley Square, she knew that left to herself she would not have done so. But Lord Palmer, a good friend of Felicia's aunt's, had promised her to look after her niece, and it was he who had brought Felicia to Berkeley Square after her aunt's funeral. Yet Lady Palmer had appropriated the credit to herself. And her ladyship's whims and scolds were not easy to endure, let alone the condescension and the constant reminder what a great benefactress she was to Felicia.

For Darcy's sake, Felicia endured all—dreading her displeasure, fearing that a sharp retort which sometimes sprang to her lips, or a refusal to bow to her wishes, might cause Lady Palmer to ruin Darcy's chances of success. Oh, if only she could accompany Darcy as his wife on his trip to Vienna with Lord Palmer—if he was offered the post—and not be obliged to reside with Lady Palmer any longer. Or at least if she could secure a post somewhere as a schoolteacher or a governess. But neither Uncle nor Lord Palmer would hear of such a notion.

Felicia sighed. She wished she could have told Darcy of her apprehension about the earl's thirst for revenge, but she dared not. For one, Darcy would only have dismissed the danger to himself with a shrug, or even been angry that she had listened to gossip. For another, Lady Palmer did not stir from Felicia's chamber the few minutes Darcy was allowed to visit her. She wished she could have talked with Uncle Edward about her fears, but when he had called on her, she had still been in no fit state to speak up on such an important matter.

"Pay attention to what you're doing!" Bertha's admonition interrupted Felicia's musings. Bertha was scolding the maid for spilling some water and ordering her to mop up the spill.

"A bird-witted hen." Bertha snorted. "But I ain't surprised at the help here. With the wages her ladyship pays, what can you expect." She frowned. "It's not my place to say it, but Mr. Vellacort's neglecting you. He don't visit you enough, nor take you out driving."

Felicia experienced a surge of irritation. "Now Bertha, you know very well he is not welcome in Berkeley Square. He feels uncomfortable here. And Lady Palmer doesn't like me to go out much."

"Your being in black gloves just gives Lady P. an excuse not to take you anywhere," Bertha resumed her diatribe, "nor allow you to attend parties she gives herself. For all the diversions you have in London, you might as well be living in the country. Now if you'd only accepted the offer—" She broke off, seeing Felicia's countenance darken.

Felicia shifted her head on the pillow. Again she had to agree with Bertha. Her life would have taken quite a different turn had she accepted the quite eligible offer she had received at her come-out. Not to mention the offer from her cousin Jerome. But at that time she had already met and fallen in love with Darcy. And her aunt had given her consent to his suit only shortly before her passing.

Not that Felicia was pining for the pleasures of the *ton*. Though her aunt had not been a very demonstrative or cheerful person, Felicia had cared for her and was saddened by her death; but with the passage of time she felt the normal urge of a girl for a little diversion. Hence her delight at the prospect of a visit to Vauxhall Gardens. And with the Duchess of Oldenburg being fêted everywhere, and in the expectation of the tsar's and other dignitaries' arrival in June, London was offering more and more diversions with each passing day. Napoleon had been beaten at last and banished to the island of Elba, and the country and indeed the whole Continent were in a mood for celebration.

Felicia's countenance grew somber. It did not seem she would be able to enjoy the Peace Celebrations—or Vauxhall, even if she was up and about in time to take part in the expedition to the Pleasure Gardens. The worry about Lord Cleary's taking revenge on Darcy must exlude everything else from her mind. The earl's kind conduct toward her did not diminish this worry, and her talk with Jerome but added to it.

Cousin Jerome, a good and dear friend, had paid a call on Felicia and contrived to be alone with her in her chamber for a few moments—which would have been viewed by that high stickler Lady Palmer as most improper.

Jerome, wishing to spare her worry, had tried to make light of her fears, but she had seen that he was concerned also. Yet he appeared quite vexed when she expressed her doubts about going to Vauxhall.

Felicia's heart again warmed to her cousin. In his vexation he had let slip that it was he who had persuaded Lady Palmer to take Felicia along to the Pleasure Gardens. *He* had decided that Felicia should have some diversion at last. And Darcy, of course, would be included in the party. All of which made her feel dreadfully guilty, for she had refused Jerome's offer of marriage and yet he still continued to be such a good friend to her.

Jerome had also reminded her to wear the necklace, and seemed displeased when she said she did not wish to wear it, for he wished her to look her best. Good, kind Jerome. If only he had remained longer with her, so she could have discussed with him properly Lord Cleary's hatred of Darcy and her apprehension.

Still, were he in her chamber now, she could not have told him of the notion that had been forming in her mind. He might think she was doubting his account of the duel, and she could not tell him that it was the earl himself who did. She could not reveal to him, to anybody, her disastrous experience as a highwayman. Felicia still shuddered each time she recalled that frightening moment when she had pointed the pistol at the earl.

The chambermaid had mopped up the spill and left, and Bertha had finished her task and was leaving the room. She was just about to shut the door behind her when Felicia heard Lester ask in a kind voice, "How is your mistress today? More the thing?"

And Felicia abruptly thought, why not?

"Yes, I am," she called out. "Pray come in, Lester."

The round amiable countenance of Lester Winwood appeared in the doorway. "Don't believe I should visit you in your bedchamber," he muttered diffidently. "Not the thing."

"Pooh," Felicia said and waved away his objection. "We've known each other since we were in shortcoats. You didn't object to entering my chamber then. Pray come in and shut the door. I wish to ask your advice on a very important matter."

Lester Winwood, casting an apprehensive glance over his shoulder—no doubt to ascertain if his mama was within sight—entered the room on tiptoes and shut the door.

"Pray come closer and pull up a chair," said Felicia.

The gentleman reluctantly obeyed.

The Honorable Lester Winwood, some three years older than Felicia, was a slim man of medium height, with brown eyes, regular features, and an amiable disposition. He also had an inclination to dandyism, which irritated his mother. Light-brown hair brushed into carefully molded and pomaded locks, a purple satin coat and a blue-and-pink waistcoat, and the height of his cravat and his shirtcollar left no doubt in anyone's mind on that score. He tripped in, pulled up a chair, and, after inspecting it warily for any sign of dust, lowered himself into it gently.

"Shockingly bad help these days. Don't wish to spoil my togs," he explained apologetically. And indeed any spot or smudge would have been glaringly visible on his dazzingly bright-yellow inexpressibles.

"Glad to see you better, Felicia. Fever all gone?"

"Yes, but I'm still as weak as a cat."

"Not surprising. I'll wager that upstairs maid did not put away things as she ought, making you stumble in the dark and fall. I cannot conceive why we cannot obtain better help.

"Pity you missed seeing the parade, and King Louis," he said. "The king's even stouter than Prinny. Prinny invested him with the Order of the Garter. What a sight to behold. The king's knee is as big as a man's waist. But the parade to Piccadilly was quite a credit to Prinny."

"I am sorry I missed it, but that's not important. Lester, have you seen Darcy today?"

"Haven't seen him since day before yesterday, at White's."

Felicia made a clucking sound. "I collect he lost again. I wish he would stop this gaming and wagering and be a trifle more careful what he is about. He cannot afford to get into a scrape."

"Shouldn't worry too much about him. I fancy the duel has sobered him up and he's careful now not to overstep the line. He wishes to get the post—and he needs it."

"I'm very glad to hear that, but . . ." She took a deep breath. "Lester it has come to my attention that Lord Cleary thinks—thinks that Darcy did not kill his brother in a fair fight."

Lester's amiable face darkened. "I should like to know who came to you with this tale. It was certainly not Mother."

"No, no. And Lester, Lord Cleary thinks that Jerome is lying about the duel, for my sake. Would he do that?"

"He would—he is very fond of you. But Vellacort did not murder Cleary's brother, so you may be easy on that score. No need for Banister to lie."

"But why would Lord Cleary persist in believing he did? He seems obsessed with the notion."

"That's it. That's the reason—obsession," said Lester, reaching into his coat pocket and producing an enameled snuffbox. He flipped it open expertly with one finger, removed an infinitesimal pinch of snuff and carried it to his nostril, then returned the snuffbox to his pocket. "Cleary was very close to his brother. Twins, you know. Took his death very hard indeed. Daresay it will take him a long time to get over it. To a man in his state of mind, a duel—same thing as murder."

He pulled out a highly scented handkerchief—the scent vying for supremacy with the fragrance of the flowers—and dusted off a few specks of snuff from his coat sleeve. "Don't put yourself in a taking over Cleary's notions," he added kindly. "Nothing to do with you."

"But it has to do with me. He wishes to take revenge on Darcy, to destroy him."

Lester looked shocked. "Now where did you get *that* notion? Who told you that?"

"Never mind. I know it for a fact that he does," cried Felicia, irritated. "And Jerome thinks so too."

Lester gaped at her, disbelieving, while the handkerchief slipped from his hand. He retrieved it, careful that it not pick up dust or lint from the floor. "Did he say that?" he asked in an indignant tone. "Shouldn't have said it. Not to you!"

"He didn't precisely say it. In fact, he assured me it was no such thing, but I know that's what he thinks. I could see he *was* concerned."

"Of course he was concerned, and so am I," said Lester, "that you're worrying yourself into a fever with such silly notions." He began to rise from the chair. "You'd best take a nap," he said soothingly. "Feel more the thing. I'll talk to you later."

"Lester Winwood," shrieked Felicia, "if you don't sit down and pay attention to what I'm saying I shall have such a fit of the vapors that everyone will rush into the chamber to see what has occurred."

Lester dropped back in his chair. "No, no," he said

hastily. "Happy to listen to you anytime. Shouldn't have entered the chamber," he muttered to himself.

In spite of her fears, Felicia gave a low chuckle. "I have *not* lost my senses, Lester, and I don't have the fever now. I know Lord Cleary wishes to take revenge on Darcy. Surely *you* must have heard him say so," she hazarded. "And it worries me a great deal."

"You may rest easy on that score. He is still grieving for his brother, to be sure, and he is angry at Vellacort, that's understandable. And he may—mind you, may—say he wishes to take revenge. But he won't. Not the thing. Not the man to do it, either. Don't pay any heed to the gossips. Assure you there is no danger. Cleary's not the man—"

"Yes, but you said yourself he's obsessed. What if he—"

"Well, he won't. Take my word for it."

Felicia felt somewhat reassured, but she was still uneasy. What if both Lester and Jerome were wrong and Lord Cleary's obsession overrode his sense of fair play? The grim countenance of the earl floated before her eyes. She shook her head. No, she must not take any chances with Darcy's life or happiness.

"Oh, how I wish I had contrived to arrive at Barnet sooner," she abruptly exclaimed with vexation. "I rushed there wishing to stop that curricle race, worried that Darcy would kill himself racing against Marcus, and instead—I cannot help wondering if, had I arrived there in time, I might have prevented the duel."

"Now don't you go worrying yourself over what's past and done with," said Lester with some asperity. "Ain't no sense to it at all. No sense blaming yourself, either."

Felicia sighed. "You're right. And it's not what I wished to talk to you about." She took another deep breath. "Don't you think, Lester, if somebody impartial could assure the earl that the duel, though a trifle irregular, was a fair fight, it would relieve his mind and quite banish my worry?"

"Yes, I daresay it would."

"Well, you know there was another witness to the duel, don't you?"

Lester pulled absently at his earlobe and nodded. "Yes, I do recall now hearing of it. What of it?"

"I collect it was a servant at that inn, in Barnet. And *he*, I'm sure, would have no reason to lie to protect Darcy. What if he were to tell Lord Cleary what he saw? The earl would believe *him*."

Lester nodded again. "One would think Cleary would have wished to ask him himself."

"He did wish to ask." Lester looked startled. "At least, I am persuaded he must have," she amended, "but—but it seems that witness has disappeared. If we could but find that man and—"

"Who's the *we?*" Lester asked quickly, staring at her, half frightened, half surprised.

"We—you and I. Of course, I can't do anything now. But I shall be up and about soon, and then we can go to Barnet to discover what happened to that other witness."

Lester seemed quite revolted at the notion. "Traipsing to Barnet on a wild goose chase to look for a witness months after the event? That don't make sense."

"Well, I had no reason to look for him before," said Felicia. "But now I have. Oh, please, Lester. I should be so much relieved if we found that witness."

Lester shifted unhappily in his chair. Then his countenance brightened. "Ask Banister to go with you. Good man to find out things, Banister. Always clever to seize on a chance, too. Bought a pair of bays once, heard Merton was obliged to sell them and bid for them before anyone else was aware of what was in the wind."

"I—I don't wish to ask him."

"Think he'll renew his suit if he does this favor for you?" asked Lester sapiently. "Can't do that very well when you're engaged to Vellacort."

"No, but—anyway, I'm sure I shan't be able to talk to him in private again until I'm on my feet, and— and I wish to settle this *now*."

"Always impatient to get things done. Might get you into trouble someday. Better think it over."

"There is nothing to think over. I wish to find that man."

"Why not just send Bertha or a groom?"

Felicia pondered that for a moment. "I can't send anybody from the household. He might tattle. I *could* send Bertha, but I think a gentleman or a lady would have a much better chance of discovering this man's whereabouts than a mere servant."

Lester sighed. "Daresay you're right."

"Well then, couldn't you go with me? Or better still, go *now* yourself?"

"What? Really, Felicia—"

Felicia rushed on. "Of course, if you feel you cannot perform this service for me, I perfectly understand. I—I'll go alone as soon as—"

"No, no, no." Lester mopped his perspiring face with his scented handkerchief. He heaved a deep sigh. "Oh, very well, I'll go with you."

Felicia's green eyes sparkled with joy and gratitude. "Oh, Lester, how very kind and obliging of you. I think I shall be well enough to go in a few days, and—"

Lester held up a hand, and she broke off, startled.

Voices could be heard on the corridor. "Mother!" Lester whispered, terrified.

And indeed Lady Palmer's strident voice could now be clearly heard. And the voice was getting louder—coming closer.

Lester's eyes started from their sockets. "She's coming here!" He glanced about desperately for a means of escape. "She mustn't find me here."

"The dressing room, quickly," Felicia said.

Springing precipitately out of his chair, Lester bolted through the door of the dressing room and shut it just as the door from the corridor opened and Lady Palmer, with a swish of her lavender silk gown, sailed into the room.

# Four

Lady Palmer was a handsome, rather imposing woman with light-brown hair sprinkled with gray. Her prim lips, wont rather to scold than to smile, were now folded into a grimace which she no doubt thought was an adequate expression of pleasure. "Felicia, child, I hear that you are much improved today. That is splendid news. It's a pity, though, that—

"Sniff, sniff." Her ladyship's patrician nose went up, as she sniffed the air repeatedly. Her sharp dark eyes grew wider, then narrowed in suspicion. "Has Lester been *here?*" she asked in an angry and ominous yet disbelieving tone. "I detect his scent."

Felicia's heart sank. It took all her willpower not to glance in the direction of the dressing room. If only the dressing room had a door to the corridor! But this space has been partitioned off from the bedchamber and turned into a dressing room. There was no way out for Lester.

Felicia hoped her quavering voice would not betray her as she said, "Lester, ma'am? Why, no."

"But his scent?" said Lady Palmer sharply.

"I ran out of my lavender water and begged leave to use a few drops of his scent to sprinkle on my handkerchief. I hope you don't mind."

"Mind? Why should I mind?" But she still looked suspicious. "Did Bertha obtain the scent from Cassel?"

"Why, I fancy it must have been from Cassel." Now Felicia was glad that Lester's valet and Bertha seemed to be sweet on each other, so the borrowing of Lester's' scent, which gave Bertha an excuse to see Cassel, would seem believable to her ladyship's suspicious mind.

Apparently it was so, for the suspicious look slowly faded. "Well, you must not be too liberal with scent. Just a few drops is quite enough. Where was I? Oh yes—it's a pity that you cannot wear your black gown to Vauxhall, but since you're out of black gloves now, a black gown would hardly be suitable for a festive occasion. Toller shall go over your old gowns to see if one of them couldn't be improved upon. If not"—her lips folded into a grimace of dislike—"we shall be obliged to have a new dress made, though I own this additional expense will make it necessary for me to practice even more stringent economy."

"It's of no consequence what I wear to Vauxhall," said Felicia in an expressionless tone. "One of my old gowns will do."

"Nonsense. Lord Palmer wishes you to be suitably dressed. He isn't perfectly sure if he'll return to town for the occasion, but he might. I don't suppose your uncle—no, no use asking *him*. I hope you wear the necklace. Such a magnificent jewel needs a plain simple gown to show it off."

"I'd rather not wear it this time," Felicia dared.

Lady Palmer's brow furrowed. "Why not?" Then she tossed her regal head. "Nonsense. You shall wear it. A plain white muslin—no, after all, you're not a debutante. It will have to be yellow."

Not with my red hair, thought Felicia, half in amusement, half in dismay. Still, no use disputing this now.

"I don't know why you have refused Banister," Lady Palmer said, playing her familiar tune. "He could have provided for you much better than Vellacort ever will—and would have married you long since." Felicia could never understand how Cousin Jerome had contrived to turn Lady Palmer up sweet. He wasted his money gaming, as did Darcy. Lady Palmer disliked Felicia, detested Darcy, and barely tolerated Uncle Edward, but Jerome to her was a paragon of all virtues—which he was, in a way, conceded Felicia. The trouble was, she was not in love with him, but with Darcy.

"I collect you haven't found the address of your relative in Jamaica?" her ladyship asked next.

Felicia sighed. "No. I couldn't find it anywhere among my aunt's correspondence. Jerome helped me look, and he couldn't either. Perhaps Aunt threw it out. After all, he never answered her letter. For all we know he might not be alive now either."

"I daresay you're right. Though from what I've heard about him, I take it he is quite respectable and proper," continued Lady Palmer. "*He* wouldn't countenance anyone, I'm sure, who engaged in a scandalous conduct; so I don't blame him for not being on good terms with your branch of the family."

Felicia bristled. If Lady Palmer was going to cast aspersions on her aunt and parents again, she wouldn't be able to keep a still tongue in her head.

"Papa and my aunt should not have been held accountable for Grandfather's shortcomings," she said, trying to keep strong indignation from her voice.

"Like father, like son. Your papa took after Sir Avery in everything. And had he not been killed in the war he would have—"

"My papa was an upright honorable man, and he died a hero's death," exclaimed Felicia hotly, jerking up to a sitting position. And cried out at the sudden pain in her arm.

Lady Palmer recollected herself. "Nobody gainsays him that," she said crossly. "I'll own *he* at least had some sense of duty, which is more than can be said of Vellacort. I fancy he must regret now his betrothal to you. I'll wager he wouldn't have offered for you today, not when he's run through all his inheritance and is as penniless as yourself."

"Darcy is in love with me," cried Felicia in an indignant voice.

"I daresay. You have that about you which seems to attract men of a certain stamp. I'm glad to say that Lester isn't one of them. But I did not come here to talk of Vellacort." And Lady Palmer turned the subject back to dresses, and for the next few moments kept up a monologue about Felicia's new gown.

Felicia, quite exhausted when at last she ran down and took herself off, lay back against the pillows, closing her eyes.

A faint noise coming from the dressing room caused them to fly open.

From behind the dressing-room door peered the pale anxious face of Lester, a finger to his lips, his frightened brown eyes darting to the door leading to the corridor.

Felicia gazed at him with amusement and warmth. "It's safe to come out now. She's gone," she said, beckoning him in.

Lester tiptoed in, casting fearful glances about him, as if expecting his mother to pop out from inside the wardrobe or from under the bed. His face was bathed in perspiration. He tiptoed to the outer door, opened it a crack, cocked his ear and listened, then peered very cautiously out. Satisfied, he shut the door, glanced around, and, espying a chair nearby, propped it under the doorknob. Then came back to the chair by the bed, plopped into it, took out his handkerchief, and mopped his brow.

"Phew! What a close-run thing that was. I shudder to think what she would have said had she caught me here with you. Besides its being dashed improper, I'll wager she would have thought I was dangling after you. In fact, she would be bound to think so. And it wouldn't make a ha'p'orth of difference that she knows I ain't in the petticoat line or that you're already affianced to Vellacort. Be very careful, Felicia, that you don't let on to her I'm doing this favor for you. She mightn't like it. Mightn't? She dashed well *wouldn't* like it."

Felicia's eyes were brimful with amusement, but also with concern. "Lester, couldn't you somehow manage to gain control of your money? It's very vexing for you to have her control your purse strings."

Lester sighed and shook his head glumly. "Can't break the trust. That's how it was set up by m' uncle."

"And Lord Palmer? Can't he do anything?"

"He says I'll have plenty of the ready to waste when I step into his shoes. Meanwhile he allows Mother to do as she pleases. Well, stands to reason he ain't complaining. Mother manages the household very well," he said with a tinge of pride. "Not one household bill unpaid, not to my knowledge, and her toggery's all paid for too. Father won't complain about that. His best friend shot himself because his wife and son squandered away all his money. So mind, keep my going to Barnet with you to yourself." He rose from the chair. "Better leave now."

"Lester, we must talk again before long. I shall be able to go to Barnet very soon, I'm sure."

Lester shook his head vehemently. "No, no, no. I ain't traipsing with you to Barnet before Vauxhall. Dashed fool thing to do. You can't go there the minute you get out of bed. You'd only get knocked up by the jaunt, and what then of your outing to Vauxhall? What's the odds to go now or later?"

"But I wish to go as soon as possible. It's Darcy's life I am thinking of," Felicia cried in an indignant voice.

Lester looked at her with concern. "You know, Felicia, I don't think you're quite the thing yet. You're talking as if the earl were about to set upon Vellacort somewhere in an alley and finish him off. I own Cleary is a trifle obsessed about his brother's death, but he ain't queer in his attic yet. And I shall endeavor to find out exactly what his sentiments are in this matter. When I do, when I find out there is a reason for worry, then we shall do something about it—at once. But it don't do anybody any good for you to be working yourself into a fever on account of some fears which reason tells me are quite groundless."

Felicia fell back against the cushions. "Oh, Lester, you think I'm being very silly and overwrought."

"No, no, it's natural. That fall must have been nastier than we suspected. Don't give it another thought."

He gave her a graceful bow, which, however, was spoiled by a sharp jerking up of his head when he heard steps in the corridor. Frightened, he was ready to bolt back into the dressing room, but the footsteps passed and receded, and then there was silence.

Lester bowed again, tiptoed to the door, peered out, nodded a sign of "all clear" to Felicia, and slipped quickly out of the chamber.

*Five*

Felicia had no occasion for a tête-à-tête with Lester again; in fact, she hardly saw him until the day of the expedition to Vauxhall Gardens. And then it was in the Blue Drawing Room in the company of his mama, Darcy, and Jerome. But Felicia, kept busy by Lady Palmer in the intervening days, and somewhat reassured that nothing dreadful could happen to Darcy in the immediate future, was again looking forward eagerly to the pleasure in store for her. Even Lady Palmer's acid comments failed to dampen her good spirits. Only when her ladyship let loose her tongue on Darcy again did Felicia bristle with indignation.

Lady Palmer took Darcy to task for wasting money on his new plum-colored coat. Yet Darcy was not a dandy, he did not spend a fortune on clothes, and Lester's russet coat was new also, and so was Jerome's. Darcy, seething with resentment, spoke sharply to her ladyship, and the situation threatened to become ugly. It was Jerome who, in his calm soothing voice, trying to keep peace between the two, at last contrived to ease the tension-filled atmosphere.

"Perhaps, my lady, Vellacort may be excused his new coat upon this occasion," he said placatingly. "After all, this is our dear Felicia's first real appearance in society since her bereavement—not to mention her recovery from her recent illness. Surely it is a time for celebration. I myself am wearing a new coat today. And, if I may be so bold as to say it, that lilac lace gown of yours must be a new one also. So becoming. How dashing of you to choose that white underdress and that lilac turban. I've always said, ma'am, that you have an impeccable taste in clothes. I'm sure I detect your unerring hand in choosing this delightfully simple gown for Felicia. White indeed is all the rage now, since the restoration of the Bourbons. I'll wager it was *your* notion, not the modiste's, to have it adorned with just that silver ribbon at the waist and neck. Left to herself, I'm sure the modiste would have put ells of frills and flounces on it. You, ma'am, are an example to us all in taste as well as in deportment."

Lady Palmer preened herself, the angry flushed look fading from her face to be replaced by a smug self-satisfied expression. "You dear boy," she tittered, giving Jerome a benevolent look. "I daresay you're the only one who really appreciates my worth and my economy. So refreshing in a young man."

Felicia stared at Jerome in awe, Darcy looked at him sullenly, Lester gaped at him in admiration. Then Lester muttered to Felicia, who was sitting next to him, "*He* should be a diplomat."

Felicia could not help being amused by the comic expression on Lester's face, but she concurred with his view. Jerome was a most complete hand in any situation. She frowned. If only Darcy could be a trifle more diplomatic with Lady Palmer. But he couldn't help himself; Lady Palmer always rubbed him the wrong way. Feeling almost a traitress, Felicia chided herself mentally for this uncharitable thought about her fiancé. After all, Darcy was only two-and-twenty, while Jerome was almost forty and much more experienced in handling a difficult situation.

She cast an appraising glance at her cousin. She could understand partly why Lady Palmer found her choosing Darcy over Jerome incomprehensible. Jerome was quite a presentable man. He was tall—taller than Darcy, who was slim and graceful—and he had a good figure. He could have worn extravagant clothes with grace without making himself look ridiculous, yet he preferred quiet elegance to ostentation. His olive-green coat was of a perfect cut, but his pale-green embroidered waistcoat did not dazzle the eye as did Lester's. And his cravat was not as monstrously high as Darcy's. His ash-blond hair, stylishly cut, was slightly graying at the temples, giving him a rather distinguished appearance. Oh yes, he was all that was admirable—but of course he was *not* Darcy.

Her eyes softened as she gazed fondly at her betrothed. He was *so* handsome, with his perfect classical features, his deep blue eyes fringed with dark lashes, his guinea-gold locks, and the most charming smile imaginable.

She sighed. The smile was not in evidence now, and the fine-shaped lips were pouting. Lady Palmer always did that to him, always made him cross, thought Felicia with resentment.

But Jerome was rising from his seat. "Perhaps we should be on our way, ma'am," he said deferentially. "I do wish to procure a box for us before all the best places are snapped up."

Lady Palmer gave him a gracious nod, then frowned at Felicia. "I wish you had worn that necklace. I am really disappointed." Jerome was disappointed also, but Darcy did not seem to mind.

"But I have explained to you, ma'am, why I don't wish to wear it," protested Felicia.

Lady Palmer gave a contemptuous snort. "If I told you once, I have told you a dozen times, there is very little danger of your losing it or having it stolen—unless you are grossly careless. You stand in far greater danger of being accosted by inquisitive bucks. On no account are you to wander off into a dark alley by yourself, for you might be subjected to the sort of advances that can draw shame and scandal on your head. So don't let your head be turned by all the sights and excitement.

And do not let the lax deportment of some females there set an example for you. For, mark my words, one hint of scandal and I'll wash my hands of you. And you may be sure Vellacort *shan't* get his post with Lord Palmer. I shall see to that." Her ample lilac-draped bosom quivered in outrage at even the possibility of Felicia's disgracing herself.

"Felicia's conduct is always above reproach," said Darcy quickly. "As for being accosted by inquisitive bucks, they will not dare to make improper advances to her, not when she has *me* to protect her."

Lady Palmer harrumphed, not looking reassured, but she rose majestically from the sofa, while Lester hurried to place her purple velvet cloak round her shoulders. Darcy helped Felicia to don her cloak of green silk, and in a few moments they were on their way to Vauxhall Gardens.

It was a lovely evening in May. Felicia's new gown, though of a simple design, showed up to perfection her graceful figure and, having shaken off her resentment of her ladyship, she was anticipating the pleasure of being in the company of Darcy and the excitement the diversions of the Gardens would provide.

In the event, she was to have a trifle more excitement than she had bargained for.

As Felicia stepped off the boat at the landing stage in front of the water gate to Vauxhall Gardens, she saw three beautiful ladies in exceedingly low-cut muslin gowns.

All three were blond, with heavily painted faces. One of the three, the blue-eyed one, was slightly plumper than the others and was wearing an enormous yellow rose in her hair; one was slightly older, taller, and more elegant.

"Brazen hussies," said Lady Palmer with a snort. "Plying their trade under the noses of the *ton*."

"Do you know them?" wondered Felicia.

"Know them? I should say not. *I* am not in the habit of associating with common Cyprians. It's a pity some gentlemen of the *ton* do." She cast an uneasy glance at Lester, but he was carefully removing an invisible speck of dirt from his coat sleeve, while Darcy, after one quick look, kept his eyes studiously averted from the sight, which seemingly had made him uneasy.

A slightly foxed gentleman, hearing Lady Palmer's remark, tipped his hat to her and said, "No, no, ma'am. There is nothing common about *them*. The tall one is Zemelda, a diamond of the first water, one of the leading Fashionable Impures and expensive as they come. I am surprised she is without an escort today. But that's all to the good. Now's my chance to try my luck with her." And he tottered off toward the three, while Lady Palmer glared indignantly at his retreating back.

As their little group passed the Fashionable Impures, Felicia fancied she saw one of them cast a wink in their direction, but couldn't be quite sure. Perhaps she was winking at the foxed gentleman.

Once through the gate, Lady Palmer's party entered a long graveled walk, lined with stately trees, and the sights and sounds of Vaxhall assailed Felicia's senses in full force. From the rotunda on the left the sounds of dance music could be heard. From the right, where through the trees she could see an orchestra stand in the middle of a clearing, a classical melody floated on the cool fresh evening air.

Straight ahead and all around her, visible as far as the eye could see, was a multitude of colored lights, winking in the gathering twilight. Succulent fragrance from the supper boxes on the right indicated that some guests had already chosen to sustain themselves, while the scent of perfume wafted to her nostrils from the strolling groups of ladies and gentlemen, their colorful garments vying with the spring flowers.

After strolling a few yards down the Long Walk beside Felicia, Jerome excused himself and went off to secure a supper box for them. "Pray wait for me beside the orchestra," he said before he hurried off. The rest of them continued on their leisurely way. Abruptly Lady Palmer spotted something and stopped.

"Well, I declare, if it isn't Hermione Silverdale," she said. "And she is as indecently clad as those three hussies by the gate."

"It's the latest crack of fashion from Paris. Soon all the ladies of the *ton* will be wearing those gowns," said Darcy. "And after all, there really isn't that much difference between her and them. Only that she is of good birth."

Felicia's eyes widened. "You mean she—but she *couldn't* be."

"She is Cleary's current mistress," snapped Darcy, his brow darkening.

Felicia experienced an unpleasant shock.

Lady Palmer favored Darcy with a frosty glare. "You forget yourself, Vellacort. You are speaking in the presence of ladies and of his relation."

Darcy shrugged. "All the world knows Hermione took up with Cleary the minute old Silverdale popped off, leaving her with a pile of debts. Cleary can afford to keep her in style."

Felicia stared at the tall turbaned young woman with something like resentment stirring in her breast, a feeling she was quite at a loss to comprehend. After all, the earl's affairs were none of her concern. And she *did* know he had a *chère-amie*. It must have been for her that he had bought the necklace, she mused. Yes, it would have looked well on that long smooth neck.

Lady Palmer would have rebuked Darcy again, but fortunately an acquaintance came up to them, and Darcy escaped her sharp scolding.

In a short while Jerome returned. "I have procured for us a box," he said a trifle breathlessly. "And I also have a surprise for you, ma'am." And he waved a hand. A lady in a lavender gown and a turban with so many ostrich plumes that they threatened to topple the headgear from her head was leisurely advancing on their group.

"Barbara Planchard!" cried Lady Palmer, overjoyed. "Well, I never!"

"I took the liberty of inviting her to sup with us. I hope you have no objection, my lady," said Jerome.

"Objection? Objection?" Lady Palmer's countenance wreathed in smiles. "You dear boy, you know perfectly well I am delighted. One of my best bosom bows. But when did she return to town?"

"But recently, ma'am. I chanced to see her this morning and daringly offered to include her in our party."

The stately lady sailed up to them, and there was a brief moment of introductions and greetings, after which Lady Palmer happily withdrew with her friend a few feet away, while Jerome became engaged in conversation with a military gentleman.

Lester said to Darcy, "You know Lady Planchard, Vellacort?"

Darcy shook his head.

"She is a frightful quiz and the worst gossip in town, but she and m' mother are as thick as thieves. Once the two start chattering, they'll forget the world. Now ain't that clever of Jerome," he added with admiration and respect. "Hit upon the one notion that would give us all a chance to slip away unnoticed. What's more, she'll be too busy to wonder much where we are."

"You mean Jerome invited her on purpose to allow me—us—some freedom? Oh, isn't he the kindest person," Felicia cried, her heart warming again to her cousin. Indeed, she had so many things to be grateful for to Jerome.

Lester glanced about. "Think I shall toddle off now."

"Don't forget to join us for supper," said Jerome. "Our box is on the other side of the orchestra, quite close to the Cross Walk."

Lady Palmer began to stroll with her friend in the direction of the Cross Walk, casting backward glances to see if her charges were following her. But presently she forgot to turn back, and Lester began slowly to edge away from the group. Soon he was lost among the crowd surrounding the orchestra.

Jerome went off again, saying he had to speak to the waiter serving their booth, and Felicia and Darcy were left comparatively alone, lagging behind Lady Palmer and her friend.

"It was quite sporting of Jerome to go to all that trouble just to give us a chance to be together alone," said Darcy with appreciation. "Especially as I know he still has a *tendre* for you."

"Oh no, I wish you wouldn't say that," cried Felicia. Then she sighed. "Though I own I do think so also. And it makes me feel so dreadfully guilty. For he *is* such a good friend. I wish I could have returned his affection. But alas, I have none to spare. All my affection is . . . for you." She glanced down, then lifted her head to gaze shyly and lovingly into his eyes.

Darcy clasped her hand and carried it reverently to his lips. "That I should deserve your love," he said fervently.

"Alas, it is all that I have to give," said Felicia. "I am only too painfully aware how much better off you would be if you could marry someone with a fortune, or at least with a comfortable competence."

"Never, never say such things, Felicia. You know how much I love you."

"Yes, but that's just it. You're giving up so much for love. Think how comfortable you would be with a rich wife."

Darcy wished to protest again, but a friend of his came up and engaged him in conversation about curricle racing. Felicia, a trifle bored by the topic, wandered off a little, fanning herself and listening to the music of the orchestra.

Suddenly she dropped her fan. It fell into some shrubbery, and she was obliged, with a wary eye on her white gown, to go down on her knees in search of it.

When she finally retrieved it and lifted up her head, she found herself staring into the hard gray eyes of the Earl of Cleary.

# Six

Felicia's cheeks flooded with color, and her heart gave a disconcerting leap. From her kneeling position, Lord Cleary seemed to her like a giant towering above her—a handsome, powerful giant. She could not help noticing the rippling muscles of his thighs and legs, the broad shoulders under the bottle-green coat. Today he was sporting a moderately high cravat in place of his Belcher handkerchief, but it could hardly compare with Lester's intricate creation. Further proof that his lordship did not aspire to dandyism.

The earl reached down, clasped her hands, and helped her up. "Good evening, Miss Mannering," he said in an even tone. She felt his great strength in the pressure of his grip. "I hope you have quite recovered from your—er—indisposition," he asked politely. "You look the picture of health."

Felicia blushed even more, stammering her thanks. "Yes, I am fully restored to health. And I must thank you, my lord, for your kind interest in my welfare and for the flowers."

The earl bowed. "I trust Lady Palmer was not too surprised on finding out we had met already?"

"Well, she was, but I—I explained to her that I owe meeting you to my uncle."

An amused smile lit up Lord Cleary's gray eyes. "That was quite a clever way of putting it. I admire your sharp wits. Are you never at a loss in a tricky situation?"

"Oh, I am, frequently, but during my stay with her ladyship I have been obliged to sharpen my wits. It wouldn't do for me to make her cross."

"No, indeed. And I wish you were not obliged to live with her."

A thunderous applause as the orchestra finished a piece distracted their attention, and in the comparative lull that followed, above the hum of conversation, the strains of the dance music from the Rotunda were quite clearly heard.

The earl bowed. "Are you in the mood for dancing, Miss Mannering?" he asked with a quizzical expression on his countenance.

Felicia stared at him, astonished. "Are you—are you soliciting me to stand up with you?" she said.

He nodded. "I would be delighted if you could grant me the honor of allowing me to lead you out."

"Sir, you are forgetting that I am betrothed to another," Felicia cried indignantly, but she felt her heartbeat quicken.

"I'm just asking you to dance with me—a quite unexceptionable request, I assure you."

"And I have come here under the protection of Darcy and Lady Palmer. We are on our way to our box, and you are asking me to walk with you all the way back across the Grove to the Rotunda? No, no. You couldn't expect me to agree to *that*."

The earl sighed. "Alas, I knew asking you to dance would be an exercise in futility. Though you must believe me, leading you out would give me the greatest pleasure."

"Oh no! Not you too making up to Felicia. I won't allow it!" Darcy, an angry flush on his cheeks, rushed up to them. His countenance was so full of wrath, it wouldn't need much for him to call the earl out. Felicia's heart leaped with apprehension.

A tiny frown of puzzlement had creased the earl's face for a moment, then his countenance hardened. "It would give me great satisfaction to call you out, Vellacort," he said through his teeth. "But unlike you, I do have a sense of what is fitting, *and* a consideration for others. This is not the time or the place to embark on settling old scores, regrettably enough."

Felicia heaved a sigh of relief, and gratitude for the earl's forebearance welled up within her. Another duel would destroy all chances for Darcy's career—if he survived it.

The earl bowed to Felicia. "Do not let this altercation spoil your pleasure in the evening, Miss Mannering." He turned on his heel, strode off, and was soon lost among the crowd.

"How dare he ask you to dance?" Darcy cried, grinding his teeth. "You may be sure he did it just to provoke me. And I was not aware that you knew him," he added with deep suspicion.

"I—I met him through Uncle Edward," said Felicia, hoping Darcy wouldn't tax uncle with this information.

Darcy scowled, but the approach of Lady Palmer put a temporary halt to his angry outburst. However, as soon as they resumed their walk, Lady Palmer now ordering Darcy and Felicia to walk in front of her, Darcy, still seething with resentment, flared up at Felicia. "How could you even contemplate dancing with that man?" he snapped.

Felicia, strangely disconcerted and disturbed by her meeting with Lord Cleary, felt Darcy was being unjust. "I didn't contemplate it," she protested. "Oh, Darcy," she cried, "you must not let yourself be provoked to a duel. You must take care. You—"

"How *could* you encourage him?"

"But I didn't," she uttered with hurt and indignation. "I didn't. How can you ever think so?"

Darcy was immediately contrite. "Of course you didn't. Pray forgive me. I—I cannot help feeling jealous, for I love you so. Pray say that you forgive me."

"Yes, yes, I forgive you. But you must promise not to allow yourself to be provoked."

Darcy gave her a rueful winning smile. "I shall try. I must avoid any scandal," He heaved a sigh. "Let's forget Cleary, and hope that once Lady Palmer is ensconced with her friend in the box, she'll allow us to take a stroll, and while she isn't paying attention we can sneak off into the Lover's Walk. It's a splendid place for a tryst—no illumination at all. And I shall have you all to myself at last. How I have been waiting for such a moment!"

More he could not say, for Jerome joined them at this point, and Lady Palmer with her friend approached closer. They walked in a southeasterly direction, passing by some tumblers and magicians performing their feats, and emerged onto the walk adjoining the second crescent of supper boxes.

Now Jerome took the lead, guiding them past the row of booths almost up to the Cross Walk and to the box he had procured.

All the boxes were gaily painted and lighted by many colored lamps, giving them a festive appearance.

Lady Palmer was vexed at Lester's continuous absence, but once the refreshments arrived and she again became immersed in conversation with her friend, she relaxed and generously gave her consent to Darcy and Felicia's taking a stroll, only admonishing them not to stray from her sight.

Felicia and Darcy strolled about for a while, Felicia enjoying the sounds and sights of the Gardens. By then twilight had faded into night, the moon peeped from behind the clouds, and Darcy judged it safe for them to slip away.

Holding her arm, he propelled her quickly out of sight of Lady Palmer, then at a more leisurely pace led her toward the darkness of the Lover's Walk.

The Gardens now presented indeed an enchanting appearance. The myriads of colored lights twinkling in the darkness rejoiced the eye and the strains of the music and merry laughter the ear. But now also Felicia began to perceive what Lady Palmer had warned her about. A group of giggling girls passed by them hurriedly, pursued by two bucks. And two men already quite the worse for wear were weaving along the Cross Walk and singing in exceedingly unmelodious voices.

The tempo of merrymaking was increasing.

The Lover's Walk, at right angles to the Cross Walk, loomed shadowy and mysterious. Tall trees, meeting overhead, formed a thick canopy, further increasing the darkness. Darcy turned left, and soon they were swallowed up in the night. Only through the trees could they discern the winking colored lights in the rest of the Gardens. Here the darkness was deep—inviting intimacy and secrets.

Darcy gave a deep sigh. "At last. Now if we only can find a secluded spot."

At first, surprisingly, this seemed to present a problem. They encountered more giggling girls and rowdy bucks, and espied several couples in the shadows of the trees. But turning off into one of the smaller alleys, Darcy found an isolated bench, seated Felicia, and collapsed beside her.

"I don't know how I contrived for so long not to take you in my arms," he exclaimed. "Never have I seen you look lovelier or more desirable." And he promptly proceeded to embrace her.

As his lips melted into hers, Felicia allowed her repressed emotions free rein and returned Darcy's kisses with eagerness and abandon. After all, was he not her fiancé and would he not marry her soon?

But when Darcy's ardor seemed to get the better of him, and his kisses wandered below her neck and his hands became a trifle too free, Felicia recollected herself.

"No, no, Darcy, we must not," she cried, tearing herself away from his grasp. "It would be improper. We must wait until the wedding. And that is what I wished to talk to you about."

Darcy's arms, in the process of entwining themselves around her again, suddenly fell to his sides. Felicia could not see his face clearly, but she fancied he was frowning.

She rushed on quickly. "Darcy, I live in dread all the time, fearing I might say or do something that would incur Lady Palmer's displeasure, for she would take it out on you, influencing Lord Palmer not to give you the post. I cannot stand it any longer. Oh, how I wish we would marry and I could go to Vienna as your wife. In fact, I wish to marry you right now, even before you go to Vienna."

"Now, Felicia," Darcy cried in an irritated voice. "We have been through that before. I cannot afford to give you a proper home until I get the post. And even then, marriage for us would be out of the question. Don't you think I chafe under the present arrangement as much as you? But we must wait until I find my feet first in my post, see if Lord Palmer likes my work . . . oh, a thousand things must happen before we can tie the knot."

"But Darcy," protested Felicia, "it might be months before you get back from Vienna. I could not bear to be separated from you that long. As it is, I see you only occasionally. Why, one could almost say we are hardly acquainted."

"Well, we shall have a whole summer to get acquainted," soothed Darcy. "What with all the celebrations, the dragon cannot object if I take you to see all the parades and festivities, and who's to prevent us from slipping away somewhere to be by ourselves?"

"Oh, Darcy, clandestinely! It smacks of vulgarity. I wish to be free to be seen in your company whenever it pleases me."

Darcy was getting impatient. "So do I. But it is impossible at the moment. And we shouldn't now be wasting time on mere words." He wished to take her in his arms once more.

But Felicia was highly dissatisfied with him. "Darcy Vellacort," she said crossly, pushing away his encroaching arms. "I begin to suspect that you don't wish to marry me at all—that you just find it convenient to be betrothed, and you don't love me at all."

"Felicia, you hurt me deeply by such words. Of course I love you. I loved you from the moment I first clapped eyes on you, and I still do. Do but allow me to show you how much."

With a rustle of her cloak, Felicia jumped up from the seat.

"No, I don't wish any more of your lovemaking, not at present." She shouldn't be so cross with Darcy, she chided herself; but she couldn't help it. "Let us return to the box."

Darcy demurred, but Felicia was adamant, and reluctantly he followed her down the alley. They hadn't gone very far, however, before they encountered a girl in a low-cut muslin gown. Felicia couldn't be perfectly sure, for the moonlight penetrated here but little, but she fancied it was one of the three Cyprians they had encountered by the gate.

"Are you Mr. Vellacort?" she asked Darcy.

Darcy nodded.

"Your friend is waiting for you on the Italian Walk, by the first arch, wishing to speak to you at once in private, on a most urgent and important matter." And she thrust a piece of paper into his hand. "Here is the message."

"As if I could read it here," muttered Darcy, quite vexed. "Tell this friend to take himself to the devil."

But the girl was quite persistent. "I don't think it will serve. It's someone whom you apparently know very well, and I should heed this call if I were you."

"Well, I won't. I—"

"It won't take very long, I was instructed to say. And if it will make things easier for you, I shall stay with your friend here until you return."

Felicia, thoroughly vexed with Darcy and herself, said irritably, "Oh go, go. Perhaps I shall be in better spirits when you return." She shouldn't be left alone in the company of this girl, she reflected, but after all, *she* wasn't likely to make love to her, and Darcy would soon return. "Go, but return quickly."

"Oh, very well," exclaimed Darcy, quite peeved. "I shall take a shortcut through here." And he pointed at the stretch of the alley which lost itself among the shadows of the trees. "You stay here. I shall be back directly." And he strode off into the darkness.

"Who is this friend?" Felicia asked the girl. She wasn't the one with the yellow rose and she wasn't the elegant one, but she could have been the third one by the gate.

The Cyprian shrugged. "I'm sure I couldn't tell you. But you needn't fear. He won't be long. Is this your first visit to Vauxhall?"

Felicia nodded.

"And are you enjoying yourself?"

Felicia answered that she was. A few minutes of desultory conversation followed, after which Felicia's impatience got the better of her. "I think I should like to seek out Darcy," she said. "Why don't we stroll to the Italian Walk and meet him coming back?"

The girl shrugged. "As you wish, but I would advise you to wait."

"Well, I don't wish to wait," snapped Felicia. Her first taste of freedom in months, and she was to spend it thus? She felt very ill used. And why hadn't Darcy come back? "Pray tell me which way should I go. I would rather go by the main walk, but then we might miss him."

"We'll take the short cut," said the young woman, and led Felicia deeper into the dense grove.

They had gone a few yards up the alley when abruptly a loud clanging of a bell shrilled through the night, drowning out all other sounds.

Startled, Felicia stopped in her tracks. "What in the world?" she cried. But the girl grasped her by the hand and began to drag her off the path and in among the trees.

Felicia tried to wrench free. "What is it? What are you doing?" she cried, alarmed and bewildered.

"It's the nine-o'clock bell for the Cascade. We must

rush to be there on time, or we'll miss it. Everybody must run when the bell clangs."

"But I can't ... what is the Cascade?" she gasped out, running and trying to free herself.

"It's a water spectacle," shouted the girl, still running and dragging Felicia along. "There is a miller's house and a waterfall. We must hurry, or we'll miss it."

"But I don't wish to go there. Not without Darcy. I must find him first."

The girl abruptly released her hand. "As you please," she shouted, "but I won't be deprived of seeing the spectacle."

And she rushed off through the woods, heedless of Felicia's frightened call, "Wait, wait, don't go. Don't leave me alone."

Following upon the clanging of the bell Felicia now could hear the stamping of many feet, as other people apparently rushed to see the spectacle. What should she do? she wondered, worried and apprehensive. Yet Darcy must also have heard the bell and would be coming back to her. She would go to meet him. And she started on the run up the alley.

Soon she heard the pounding of feet behind her. Her heart leaped to her throat and began to hammer uncontrollably. It was very dark here, and she was alone. What if she was accosted by someone? Too frightened to glance back, she increased her pace.

The running footsteps behind her were gaining, and suddenly a heavy hand was clamped on her shoulder, spinning her around.

"Not this way to the Cascade, my pretty. Not this way," a rough masculine voice boomed. Terrified, Felicia tried to peer through the gloom. She could discern a tall figure in plain coat and breeches, a round face hiding behind a mustache and whiskers. Not a genteel person, of a surety. Felicia began to shake violently with fright. "P-pray, l-let me go, sir. I'm not trying to reach the Cascade," she gasped out.

The viselike grip did not slacken.

"You're right. Never had a fancy for it meself. What's

a stream of water compared to the sport we can have here?" And he laughed. Both the voice and the laugh were coarse and menacing. And the unmistakable fumes of alcohol assailed her nostrils.

Felicia's teeth were chattering with cold. It was this sort of thing Lady Palmer had warned her about. Oh no! Frightened as she was for herself, she instantly thought what this scandal would do to Darcy. It could, nay it would, ruin his career.

"Pray, pray, let me go," she begged. She might have saved her breath.

"No, no, my pretty. I have a fancy for some sport. I can see you've never been broke to bridle. It'll give me pleasure to train such a fresh young filly as you."

"I am *not* a horse, and you are revolting," cried Felicia, and immediately was aghast at what she had said. Fear and despair lent her strength. She gave a mighty wrench and tug, tore herself free, and, terror-stricken, fled down the dark garden path.

But the amorous villain was hard at her heels. In no time at all he had overtaken her, and his rough meaty arms wrapped themselves around her body. Mindful not to attract attention to herself, Felicia still could not help emitting a piercing shriek before he clamped his hand over her mouth.

From somewhere close by she suddenly heard sounds of laughter and shouts and squeals of fright and delight. The man freed her mouth, thinking the revelers might come this way. "One peep out of you, and I shall knock you out," he hissed.

Yet Felicia, trembling, screamed "Help!" In vain . . . the laughter and squeals were receding.

"Ain't no use screaming. They'll just think it's all pretend, like theirs," the man said savagely. "So you might as well resign yourself to your fate."

"Never!" cried Felicia and shrieked again for help. But other cries were now mingling with hers. The sound of music had picked up also. And the intoxicated ruffian was holding her fast, his strong bearlike embrace pinioning her to his body.

Where is Darcy? The question flashed desperately through her mind. She struggled furiously trying to escape, kicking and clawing to break free.

Pressing his hand over her mouth, the man began to drag her deeper into the woods. Felicia felt her senses reel. Panic and despair held her in a firm grip. It seemed she was powerless to free herself. There was no escape, no rescue for her. She was doomed—doomed to a dreadful scandal, and Darcy was doomed to ruin. Everything began to whirl about her, then went black. And she went limp in the arms of her assailant.

# Seven

Lester Winwood, glad to have escaped his mother's eagle eye and having spent some agreeable time with his cronies, suddenly recalled the Cascade and thought it behooved him to return to the box, to help guard the ladies during the rush to see this water spectacle. Though why people should be in transports over such a trifle, he couldn't fathom.

He was sauntering along and had just rounded a corner when his eyes started from his head at a sight, and he blinked. Was it possible? Or were his eyes deceiving him? After all, the two engaged in a somewhat heated conversation were quite a distance away. Yet he was almost certain the man was Vellacort. Yes, now he was sure it was Vellacort. But the girl with him was definitely *not* Felicia. She was one of those three high-flyers they had seen at the gate, the plumper one, with the yellow rose in her hair. A pretty enough filly, but not, of course, to compare with Felicia.

What was he—oh, no! *Now* he knew why the girl had seemed familiar to him before. She called herself Tessy and she had been Vellacort's inamorata. No, it was the outside of enough! Poor Felicia. Still, the fellow wasn't married to her yet, and he definitely was not a monk.

But where was Felicia? Banister had told him that

Vellacort had taken Felicia into the Lover's Walk. So what was he doing *here*, dallying with his former inamorata? And who was looking after Felicia?

Lester Winwood had stopped in his perambulations, frowning, tugging at his earlobe, and wondering whether he should go ask Vellacort what he had done with Felicia. Then an acquaintance interrupted his musings, and when he extricated himself from the conversation and looked around for Vellacort, he and the girl had disappeared.

Lester swore and stood there helplessly, frowning and wondering what he should do next.

"Why the frown?" a familiar voice hailed him.

Lester, startled, looked up at the handsome countenance of Lord Cleary. There was a sardonic glint in the earl's gray eyes. "Are you contemplating returning to your estimable parent? I assure you there is no need. She is amusing herself tolerably well with her friend."

Lester shook his head impatiently. "It's not m' mother I'm thinking of, it's Felicia—Miss Mannering. Look on her as m' sister. Don't wish her to get into a fix."

The earl's dark brows snapped together. "How so? Why should you be concerned? She is in good care. Vellacort is looking after her."

"That's just it, he ain't. Saw him just a moment ago with—with—now don't blab about it—" the earl raised a brow sardonically—"with the dasher he was once involved with. And Banister has told me Vellacort had taken Felicia to the Lover's Walk. So if Vellacort is not with her, where is she? Alone in the Lover's Walk, with all those foxed bucks and cits on the loose, accosting her, and she as much fit to defend herself as a lamb. Could he have taken her to the box first?"

The earl's countenance grew stern. "We must make sure if he did. Much obliged to you, Winwood. Keep this matter to yourself but tell Banister. Get him to help you search for her. Above all, don't let on about your misgivings to Lady Palmer or that gossip bosom bow of hers. Or the whole town will be aware of Miss Mannering's 'indiscretion' yet tonight." And he strode purposefully off down the walk.

"Where're you going?" called out Lester Winwood after him.

"To do Vellacort a good turn," the earl replied and hastened off.

Lester Winwood stood in the middle of the walk, deliberating where to go next, unconscious of being jostled by revelers. Then suddenly the nine-o'clock bell began to clang and he was almost knocked off his feet as the surge of humanity made for the Cascade.

"They'll mill her down in their mad rush," he muttered worriedly, thinking of Felicia in the midst of the wild charge.

He stood a trifle aside, letting the stream of people rush past him, trying to recall which way Banister had been heading when he had seen him last. He must have been making for their box. And Lester set off at a fast pace toward the box also, reflecting with some dismay that his mother would be vexed that he wasn't there to escort her to the Cascade.

Halfway there, he espied Jerome Banister in conversation with a lady. Lester's eyes widened as he recognized Zemelda. Is she casting lures at Banister? he wondered. She'll catch cold at that. Even if he were the type to keep a ladybird, he could hardly afford *her*.

The next moment Banister detached himself from her and hurried forward. Lester buttonholed him. "The very man I wished to see. I must speak to you."

Banister seemed unwilling to be stopped. "Very well, but I am a trifle in a hurry. Already I was detained by a chatterbox I couldn't get rid of. So be quick about it. And if it's Lady Palmer you're worried about, she has decided against going to see the Cascade."

"Glad to hear it," Lester said with relief. "Banister, have you seen Felicia?"

"No why? I told you Vellacort has taken her to the Lover's Walk. I doubt if we shall see them before supper."

"He *may* have taken her there," said Lester with some

asperity, "but he ain't there with her now. I just saw him now with that former high-flyer of his. I don't know what he was about, but he must have left Felicia unattended. We must find her."

Banister's countenance grew long and concerned. "Yes, we must find her before—before it's too late." He bit his lip. "I'm off to Lover's Walk to search for her." And he hurried off.

"Banister. Oh, I say, Banister . . ."

But Banister was not paying him any heed.

"I only wished to tell you," muttered Lester unhappily to himself, "that I fancy Cleary is looking for her there already." He shrugged and also made as fast as he could toward the unlighted part of the Gardens.

Felicia regained consciousness to the sensation of being carried in an ungentle way. She stirred groggily, and at once the person who was carrying her stopped. Raising her head, she stared into a shadowy bearded face. Memory rushed back, and terror flooded her heart. No, no, it could not be. It was a nightmare and she would wake up from it presently. "P-pray let me go," she croaked, a fit of shudders raking her body.

"Oh ho, so you have come to, my fine lady. No, no. I shan't let you go. Not yet. But no need to be in a quake. I shall treat you gently."

Felicia's horror knew no bounds. His hot alcoholic breath was on her face. *He* would treat her gently! Oh God! She would be disgraced forever. Lady Palmer would cast her off, Lord Palmer would be forced to wash his hands of her and of Darcy. Darcy's life would be ruined. No, no!

"Help!" she screamed in panic, kicking out and pummeling the man with her fists. But her blows did not seem to have much effect. 'Oh ho, so you still want to fight, do you?" he roared.

Summoning all her strength, Felicia contrived to land a trifle stronger blow, to his eye, and while he howled with pain and relaxed his grip for a moment, she tore herself away and slipped to the ground, stumbling and falling and picking herself up. But he pounced upon her the next moment, his arms twining themselves about her again.

Felicia screamed once more and kicked and flailed her arms, struggling to break free. She could taste the panic in her mouth. And as he was about to stifle her cries with his meaty hand, she jerked her head and sank her teeth into its flesh. The rogue cried out with pain and swore at her, but his hold on her did not slacken.

"You little redheaded vixen. I vowed to treat you gently, but I've just forgot my vow."

"Let me go," panted Felicia, as she struggled on. Her cloak had fallen off in the struggle, and now the flimsy cloth of the bodice of her gown gave way. "No, no!" she cried. And the next moment she went reeling back, landing up against a tree, banging her head painfully. Stunned, her chest heaving, she grabbed at the tree for support.

When she caught her breath and contrived to look up, she saw her assailant being felled with a well-directed blow to the jaw from none other than that great sportsman the Earl of Cleary.

"Lord Cleary," she gasped out in gratitude and surprise. She could just discern his features in the moonlight, and she fancied he looked rather grim.

"Miss Mannering, are you hurt?" He was by her side in a trice, supporting her in his strong arms.

"I—I—no. But my gown . . ." she managed to stammer out.

"Have you a wrap or a shawl with you?"

"My cloak. But—but I don't know where I've lost it." She was still shaking violently. Quickly Lord Cleary removed his elegant coat and wrapped her gently in it, then seated her on the ground beneath the tree. "Don't be afraid—he won't come around for a while. I'll look for your cloak. Call me if you hear someone approaching."

"Don't, oh, pray don't go away," Felicia said in a weak voice. But her shudders were abating somewhat.

Lord Cleary's movement was arrested. He turned back to stare at her. This time she could not see the expression on his face.

"Pray be easy. I shall remain within hearing. If I can't find your cloak soon, we shall have to do without it."

Fortunately he soon found her cloak, and he lifted her up and slipped it around her shoulders. "Can you walk?" he asked her gently.

"Yes, yes. I think so. I daresay I am bruised, but nothing to signify. Oh, Lord Cleary, pray help me to avoid a scandal. It would ruin Darcy's chances forever."

"I shall help you to avoid a scandal," the earl said grimly, "not for his sake, but for yours. That *he* should possess your love!" he said savagely under his breath. "Leaving you alone here, at the mercy of any drunken yokel."

"It's not Darcy's fault, truly it isn't. You must believe me," protested Felicia. "It—it just happened." She began to shudder violently again.

"There, there, it is all over, you mustn't be afraid anymore," he soothed. But when her shivers would not stop, he gathered her in his arms, cradling her against his strong body, and the warmth and the strength of him seemed to flow through her, bringing soothing relief. And slowly her shivering subsided. She heaved a deep sigh and stepped out of his arms.

"Thank you, my lord. I am better now. I am very much obliged to you for coming to my help. If you hadn't chanced to come by at this precise moment . . ." She shuddered anew.

"Don't think on it," he admonished her quickly. "Try to act a trifle collected. Now remember, you have become separated from Vellacort during the rush to the Cascade. And I hope that damned idiot will have thought of the same excuse. I beg your pardon, but this is intolerable—his placing you in this situation."

"But it was not his fault," insisted Felicia, fretting at the earl's misapprehension. "Truly it wasn't. It was the fault of some friend of his who wished to speak to him. And my fault for urging him to go."

The earl gave an impatient oath. "One thing you have said that I'll wager is true. It was partly the fault of that so-called friend of his. However, it's beside the point now. We must reach your box before Lady Palmer becomes aware that something went amiss."

"Oh yes, pray take me there with all speed. But—but what if Darcy comes looking for me here?"

"Do you know the place where he left you? He would return there."

"Not precisely. We were in one of those side lanes, but I'm not certain which one."

"Then there is no point waiting for him here. It would be best if we could intercept him, but we can't start looking for him now." He was piloting her toward the winking lights of a lighted walk.

"You should do something about your hair. It is a trifle disheveled." He was looking at her critically in the darkness.

Felicia bethought herself of her small reticule, which was still hanging at her waist. "If only I could have some light. I have a small brush and mirror with me."

"This place is dotted with summer houses. I shall take you to one of them." And as Felicia involuntarily cried "No!" he added sardonically, "Surely you won't ascribe to me the motives of that drunken rogue who attacked you? I know it's improper for you to be found with me alone here, but it cannot be helped. We must just hope that we are not observed."

Felicia sighed. "Pray forgive me. My thinking is still a trifle muddled."

"And it's not to be wondered at."

They traversed the garden in silence, and in a very short time the earl was guiding her to a kiosk. He lifted off a lamp which was hanging outside of it and lit up the interior. Felicia, sinking gratefully onto a bench, tried to straighten her disordered hair, but her hands trembled so much that she couldn't quite manage it.

The earl hung up the lamp on one of the ornaments decorating the kiosk. "Pray allow me," he said gently. And taking the brush from her, he proceeded, with an expertise which betrayed an indecent knowledge of feminine matters, to set right her coiffure.

Felicia's pulses quickened. For some inexplicable reason she found the feeling of his hands in her hair exceedingly pleasant.

Working in silence, his hands gentle and deft, the earl quickly and efficiently brushed Felicia's tumbled locks and confined them with the silver ribbon. Only once he spoke up. "You have very beautiful hair, Miss Mannering. Any dresser would be proud to take care of it," he said.

The coiffure completed, he turned to the gown. Gently pulling away the folds of her cloak, which caused her to shrink back involuntarily, he observed the torn bodice. "Do you have some pins in that reticule?" he asked. "If you were to pin up the rip I fancy it would not be so noticeable, and with the cloak over your shoulders, you will be quite passable."

Felicia did as he advised her, and very soon she pronounced herself tolerably well groomed. The earl pulled the cloak closer about her, returned the lamp to its place, and led Felicia, now much more composed, out of the summer house.

But though outwardly she was composed, Felicia's heart was still tumultuous, her breathing a trifle fast. Gratitude toward the earl overwhelmed her. Indeed, having had another example of his kindness and generosity, she could not now believe that he would treat Darcy in an underhanded way. No, his threats of revenge must have been just empty talk, coming from a grief-stricken heart. As for Darcy, she was somewhat vexed with him for not showing up in time to rescue her, though no doubt he had a good reason for it.

They had emerged now on what she recognized as the Cross Walk. The merrymaking was continuing, and the groups of revelers were growing more and more boisterous. But nobody seemed to mind, except perhaps people of Lady Palmer's stamp, thought Felicia.

"I do hope they have not yet set up a hue and cry for me," she said worriedly. Lady Palmer would be very angry indeed. "You see, she had warned me—" She broke off and bit her lip.

He pressed her hand reassuringly. "Don't be so cast down. We shall brush through it tolerably." Then he added savagely under his breath, "If somebody had told me yesterday that I would be doing Vellacort a favor, I would have told him he was all about in his head. I doing a favor for my brother's killer."

There it was again, thought Felicia in despair. Though she didn't think now he would harm Darcy, she fervently wished he would disabuse himself of this notion that Darcy had killed his brother deliberately.

"I wish I could make you believe—"

The earl stiffened. "No. Pray don't try to convince me."

"I know perfectly well I cannot. Only somebody who had seen it all could convince you."

"Are you still thinking of that nonexistent servant in Barnet?"

"Yes. And I am persuaded he does exist. I shall soon go to Barnet myself. I'm sure I can discover where that man, that witness, is living now."

The earl stopped to look at her. In the light of the lanterns she could see that his handsome countenance was set in a heavy scowl. "You would go to all that trouble for him?"

"He is my fiancé, and I love him," she said simply.

The earl uttered a savage oath. "He does not deserve your love—but I know we shall never see eye to eye on *that* score. Damnation! I wish there were somebody that could take care of you," he burst out.

"Well, I do have Uncle Edward and Jerome. They both do what they can for me, though I own it would be more comfortable to reside with kin. But alas, the only other relation I have is in Jamaica, and he may be dead for all I know, for he never answered my aunt's letter."

The earl pricked up his ears. "Jamaica, Jamaica . . . yes, now I do seem to recall. A distant relation, but a trifle closer connection of yours than Banister is. It would be to your advantage to become acquainted with him. Why don't *you* write him a letter?"

Felicia gave an amused chuckle. "Oh no, now you sound just like Lady Palmer. She has been after me to find his address among my aunt's possessions."

"And have you found it?"

"No. Try as I might, I couldn't. But it's of no consequence. Darcy will take care of me when I marry him."

Lord Cleary's mouth tightened. "And when will be that happy event?" he asked with heavy sarcasm.

"I—I'm not perfectly sure. But soon, I hope. It would be difficult for him to marry me now, at once, before he gets his post."

"Impossible," said the earl categorically. And added, but in such a low voice that Felicia wasn't sure if she had heard right, "Thank God."

The lights of her box loomed in view. And Felicia shivered with nervousness as she and Lord Cleary approached closer. Lady Palmer and Lady Planchard were still talking, seemingly not unduly perturbed. Lester was standing beside them, and on seeing him, the earl frowned.

"Good evening, Cousin Beatrice, Lady Planchard," the earl said, bowing and leading Felicia into the box. Felicia noticed that Lester, catching sight of them, visibly relaxed, mopping his face with his scented handkerchief.

"Evening, Cleary," said Lady Palmer, while Lady Planchard gave a nod. Lady Palmer's sharp eyes bored into Felicia. "You were supposed to remain within my sight all the time," she said severely. "And where have you lost Vellacort? I trust you two men did not come to cuffs?"

"Nothing of the sort," answered Lord Cleary lightly. "I don't know where Vellacort is. Miss Mannering became separated from him during the rush to the Cascade, and I, chancing to see her alone, thought I should fetch her to you."

"Very proper, and very remiss of Vellacort not to watch over her," her ladyship said with strong censure. "But that is so like him. No sense of responsibility at all. And he wishes for a diplomatic career!"

Felicia's heart leaped in apprehension. Oh, if only Lady Palmer would not cause trouble for Darcy.

"This Cascade thing is nothing but a take-in," Lester said. "Grossly overrated. As for Miss Mannering's becoming separated from Vellacort, I shouldn't wonder at it at all. I'm glad, Mother, that you haven't tried to see the Cascade today. Why, I was fairly knocked off my feet and trampled upon when the bell started clanging."

Lady Palmer looked slightly mollified, and Felicia sighed with relief, casting Lester a grateful look. Perhaps the punch had mellowed her ladyship temporarily, she thought.

But Lady Palmer hadn't finished yet. Taking a sip of her punch, she again condemned Felicia's fiancé for not taking better care of her and Felicia for allowing herself to be led out of her sight, and then thanked Lord Cleary for looking after her charge.

"I would invite you to sup with us," she said to the earl, "but I doubt you would accept."

"Sup at the same table with Vellacort? I should say not," he said harshly. Yet he seemed loath to depart, though he took his leave of the ladies. He was still asking Lester some questions about horses, when a breathless Jerome rushed up to the box.

"Lady Palmer, my lady—" he began, his usually composed demeanor betraying his agitation. Then he caught sight of Felicia and blinked. "Felicia, thank God," he exclaimed. "I—I saw Vellacort alone, and I—"

"Felicia!" Darcy's anguished voice was heard, and they all transferred their gaze from Jerome to him.

Darcy seemed breathless and disheveled and very distraught. "What has occurred? I have been looking everywhere for you." His gaze turned from her to the interested circle of faces in the box, and he frowned at the sight of Cleary.

"After we became separated during the rush to the Cascade," Felicia said quickly, forestalling any other explanation on his part, "Lord Cleary, fortunately passing by, restored me to Lady Palmer."

"But—but—you were sup—you should have waited for me," Darcy said, his countenance turning red with anger. He glanced at the earl again, and the two men exchanged angry looks, before the earl, bowing once more to the company, strode off.

"If you had looked after Felicia better, Cleary wouldn't have been obliged to step in," Lady Palmer said sharply. "So let us hear no more of that. *You* were at fault and should count yourself lucky that Felicia met up with Cleary and not with some drunken rogue." There were a few more words in that vein, as Darcy grew even angrier and was unable to put a word in edgewise. Then Lady Palmer, refreshing her throat with another sip of punch, said, "And now, Banister, I wish to have my supper. Summon the waiter."

But Jerome, before doing so, said in a low voice to Felicia, "You have given me such a turn. I was frantic with worry about you. I knew where you and Darcy had gone, and I was extremely concerned. I was looking for you, and—"

"Dear good Jerome," cried Felicia, warming up to him. "How kind you are to me. But nothing untoward has happened. Lord Cleary saw to that."

"But how did it come about? For I do not believe—"

"Pray, Jerome, not now. Later."

Jerome nodded. "Just be assured that your welfare is very close to my heart," he said earnestly.

"Your heart and Cleary's," Darcy, overhearing him, said with a sneer, before collapsing onto the seat beside Felicia, while Jerome moved off to confer with the waiter.

"You should have waited for me," Darcy said in an irate whisper to Felicia. "You should not have gone off.

Never do so again. You could have spoiled everything with your heedlessness."

"I, heedless?" No, this went beyond all bounds. Never had Felicia felt less in charity with Darcy than at this moment. Here she was doing all in her power not to bring disgrace upon his head, and it had been *she* who had been the injured party, *she* had been left alone and unprotected.

She took a deep breath. "I shall explain later," she said, casting a meaningful glance in the direction of Lady Palmer. "Truly the whole thing was not my fault."

Darcy relaxed. "Of course it wasn't. Pray forgive me. But seeing you again with Cleary . . . and where did he find you?"

*"Darcy!"*

"Oh, very well, said Darcy sullenly. "But if that fellow is to turn up every time I take you out somewhere—"

"Darcy, you are jealous," cried Felicia.

"Of course I am jealous. Who wouldn't be? You are so dashed desirable, Felicia." He cast an uneasy glance at the two older ladies and, fearing to betray what they would call unseemly ardor, steered the conversation to a safer subject.

Soon, the waiter came with the food, and the supper part of the evening passed uneventfully. Lady Palmer wondered a little why Felicia had chosen to keep her cloak on, but she paid more attention to the ham shavings and the green goose than to her. The rest of their time was spent in strolling about, admiring the paintings of Hogarth and Hayman in the Great Room, listening to a singer, and watching the fireworks explode in the night sky.

The orchestra from the Rotunda beckoned Felicia to take a turn on the dance floor, but she did not dare to throw off her cloak. In any case she was in no mood for dancing, and could not enjoy herself now as she had hoped to. Her terrifying ordeal was still fresh in her mind, as were Lord Cleary's and Darcy's actions.

Not feeling the least bit grateful to the earl, Darcy found his rescuing Felicia extremely irritating. Since this irritation obviously arose from strong feelings of jealousy—even though there was not the slightest need for him to be jealous of the earl—Felicia should not have found fault with it. Yet it irritated her that though he professed his impatience to have her to himself, he did not offer to curb his gaming and practice a little economy so as to be able to marry her at once.

Above all, it vexed her to own that her beloved Darcy had shown himself in a poorer light than the earl. True, she herself had urged him to see this friend, so she had no cause to complain about being abandoned. Yet when she had told him that she had been accosted by a drunken brute, though he was properly shocked and angry and begged her pardon, he seemed to be more concerned with the potential scandal than with her hurts.

But perhaps it was just her overwrought nerves that made her think he was not properly concerned. After all, he could hardly take her in his arms and kiss away her fears and hurt, as he reasonably pointed out to her. And there was no opportunity for them to be alone and unobserved. If it wasn't Lady Palmer, it was Jerome or Lester, who constantly kept her in sight, and Lord Cleary's tall figure hovered disturbingly somewhere on the perimeter of her vision most of the time. Only when the fireworks started did she lose sight of him. So it was quite worn out with vexing and conflicting emotions that Felicia at last and thankfully returned after midnight to Berkeley Square.

The only comforting thought she had brought with her from this outing was the feeling that Lord Cleary would not deliberately seek to destroy her fiancé.

Alas, she was soon to discover that her comforting conclusion was much too premature.

# Eight

Felicia, in her blue sprigged muslin gown and blue spencer with her Lavinia chip hat tied with a blue ribbon in a bow under one ear, was standing by the window of her bedchamber, waiting for Lester's soft tap on the door.

Having convinced herself she had shown too much pique, she was no longer vexed with Darcy, and their good relationship was reestablished. But she was going to Barnet, for though she did not think now that Lord Cleary would deliberately seek revenge on Darcy she still deemed it important to erase the enmity and misunderstanding between them. If she did not, sooner or later the two men would come to cuffs, and she shuddered at what the consequences of this would be for Darcy's chances for a political career.

And she had not much time to track down this missing witness, because the royal guests would be arriving in London on the seventh of June, and there would hardly be an opportunity for any searching then.

Yet Bertha was not enamored of the venture. "It's not my place to say it," she said after a loud sniff, "but I do hope Lady Palmer won't discover that you're driving out with Mr. Winwood. It wouldn't do to set up her ladyship's back. And her as cross as crabs already, on account of being obliged to have all those new gowns made for you—even though his lordship has ordered her to do so and it's he who will pay for them. It must have quite astounded her ladyship that he wishes you to go to the Carlton House banquet. One would think with all the fittings and shopping and the prospect of dining at Carlton House and being presented to royalty, you wouldn't have a thought to spare for this notion of Barnet."

A hardly audible knock on the door prevented Felicia from responding to her maid. Bertha, with a sigh, went to the door, opened it a crack, then nodded to Felicia.

Clutching her reticule, Felicia rushed to the door to meet Lester, nattily attired in a coat of blue superfine, pale primrose pantaloons, and a green-and-pink embroidered waistcoat. But though he obviously had taken pains with his attire, he was ill at ease and kept casting glances over his shoulder.

Bertha, who had instructions to say her mistress had a headache and not to allow anyone into the bedchamber, shut the door, while Lester, taking Felicia's arm, tiptoed with her toward the servants' staircase.

Abruptly, from below Lady Palmer's strident voice could be heard, and Lester froze in his tracks. Felicia could not make out her words, but leaning over the railing, she observed the butler's stately walk and heard him say, "No, madam. I believe Mr. Winwood has already left." Whereupon he passed out of sight and the door from the saloon was shut.

Lester went limp with relief at their narrow escape. Felicia, peering over the railing once more, couldn't see anyone. And silence again settled in the hall. "Come, let us go quickly," she whispered. And she pulled the unnerved Lester down the servants' stairs. But they haven't passed all the danger points yet. As they were nearing the kitchen they heard footsteps and were obliged to retreat hastily up the stairs.

Once the sound of footsteps died away, they made a run for the side door, and emerged onto the alley, Lester bathed in perspiration and blinking both ways to check if somebody was watching them. But for the moment nobody was within sight, and he hastened with Felicia toward his curricle, waiting in the lane with his groom, who could be trusted to keep quiet.

With less gallantry than was his wont, Lester helped Felicia to climb onto the box of the curricle and sprang up himself. Then, dismissing the groom, he gave the horses the office to start. Not until they were well out of sight of Berkeley Square was he able to relax.

But their exit was not as unobserved as they had supposed. A caller at the front door of Lady Palmer's house was watching them drive off with a puzzled frown, before the door opened to admit him and he disappeared from view just as Lester turned his head to glance back.

Lester sighed with relief. "Phew! That's over! Now if only we don't meet up with an acquaintance."

But though the streets were thronged with people, Lester and Felicia were spared the embarrassment of seeing someone who knew them.

The signs of the oncoming royal visit were everywhere. Streets were being swept; pennants, flags, bunting, and welcome signs were put up; people from out of town, arriving early for the festivities, thronged the streets. The city was acquiring the air of a country fair. A troop of colorful dragoons was marching somewhere, and mailcoaches and stagecoaches bursting at the seams with people and luggage were arriving constantly.

"Such a bustle already," complained Lester. "It will take us longer to reach Barnet than I had thought."

"No need to fret," soothed Felicia. "Lady Palmer will be too busy to look for me before evening. We shall be home long before that, I daresay."

"Let us hope so. I shudder at the consequences of Mother's discovering our jaunt. We both would be in the basket then. Why, she would think I was making up to you then for sure. And now more than ever I need to be in favor with her. I've just ordered two more coats and waistcoats, and the tailor wishes to see some blunt. You know how hard it is to make her loosen the purse strings. And I've just contrived to cozen her into giving me a larger allowance next month, on account of all the expenses incurred because of the state visit. Can't have her go back on her promise now."

Felicia cast him a sympathetic look. "Poor Lester. I do wish you had control of your own money."

"No use wishing for what can't be. Waste of time. But that's why we must be very careful and return as speedily as we can. Don't think we shall tarry long in Barnet. Dashed waste of time going there."

Felicia had her own notions about that, but declined to dispute with him the value of their search.

Once out of town, she enjoyed the drive and the fresh country air, and though the roads were more crowded than usual, they made good progress without meeting anyone they knew. Sooner than Lester expected, they turned into the yard of the posting inn in Barnet, and Lester helped her to alight from the curricle.

It must have rained just before they arrived, for deep ruts crisscrossed the yard and large puddles glistened in the bright sunshine. Several vehicles stationed about the yard gave the place an air of bustling activity.

While Lester was relinquishing his curricle and horses to the care of a groom, Felicia whispered, "Oh, Lester, do ask him about this witness now."

"What? Here in the yard?"

"Why not? There's nobody within earshot."

Lester grimaced. "Oh, very well. But I'll feel dashed silly."

"Then I shall—"

"No, no." He cleared his throat. "One moment, my good man."

The groom turned around. "Yes, sir?"

Felicia tapped her foot impatiently while Lester went about his questioning in what she thought was much too painstaking a way. In the end all they discovered was that though the man had been working here on the day of the duel, he hadn't witnessed the event. Two other men, Johnson, an ostler, and Sam, the tapster, who might have witnessed the event, were no longer working at the inn, and he did not know their directions. But the landlord should. And the maid, Nancy, who had been sweet on the tapster, might know his address too.

"You talk to the landlord and I'll question the maid," said Felicia, her green eyes sparkling with excitement.

"It wouldn't hurt to have some refreshments first," said Lester. "My throat's dry from all that talking."

The rumble of an oncoming vehicle was heard, and a lumbering post chaise rounded the bend. An ostler ran forward to meet it. As he made a dash across the yard past Lester and Felicia, paying no attention to the mud puddles, his big boots hit in the middle of a particularly large muddy pool, splashing water and mud over Lester's impeccable primrose pantaloons and Felicia's gown.

Lester gave a cry of horror, throwing up his arms. "My pantaloons! They are ruined! That dashed clumsy oaf!"

Felicia, calmly taking out her handkerchief, dabbed with it at the mud on her gown. "Use your handkerchief, Lester," she said, biting her lip at his tragicomic countenance.

"A handkerchief won't help," moaned Lester, producing it nevertheless and touching it delicately to a mud spot. "Must get somebody to clean them—at once." He started for the inn with Felicia. "You can wait for me in the private parlor."

But a maid at the inn, promising to fetch the landlord, informed them that the private parlor was occupied by a gentleman having his meal. "Be pleased to come into the taproom," she invited.

The taproom was noisy with guests and travelers, and Lester, eyeing it with disfavor, said, "Can't leave you here alone. I'll just nip across to the private parlor. Perhaps the man is almost finished with his meal. You take a seat here by the door." And he trotted off, casting a dismayed glance at his muddied pantaloons.

It was then Felicia realized that Lester knew his way about the inn. He must have stopped here when calling on Darcy at his estate near Barnet.

She beckoned to a passing waiter. "Is Nancy, the maid, on the premises?" she asked.

"She's in the kitchen, ma'am."

"Pray fetch her to me," said Felicia. She couldn't just sit and wait and do nothing.

In the meantime, while Felicia was getting ready to question the maid about the missing witness, Lester was opening the door to the private parlor across the hall.

As he pushed open the door, he sucked in his breath and his eyes started from his head in consternation. A voluptuous demi-rep in a low-cut yellow transparent gown, an enormous yellow rose in her hair, was being fondled and kissed by a gentleman in a wine-red coat, fawn pantaloons, and gleaming Hessians. And that amorous gentleman was Darcy Vellacort.

# Nine

Lester Winwood slammed the door shut, the noise startling the two, and they sprang apart.

"What the devil are you doing here?" Darcy Vellacort said, surprise and anger ringing in his voice.

"More to the point, what are *you* about?" said Lester with asperity and a censorious expression on his usually amiable countenance. "Felicia's in the taproom."

"Felicia? Here? Were you bringing her to call on me?"

"No, no. No time to get into that now. You get rid of *her* fast, before Felicia pops in here. Ain't never seen her in a fit of the vapors before, but I shall if she casts her eyes at you two." He shuddered dramatically, then glanced at the remnants of a meal. "Now ain't that just like you. Why don't you dine at home?"

"You know damn well I can't afford to keep a cook at the manor. The only servant I have is old Dobbs, who has nowhere else to go."

Lester now rounded on the Cyprian. "And you shouldn't be chasing after him. Leave the fellow alone. He's betrothed now."

The blond girl tossed her head pertly. "What concern is it of yours?"

"Vellacort, get her out of here, *and* out of town," cried Lester Winwood, much incensed.

Felicia's betrothed seemed to have realized at last the danger of the situation. He grabbed the Cyprian by the arm, then hesitated. "I wish to know what Felicia—"

"Yes, yes. You stash *her* away somewhere out of sight, then come back. We'll still be here." But privately he was hoping for the opposite. Really, Vellacort was beneath contempt, thought Lester, as Felicia's betrothed disappeared with his *chère-amie* through the window of the parlor. Couldn't even conduct his affairs with discretion. Dashed loose screw.

His glance fell on his pantaloons, and he promptly forgot Vellacort. He trotted out to get help and to tell Felicia she could now stay safely in the parlor.

He almost collided with her in the corridor. "Oh, Lester!" She pounced on him in excitement. "I've talked to that maid, Nancy, and it's the tapster who witnessed the duel. And he is the innkeeper's son. She wouldn't give me his direction, but the innkeeper will give it to you, I'm sure. He must know you. Let's talk to him right now."

Lester gazed at his mud-bespattered pantaloons. "They are ruined," he moaned.

"Lester Winwood, are your pantaloons more important to you than Darcy's welfare?" cried Felicia.

And to her surprise she heard Lester exclaim in an unwontedly angry tone, "I wish you wouldn't be so dashed concerned over his welfare." He was immediately contrite. "Beg pardon, but—but—" He couldn't tell her that her precious Darcy wasn't worth her concern. "Ain't no reason to be so worried, and here my pantaloons are ruined, and we must hurry back before Mother discovers what we have been up to."

Felicia relaxed, giving him a rueful smile. "It is I that should beg your pardon. It is because of me that your pantaloons are ruined and you stand in danger of angering your mama. Indeed, I have been dreadfully selfish."

"No, no," Lester said quickly. "No such thing. Perfectly understandable. You're in love with Vellacort. But no reason to worry. Oh, very well, let us go into the parlor and talk to old Stoddart. Then you wait for me there, while I have my pantaloons attended to."

The portly ruddy-faced innkeeper was reluctant at first to tell them where his son was working now. But at last he divulged that Sam Stoddart was now working in a tavern in London. But he did not remember the name of the place.

"And where is this tavern located?" asked Lester.

The innkeeper kneaded his greasy apron in his hands. "I don't rightly know, my lord, where it is. Lunnun is full of taverns."

"Are you telling *me*," Lester said with a snort. And in an aside to Felicia, "You don't expect me to dash from one tavern to another—with the town so crowded with people—looking for a needle in a haystack."

"But you *must* know his direction," Felicia said irritably to the landlord. "What if you wished to send a message to him?"

The innkeeper looked at the ceiling as if he could see the address of his son written there. As no inspiration came, he scratched his head, and mumbled something unintelligible.

"Speak up, man," cried Lester, who was fast getting quite tired of the whole business. "In what part of town is it situated? You must know that, at least."

"Ah yes." The innkeeper's face brightened. "That I know. Now let me see." He screwed up his eyes, then stared at the ceiling again. "Yes. Covent Garden, now I recall. Close to the market. It's . . . yes, it's the tavern on the corner of an alley off Maiden Lane."

"Thank goodness," cried Felicia. "Lester, do you know the place?"

Lester pulled at his earlobe. "Fancy I do. At least I know where Maiden Lane is."

"Much obliged to you, Stoddart," he said, and wished to pay the innkeeper for his information. But to his surprise the man refused his money. Lester cast him a suspicious glance, but pocketed the coin; and when the man left, he said, "Well, we have settled that quickly enough. Now to see to my pantaloons and then home."

"Home? Oh no. We must go to that tavern. It's in London, so it shouldn't take—"

"Oh no, we *don't*. I ain't going to that pub today nor tomorrow either. And neither are you."

"Lester!" cried Felicia, astonished and outraged.

"And don't you Lester me. I don't object to tooling you to Barnet, but I'll be dashed if I'll trust myself into the part of town full of cutthroats and pickpockets any time of year, let alone now. Why, do you know what it's like, with all the men drinking to the end of the war, and the tsar coming in a few days? It's just setting yourself up to be robbed or worse. I'd as lief take a walk at night on Hampstead Heath."

"Is it such a bad part of town? I didn't know."

"I know you didn't. For one, you haven't gone anywhere; for another, ladies ain't supposed to know things like that."

"Yes, but perhaps it wouldn't be so dangerous now, with everybody in such a good mood."

"Yes, and the pickpockets in a good mood for picking pockets, I daresay. I have no fancy to have *my* pockets picked, even though they're practically to let. Nor do I fancy being bashed on the head. As for you—showing your face among the riffraff there—why, it's unthinkable. *You* can't go at all."

"But Lester—" protested Felicia weakly.

"No. 'sides, there ain't time. You have to be fitted for your new togs, and so do I. And you have to buy hats and I don't know what else besides. Told me so yourself. And once the royal visitors arrive, there won't be time for anything but going to parties and parades and such. Much better to go after they've gone and the town returns to normal. Ain't no reason to be in such haste. I promise I'll find Sam Stoddart for you, after the royal visit."

"I suppose there really is no need to be in such a hurry to find this tapster," said Felicia, sighing. "But I *must* go with you. I wish to question him myself."

"But I just told you . . ." Lester began with exasperation. Then he shrugged. "Oh, very well. We'll go together."

"Oh, Lester," cried Felicia. "Oh, I do thank you so much. You indeed are all that is amiable and obliging. I am ever so grateful to you."

But after he had gone to attend to his pantaloons, Felicia was beset with doubts. Had Lester promised to take her along only to stop her from plaguing him, and thinking she would forget all about this notion? Did she dare go there herself or even with Bertha? Well, time enough to decide on that, if Lester went back on his word. And with this problem disposed of to her satisfaction, Felicia settled back in good spirits to wait for Lester.

Although it would be *so* good if they could go to this tavern yet today, she mused, her impatience still riding her.

She was still thinking of that possibility when a well-known tread was heard outside the door of the parlor and Darcy, after only the briefest of knocks, burst into the chamber.

"Darcy!" Felicia exclaimed, jumping to her feet and rushing to meet him.

"Felicia!" Darcy stepped forward and promptly took her in his arms. And his lips sought hers in a most satisfying kiss.

It was Felicia who recovered first, pushing away from him. "No, no, Darcy, we mustn't," she said, casting a fearful glance around the chamber. But of course they were alone.

"Why not? It's a golden opportunity. Just for that I'm glad Winwood has brought you here." He wished to take her in his arms again, but she evaded him, darting behind the table and putting it between him and herself.

"Why are you here? Winwood wouldn't tell me," Darcy asked.

"Poor Lester. All he can think of is his mud-spattered

pantaloons." She smiled, then grew serious and bit her lip. "Promise you won't be vexed if I tell you?"

"Why? What are you up to?" asked Darcy with suspicion in his voice, a deep frown marring his handsome features.

But Felicia rushed on, "Oh, Darcy, I do so wish to make sure that nothing will spoil your chances with Lord Palmer. And I have discovered that Lord Cleary believes that duel wasn't quite an honorable affair, and he doesn't believe Jerome's testimony, but I am persuaded he *would* believe this tapster who was the other witness. That's why I came here with Lester, to search for him, and we have his direction. It's a tavern, in London. And Lester promised to go with me there, but I believe he won't.· Oh, Darcy, would you go with me there—today? Think how much more comfortable we all will be if Lord Cleary is disabused of his notion."

Darcy, who was watching her with tightening lips and deepening scowl, now exploded.

"Have you lost your senses?" he shouted, all loverlike demeanor evaporated. "Must you stick your nose into something no lady should know about? Going to see this man is out of the question!"

Felicia sustained a severe shock. Never had she seen Darcy so fiercely angry. "But Darcy," she quavered, blinking, "I only wish—"

"I know what you wish. You wish to ruin me," he said bitterly. "First that thing at Vauxhall, and now this. You wish *me* to go with you to this man—"

"If I go with you, nothing very much can happen to me," Felicia said automatically, still numb with shock. "Oh, Darcy, how can you say I wish to ruin you? I love you so. And I only wish to protect and help you." Slowly she lowered herself onto a chair as if her legs were no longer able to support her.

Darcy's grim expression vanished in an instant. He knelt at her side, grasped her hands, and· kissed them passionately. "Forgive me, my darling. I know that you love me. God knows why, but you do. But don't tease yourself." He paused as if to choose his words carefully. "There is no need to go to all the trouble. I don't give a groat what Cleary thinks of me. As for that gossip about his revenge, it's just talk. He hasn't done anything yet to harm me, and he won't." His brow darkened. "Just you stay away from him," he cried irritably.

"But Darcy, you have no reason to be jealous. I love you and only you. I just don't want Lord Cleary to ruin your chances."

Darcy was immediately contrite again. "Pray forgive my insensible words. And don't put yourself in a taking over this whole matter. Let me worry about it. I shall go to see this man myself."

But suddenly Felicia knew he would not.

"Why don't you wish to see him and have him talk to Lord Cleary?" she asked, a horrible suspicion stealing into her heart. "Surely you cannot be afraid of the truth," she added on a whisper. Then she tossed her head resolutely. "No, you couldn't have killed Marcus in an underhanded way. I *know* you couldn't."

Darcy seemed to be strangely moved. "That you have so much faith in me," he said, awed. He pulled himself together and gave a lighthearted laugh. "No, I did not murder Marcus deliberately, not to my knowledge," he said jokingly, and Felicia relaxed. For a moment there she had almost committed the unforgivable, entertained a hideous suspicion of her beloved.

But she was still puzzled. "Then why don't you wish to seek this man?"

Darcy, rising, kissed her tenderly on her white brow. "Because I'm not sure if he would be willing to help me. More the opposite. You see, he was afraid that because he had helped me in the duel, he would have trouble with the law; that's why he fled Barnet and gave up his good post at his father's inn."

Yes, *that* made sense to Felicia. And if the post he had now was so much inferior . . .

"So you let me be the judge of what is best to be done. And don't worry. Forget all about Cleary and this witness, and for God's sake don't cajole Winwood into taking you to see him." His brow furrowed. "He shouldn't have brought you here, but now that he did, we can use this chance to spend some time together alone, something that I wished—"

"Oh no, you shan't!"

Lester, his amiable countenance quite red, and his pantaloons cleaned of the mud, stood on the threshold.

"And I knocked. But you didn't hear me. Felicia, you cannot allow him to persuade you into any clandestine conduct. You are under my protection, and I shan't allow Vellacort—"

"*You* won't allow . . ." Darcy took a step toward him, an ugly look on his countenance, a menacing fist raised up.

Lester Winwood paled and took a hasty step backward, bumping into the door he had just shut.

"Darcy!" cried Felicia and rushed between him and Lester. "You're not going to fight *Lester*."

Darcy's fist opened up and his arm lowered. "I beg your pardon, but he should leave us alone."

"No, I won't," maintained Lester. "It would be most improper. And we must hurry back."

"He is right, Darcy," said Felicia. "It would be improper for us to stay here, but even were I inclined to disregard propriety, I dare not incur Lady Palmer's wrath—on account of you. You know what would happen were she to discover I had driven out with Lester."

Darcy frowned, then sighed. "You *are* right. We mustn't set up her back, especially not now. I'm to present myself to Lord Palmer soon."

"Oh, Darcy, you are going to get the post!" cried Felicia, overjoyed, and she would have rushed forward to embrace him, but for Lester's presence.

"I have high hopes," said Darcy. "So much as I regret to give up such a good opportunity of being alone with you, you had better return to London with Winwood."

And return she did, with Lester springing his horses all the way, and glancing at his watch from time to time. But fortunately their arrival at Berkeley Square went unnoticed, and Felicia could congratulate herself on the relative success of her mission.

During the drive home, thinking over her conversation with Darcy, she had found another reason why he did not wish her to seek out this witness. He didn't wish her to contact Lord Cleary, because he was jealous, and he didn't wish to do it himself, because of his pride. He didn't wish to seem to be trying to appease the earl. Thus she explained Darcy's conduct to her satisfaction.

She also realized that it would be useless to ask him again to seek out this witness. She would be obliged to wait with her investigation until after the royal visit.

But to see the sense in leaving the matter of the witness for later was one thing, and to wait till later was another. And if Felicia had not been so busy with fittings and shopping and had not had such a hard time enduring Lady Palmer's megrims and scolds, she would have fretted much more about being obliged to wait awhile before presenting Lord Cleary with the proof of Darcy's innocence. But the days passed all too quickly, even for her, and at last the day all London was waiting for dawned—the day of the royal guests' arrival.

Jubilant masses had gathered in the streets since dawn with flags, banners and signs waving, and all the windows on the route of the royal procession were crammed with people too. Such a crush London had not experienced in memory. But the crowds were to be disappointed at first, for the tsar had circumvented the prescribed route, arriving at Pulteney's Hotel in Piccadilly, where his sister the Duchess of Oldenburg was staying, by a different route and unnoticed. Of course, as soon as the people realized what had occurred, a great jubilant cheer went up and the tsar, an amiable handsome man, according to Bertha, who had contrived to catch a glimpse of him, was obliged to go out on the balcony to greet them.

"Such huzzas and shouts as you never heard in your life," said Bertha. "And then General Blücher—the crowds went wild on seeing him too, so Cassel tells me."

She straightened the skirts of Felicia's gown. "It's not my place to say it, but I can't commend Lady P.'s taste. I wish she had not ordered that red velvet trimming on the gown."

Felicia, standing in front of the mirror, heaved a sigh. Those were her sentiments also.

But the gown, high-waisted, and with puff sleeves, was in every other respect the best she had ever had. Of very fine costly pale-green satin, so fine it felt like cobweb to the touch, with a delicate darker-green net overdress, the soft gown accentuated her perfect figure and went well with her red hair and green eyes. Only the trimmings of red velvet ribbon at the bosom and sleeves she could have done without. The rest of the ensemble was quite satisfactory also—long white gloves, white satin slippers, a green reticule, and a new French shawl, a present from Lord Palmer, which Bertha now draped round her shoulders.

The green gown was square over the bosom and low-cut—though not as low as those she had seen at Vauxhall—and her white neck was adorned with Uncle Edward's ruby-and-diamond necklace. She couldn't get out of wearing it *this* time. Surely, Lady Palmer had said, Felicia wasn't afraid it would get stolen at Carlton House.

"Perhaps if I cover it with the shawl, nobody will notice that it's paste, and I suppose they'll all be looking at the guests, not at me. But I still wish I weren't wearing it."

"I'm sure you don't need to worry, miss," said Bertha. "Nobody will think it's paste, and nobody will notice." Bertha straightened the ribbon threaded through Felicia's red hair, left in soft curls in the front and gathered and falling down in becoming ringlets at the back.

"And here's your fan, miss," she said to Felicia, handing it to her.

Felicia, at least outwardly, was ready for the Regent's banquet.

But she was not to attend it until the following night.

To her and everyone's surprise the banquet had to be postponed, because Tsar Alexander refused to go to Carlton House that day. With the banquet all prepared and the Regent and his retinue waiting for him for hours, he decided to dine at his hotel. So other invited guests, including a very vexed Lady Palmer, had perforce to dine at their own homes too.

Felicia thought that this action of the illustrious guest was quite outrageous. Alas, she was soon to discover that her own countrymen—at least one of them—had no match for outrageous conduct.

# Ten

Carlton House shone like a bright jewel against the night sky. Light from the many brilliant chandeliers streamed through its many windows, scarlet and yellow flares were set between palm trees in brightly painted tubs, and the pillars of the edifice were hung with thousands of lanterns. To Felicia the Prince Regent's glittering residence seemed like a fairy palace.

The vast marble entrance hall with its porphyry columns struck her as quite elegant. And she particularly liked the Crimson Drawing Room with its blue velvet carpet, depicting the order of the garter. Yet the more she saw of the residence, the more she was overwhelmed with all the glitter and could understand why some people regarded the lavish decor as a bit too much.But it did somehow conform to her mental picture of what the inside of a fairy-tale palace should be. And filled as it was now with ladies in their best attire and gentlemen in uniform or court dress, the whole presented a kaleidoscope of color and light, changing dazzlingly before her eyes. Still, after a while all the color and glitter, the gold, crystal, and shining mirrors, became as overpowering as the stifling heat in the chambers, causing her head to ache and whirl and making her wish longingly for the cool restful green of a garden.

Yet if the palace seemed to her lifted from a fairy tale, the florid-faced, portly, jewel-bedecked Prince Regent, the diamond star on his coat blinding the eye, was hardly the epitome of a Prince Charming, although his manners were quite affable and he spoke to her kindly, complimenting Lord Palmer on the beauty of his "ward."

But the protracted sumptuous meal, which had at least a hundred dishes, was a somewhat stiff and awkward affair, in spite of the prince's attempts to put everyone at his ease, for the queen cast a pall over the glittering assembly with her stiffness and adherence to her rigid etiquette.

The tsar—a young elegant blond man in bottle-green uniform trimmed with gold and decorated with diamond stars—looked bored, the gaunt, melancholy King of Prussia impatient. Only Blücher, the bewhiskered jovial old soldier, seemed to be enjoying himself.

After dinner the queen presided over the assembly in the Throne Room, an imposing chamber made even more so by the many ostrich plumes waving above the silver helmets of the high canopy. Felicia, after making her curtsies and being introduced to several members of the *ton* by Lord Palmer, was left alone with Lady Palmer, as Lord Palmer and Lester had wandered off to talk to their acquaintances.

It was only now that Felicia espied the tall impressive figure of Lord Cleary. Her heart leaped at the sight of him. How magnificent he looked in his court dress, consisting of a dark-green velvet coat, white silk stockings, black florentine silk knee-breeches, and dazzlingly white waistcoat, which Felicia much preferred to Lester's, which was also white but richly embroidered with gold. But even at the distance she could perceive how grim Cleary looked, as if he wished to run somebody through with the sword at his side. Was it because his plans had to be changed? wondered Felicia.

Somebody spoke up to her, and she turned away,

and when she looked for him again he was lost in the crowd.

Felicia, standing a trifle aside from Lady Palmer, wondering if she would see the earl again, let the flow of conversation all around her pour over her ears in an unceasing stream. And while she fanned herself, flushed and perspiring in the now unbearable heat of the chamber, she wondered if the stiff points of Lord Cleary's shirt collar were wilting just like those of the gentlemen nearby.

Abruptly she felt somebody stare at her, and turning around, she saw with surprise the tsar quizzing her unabashedly. Her cheeks grew even warmer, but the emperor's roving eye passed on to another comely young lady. Felicia turned back and found herself being ogled by the Prince Regent. Embarrassed, she strolled out of his sight, searching for a door or a French window to escape the heat.

"You are aiming high, Miss Mannering," said a hostile voice, startling her. She whirled around, suddenly breathless, her heart pounding. "I saw the tsar quizzing you, and then you were trying to catch the eye of the Regent," continued Lord Cleary. "But if you think you can supplant Lady Hertford, you are much mistaken."

Felicia's jaw dropped. Despite her bewilderment and shock she managed to say with tolerable composure, "I *beg* your pardon."

"It is a trifle too late for that," he said with heavy sarcasm and a sardonic curl to his lip. "After lying to me so brazenly, and after what I now know you did to my brother." His cold gray eyes fairly glittered with suppressed anger. "I am not surprised that Marcus was quite taken with you. You present an exquisite picture," he said with a sneer. "What a pity that such a lovely facade hides a shallow, lying heart."

Lying? She? What about?

"You must have windmills in your head, my lord," she exclaimed. Ahh. He must have been dipping even more into the Prince Regent's maraschino or the wine. How else could he accuse her of casting eyes at royalty?

As for what she did to his brother . . . she? That was the most incomprehensible of all.

"I think that the heat and the wine have addled your brain, my lord. You should seek the garden to cool off," she said acidly. Her surmise that he was quite foxed was confirmed when she caught a whiff of his breath.

He bared his teeth. "An excellent suggestion. I should like nothing better than to seek out the garden—in your company." He seemed to be laboring under some strong emotion and controlling himself with difficulty. He took a deep breath. "I'm sure Lady Palmer will entrust you to my care." And without more ado, he went to speak to his cousin.

Felicia considered fleeing. But where to? She would only run into more complications. Already she was being stared at by a portly gentleman bearing a strong resemblance to the Prince Regent. She fancied he was the Duke of Clarence.

Would Lady Palmer permit this impropriety? Should she beg her not to? She would make the attempt.

But the earl was already by her side, and taking her firmly by the arm, he began to lead her through the crowd. Felicia, who had been fanning herself vigorously, willy-nilly followed him. To resist the pressure of that strong hand, to struggle, would have meant to attract unwelcome attention.

"I'm surprised at Lady Palmer's allowing you to take me to the garden," she said in an irritated tone.

"I have explained to her that you're about to swoon from the heat," said the earl. And he was not far from the truth, thought Felicia. But it had been clever of him, she could not help admitting. Having Felicia collapse in a swoon in the middle of the Throne Room wouldn't have been at all to her ladyship's liking.

He seemed to be well acquainted with the Regent's residence, for he drew her unerringly through several splendid chambers and the Gothic Conservatory—more like a miniature Gothic cathedral—to the velvety lawns of the garden.

As soon as she stepped over the threshold and the fresh cool air flooded over her overheated body, she greedily drew in deep breaths and involuntarily cried, "Aah, this is better, much better."

"I did not take you here to make you feel better,' he snapped. "On the contrary."

"Why then did you drag me here, my lord?" she asked stiffly, freeing herself from his grip.

The earl appeared nonplussed for a moment, the moonlit sky and the lanterns allowing her to discern his features. His lips were tightly pressed together, his brow furrowed, the whole expression singularly grim and unyielding.

Why had he dragged her out here? It was a good question, Lord Cleary mused. He gave a soundless bitter laugh. Fool that he was, he wished somehow to discover what had possessed her to lie to him, above all to discover that in some mysterious way he *had* been mistaken and she hadn't lied to him after all. A futile hope.

"I want an explanation from you," he finally said. "An explanation of the fact that it was you who were primarily responsible for my brother's death."

"What?" Felicia was stunned. The man had lost his senses. No doubt about it. His grief for his brother had proved too much at last. "My lord, you are a prime candidate for Bedlam, and I won't stand here and listen to such insulting nonsense."

"Do you deny it then?"

"Of course I deny it. I haven't the faintest notion what you are talking about. I hardly knew your brother. I've met him scarcely a few times."

"Yet you cast lures to him just the same."

"I never did," cried Felicia, much outraged, sparks of wrath in her eyes. "How could you come to such an erroneous conclusion? Who could have told you such hideous lies?"

His lip curled disdainfully. "Very pretty. But you won't convince *me* with your histrionics. Fair Cyprians know well how to lie, and they *are* Cyprians whether they are of good birth or of the Covent Garden variety." But Vellacort must have blamed Marcus for the whole, he thought. And murdered him. If only that duel had been an affair of honor, he, Cleary, could have accepted the loss of his brother with less anger, though no less grief.

His hands balled into fists, the nails digging deep into his palms, but he did not feel the pain. If only he had been more interested in Marcus's affairs in those last few months. But he had been so busy on the estates. The curricle race that Marcus had undertaken to run with Vellacort—had Vellacort wagered on that race heavily and then regretted it, and being afraid of losing, killed Marcus to avoid the race? No, it could not be. And yet . . . regardless, he *had* killed Marcus. And this beautiful jade standing in this outraged pose before him had led his brother to his death.

Abruptly he realized she was speaking.

". . . for you are well acquainted with them. But I am *not* of Hermione Silverdale's stamp, and I think you're beneath contempt to utter such gross insults and absurdities." Her voice vibrated with indignation, and her large green eyes looked daggers at him.

"Absurdities, are they now? he said in biting accents. "Can you deny that you were present in Barnet on the night of the so-called duel?"

Felicia was taken aback for a moment. "How did you know of it? But no matter. Why should I deny it? Yes, I was there, hoping to prevent the curricle race. I wish to heaven I had been there in time to prevent the duel."

"A likely story. So you admit to being in Barnet. And you cannot deny that you knew my brother."

"Only slightly."

"Only slightly," Lord Cleary repeated with a sneer. "I wish to heaven it had remained that way." He recalled now Marcus's joyous face and his enthusiastic praise of Miss Mannering's beauty, his saying that it would be so easy to fall in love with her.

The earl ground his teeth in impotent rage. He knew to his own sorrow how easy it was, imbecile that he was.

She had appeared to him so innocent, so guileless, so wholly convinced the duel was a fair fight. Yet all the time she must have known the full hideous truth, all the time she had been lying—so glibly and convincingly. And he had believed her.

"I can understand Banister's lying about the way my brother met his death, but that you—that *you* could do it," he could not help exclaiming.

Felicia stamped her foot in anger, her eyes blazing with wrath. "I did *not* lie to you. Darcy killed your brother in a fair fight, and I shall prove it to you. I have discovered the whereabouts of that tapster who witnessed the duel, and I shall go to him at the earliest opportunity and fetch him to you and—"

The earl, on the point of uttering a sharp remark, was diverted, staring at her in surprise. "*You* have discovered? How is it that my groom didn't do so?"

Now it was Felicia's turn to stare. "Your groom? Have you sent him to Barnet to make inquiries? I thought you did not believe that a witness existed."

"I had changed my mind—after Vauxhall. I decided that it wouldn't do any harm to investigate further, and I sent my groom. He it was who discovered that *you* were present there on the day of the duel."

"Oh? Well, I have made no secret of it. I daresay that's why you did not get the man's address, because you sent your groom. You should have gone yourself. But you are so convinced Darcy murdered your brother, you're not really interested in making any further inquiries. You're not interested in the truth," she said bitterly.

"I know the truth," he cried. "Vellacort did murder my brother. Oh, he might have had provocation, or thought he had, but it was murder just the same. And I won't allow his murderer to go unpunished. Oh yes, I know the truth—and I know the truth about you."

Felicia wished to speak up, but he bore on inexorably in a hoarse voice, "At best, you are a shameless flirt and a liar. At worst, a heartless jade, who connived to hush up murder."

Felicia's wrath had boiled over. "No, this is the outside of enough! How dare you keep on calling me such names? You are the most odious, insulting, detestable, toplofty, stupid man of my acquaintance, and it seems to me a great pity that it was not you Darcy killed but your brother!"

A strange light leaped into the earl's eyes. "Believe me, Miss Mannering, no one regrets this circumstance more than I," he said in a quiet repressed voice. And suddenly for an instant, in spite of her outrage, Felicia could not help pity welling up within her. Obviously he was still grieving bitterly over his brother's death, and the grief must have addled his brain. And the constant drinking accompanying the peace celebrations would hardly help him to think clearly.

She took a deep breath, trying to control the quivering of her body and her wildly pounding heart. "Since, I collect, it is useless to make you see reason or endeavor to still your insulting tongue, I shall remove my presence, which is so obnoxious to you, and I trust our paths will never cross again."

And lifting her skirts, she rushed back to the palace.

The rest of that night seemed to Felicia like a nightmare. By the time she found her way back to the Throne Room, with the help of a scarlet-and-gold-attired footman, she had recalled the danger of scandal and contrived to pull herself together. But though she appeared outwardly reasonably composed, her mind and heart were in turmoil. All her worry about Lord Cleary's revenge on Darcy returned in full force. And added to it was her outrage at his unjust accusations. What made him think she had cast lures to Marcus? She should have asked him that. She had intended to ask him. But how could one converse calmly with the earl? And it was plain that only the testimony of that witness would convince him. She must seek out that tapster tomorrow. When she told Lester how urgent the matter was now, he would go with her to this tavern.

In a fever of impatience, Felicia could hardly wait for this night to end. And though she was exhausted and had a severe headache when she returned to Berkeley Square, it was only toward dawn that she contrived to fall into an uneasy slumber, to awake when the sun was high in the sky.

To her dismay she discovered that Lester, who had indulged in too many libations the night before, had incurred the wrath of his mother, and as punishment she had sent him to Palmer Court, their country estate, on a trumped-up errand. Felicia could not bear to wait for his return. Could she turn to Uncle Edward or Jerome? But Uncle Edward wasn't home. She was just on the point of sending Bertha with a message to Jerome in spite of her fears of wounding his feelings when he presented himself in Berkeley Square.

Fortunately Lady Palmer had gone out, and Felicia pounced on him the minute the footman ushering him into the Red Saloon had left the chamber.

"Oh, Jerome, I am so glad to see you," she exclaimed with relief.

Jerome bowed low over her hand. "I am highly flattered, cousin. I fancied you would be so caught up in dissipation that you wouldn't have a thought to spare for old Jerome."

Felicia reddened. "I always have a thought to spare for my best friend," she said hastily. "Lady Palmer is from home. Did you wish to see her, or me?"

"Both of you, I suppose. Although the matter concerns primarily you."

Noticing his suddenly somber mien, Felicia cried out in alarm, "Has something occurred with Darcy?"

"No, no, it's not about Vellacort. It's about Uncle Edward's necklace. Somebody who saw it last night claims it's paste. Naturally I have told Sir Edward about it, and he does not believe it. But I persuaded him to have it appraised. For if it is paste indeed, it means that somebody must have stolen it and substituted a replica. In that case we should call in Bow Street Runners."

Felicia, listening to his tale with growing dismay, said

irritably, "On no account must he call the law. That's what I was afraid would happen, once I wore it in public. *That's* why I didn't wish to wear it."

Jerome stared at her, much astonished. "You *knew?* But how could you—"

"*I* had it appraised. But Jerome, don't you see, Uncle must have done it himself—sold it and had a replica made and then forgotten about it. You mustn't cause him embarrassment and worse, by probing into the matter."

. Jerome shook his head. "No, no. He couldn't be *that* forgetful."

"Well, that is the only explanation I could come up with. But that's not important now. After all, whose concern is it if I wear a fake necklace? I have something much more important to talk to you about, and a great favor to ask of you. Pray sit down." And she seated herself on the sofa.

"I am quite at your disposal, cousin, you know that," said Jerome. "What is it? You seem overset," he added with solicitude.

"Oh, Jerome, I am so worried. I think Lord Cleary wishes to take revenge on Darcy after all."

Jerome did not seem disturbed by this intelligence. "Oh? And what makes you think so?" He seated himself on the sofa beside her, crossing his legs. "You were full of praise of him not so long ago."

"I—I talked to him last night, at Carlton House. We had words. It was something he said that makes me so worried. And he doesn't believe anything *I* say. But I know how to convince him. Jerome, I have discovered where that tapster from Barnet can be found—"

"You have what?" cried Jerome in great consternation, almost jumping up in his seat. He stared at her as though thunderstruck.

"Oh, pray, pray, do not feel offended," begged Felicia. "*I* believe in your tale implicitly. But Lord Cleary doesn't. He thinks you might be protecting Darcy. The tapster wouldn't have reason to do so. And so I conceived a plan to find this other witness, and I know where he is, but I cannot go there alone. It's a pub in Covent Garden."

"You mean he's here, in London?" asked Jerome in an even tone, relaxing back against the cushions of the sofa. He seemed to have recovered from his astonishment.

Felicia nodded. "Oh, pray, Jerome, do take me there."

"I collect you went to Barnet with Winwood to inquire after the man. It was fortunate that only I saw you drive off with him."

"Yes, oh yes," echoed a surprised Felicia fervently. And shuddered. "So do not be offended, and do go with me there now." She looked pleadingly into his face.

Jerome possessed himself of her hands and pressed them warmly. "My dear, I would do anything for you," he said earnestly. "And I am not offended in the least. I know you believe in me. But, my dear, it is out of the question for you to go to that part of town—even with me. Especially at this time. You must contain your impatience until after—"

"Yes, yes, I know, after the royal visit. Lester said the same thing."

"I assure you there is no need for such haste. Now, if we had known sooner—" He broke off, recollecting himself, and clamped his mouth shut.

Felicia pounced on him. "Known sooner? Why? What could it have prevented? Oh, Jerome, pray tell me."

Jerome said quickly, "No, no. Of course it could not have prevented anything. Besides, I cannot be sure it *was* Cleary who introduced Vellacort to Lord Berry and his set."

"Who are they? People who gamble a great deal and drink?"

"Something of the sort. But you needn't worry about Vellacort. He is steering clear of their larks. Indeed, I am pleasantly surprised at how cautious he is these days."

"Oh, you relieve my mind greatly. But I still wish to go to that tavern."

"My dear, you *cannot* go there. No lady of quality would dare set foot in those slums. But don't be in a taking over it. I shall go there myself and discover everything I can, then tell you, and we shall decide then how to proceed."

Felicia sighed, knowing herself beaten. Men were so stupid sometimes, she thought. And she didn't think Jerome would do it, at least, not without delay. She would just have to go alone with Bertha.

But Lady Palmer's claim on Felicia's time precluded her venturing out on her search, although the following day she contrived to have a word with Uncle Edward. He promised to go with her to the tavern, though he also assured her that she had nothing to fear for Darcy from such an upright gentleman as Lord Cleary and could take part in the celebrations with an untroubled heart.

Lester, when he returned to London, would not even listen to her schemes, not at all believing any urgency of finding this witness existed.

Yet in spite of these reassurances, Felicia was not in a mood for celebration. Even the intelligence that several balloon ascents were planned from different London parks failed to divert her mind or ease her agitation. But it was on the day of the Guildhall parade—a day when she had at last contrived to relax a little—that her wish to clear Darcy became a most urgent need, and her desire to save him caused her to throw all caution to the wind in order to accomplish her goal.

Most of that day was spent in an agreeable manner. First she, Darcy, and Uncle Edward went to Hyde Park to see a balloon moored there. Then they watched the splendid parade to Guildhall. It was only later in the evening, after parting from Darcy, that she accidentally discovered he would be racing Lord Cleary to Barnet the following morning, on a wager. And if Darcy lost the race and the bet, he would probably land in a debtors' prison.

Felicia, cold with fear, was sure he would lose, and

was in despair how to prevent the race. Lester, when she begged him to do something, commiserated with her, but said nothing could be done. And her urgent messages to Jerome, Darcy, and Uncle Edward as well as Lord Cleary himself went unheeded, for the men were not at home. If only she could convince the earl he had no reason for his revenge on Darcy! Felicia was sure the race was his way of revenging himself on her fiancé.

But Lester had informed her that evening—in a much aggrieved tone—that the innkeeper had deliberately given them the wrong direction of his son. The Earl of Cleary, who had gone looking for Sam Stoddart at that tavern in Covent Garden, had discovered that the man wasn't known there at all. So that meant Felicia would be obliged to go to Barnet again to obtain the right direction. And even if she could go tonight, there would not be time to seek out Sam and fetch him to Lord Cleary before the race.

Felicia, near panic, thought of Lord Palmer. But he might not like Darcy's racing on a wager, so better he never found out about it; or if he did not mind his racing, he would not try dissuading Darcy from the race. In any case, he had not yet returned home either. What was she to do?

Bertha offered a consolation. "Wait till the morning. After a good night's sleep you will know better how to go on."

But Felicia refused the laudanum Bertha had brought her. She must not oversleep. For she had decided that early tomorrow, before the race, she would attempt to plead with Lord Cleary once more. Perhaps he would be in a better mood, and perhaps she would succeed.

Thus resolved, she at last fell into an uneasy slumber—while in another part of town, Tessy, the blond Cyprian with a yellow rose in her hair, was making plans of her own.

# Eleven

Morning dawned, bright and breezy. The sun peeped in through the curtained windows of Felicia's bedchamber. Felicia arose early but did not call Bertha. Bertha had also suggested talking to Lord Palmer about the race, but he had sent word from Guildhall that he wouldn't be coming home that night, and had ordered his valet to fetch his things to him at Carlton House. And when Felicia had told Bertha about wishing to call on Lord Cleary early in the morning, Bertha had tried to dissuade her from the notion. Felicia had come to the conclusion that Bertha would not be sorry were Darcy to lose the wager and land in debtors' prison. So Felicia would not tell Bertha she was going to the earl, and would go alone. It would take too much time and bother to make Bertha obey her, and besides, Felicia was cross with her and didn't wish to see her. As for going to the earl alone, she was beneath contempt in his eyes, so one more impropriety wouldn't matter. And Grosvenor Square was not Covent Garden. Also, if she *could* persuade him to postpone the race . . . anything would be worth it. She had not been able to avert disaster the other time. She *must* do so now.

Thus she hastily donned her green muslin gown, threw her cloak over her shoulders, and let herself—

fortunately unobserved—out through the side entrance. The cool fresh air felt good on her hot aching brow, and she breathed in deeply as she hurried down the lane and into the square.

Deciding not to take a hackney, she turned left into Mount Street, then up Charles Street, and hastened toward Grosvenor Square.

Her heart pounding in anticipation of crossing swords with his lordship, she banged the knocker on his front door.

But she was to be disappointed. The butler who answered her knock at first stared at her with suspicion. Then as she told him who she was and he, blinking, recognized her, his icy mien thawed a little.

"I regret to inform you, miss, that his lordship is from home," he said.

Felicia's heart sank. "But—but—at this early hour?" she stammered. "I made sure he would be still abed. Where did he go?"

"His lordship is an early riser, but . . ." He frowned. "I shouldn't be telling you this, but this is quite singular. He received a message early this morning, which necessitated him to repair to Hyde Park, to the place where the balloon is moored."

"The balloon?" echoed Felicia, astonished. "What on earth? It's too early yet for the lecture."

"Exactly, miss. Most singular and unusual. I mislike this circumstance a great deal."

"That is a puzzle indeed. Well, thank you, Rawlins. I am much obliged to you. Perhaps I shall seek him out there."

The butler's countenance thawed even more upon Felicia's recalling his name and smiling up to him in a friendly manner. Then he glanced around. "I'm not sure—you have come alone—"

A surge of irritation welled up within Felicia. Everyone was reading her propriety, even a butler. She left the earl's doorstep and hastened along the square and Upper Grosvenor Street to Hyde Park.

Felicia knew where the balloon was moored. Darcy

had taken her and Uncle Edward there before the parade, having regretfully explained to her that he wouldn't be able to take her to see the ascension next day. Now she knew why. That ridiculous race.

She had found the experience of clambering into the boatlike basket of the balloon and the lecture the balloonist gave quite interesting, as apparently did many others. With the weather favoring him and with so many people crowding London and eager for entertainment, the enterprising balloonist was making a great deal of money from his venture. But there wouldn't be anybody there now, except perhaps the balloonist or his helper guarding the balloon against mischief-makers.

All this flitted through Felicia's mind as she hurried on to the park. A few bucks ogled her, a few people stared at her curiously, but no one accosted her, and she arrived at the gates of the park without any mishaps.

The park, shrouded in the early-morning fog, was a trifle more crowded than usual at this early hour, the populace, in the hope of seeing the tsar ride, having already congregated along Rotten Row; but the part of Hyde Park where the balloon was moored was deserted.

Normally a large crowd would have gathered at the site long before ascension, but the tsar proved a stronger attraction than a mere balloon.

Felicia could see through the mist its yellow-and-red-striped shape with the blue horizontal band in the middle. Her heartbeat quickened. She hurried forward toward the roped-off enclosure, her eyes straining for the familiar tall figure of the earl.

But she could not see him anywhere. Had she missed him, by any chance? Cold dismay struck her heart. She should have thought of that possibility before. But she had assumed he would be taking the same route as she from Grosvenor Square. Of course, he could have been here and gone already.

As she came up closer and the mist rising from the ground cleared a little, she saw a man sprawled on the grass under a tree, a bottle by his hand. The man seemed to be quite drunk.

Abruptly she heard a grunt and a cry from inside the enclosure. Her heart gave a frightened leap. She rushed to the rope barrier, climbed over it, and ran up to the balloon. Wreaths of water vapor were rising all around her, twirling about her feet, and tongues of mist were licking, entwining the basket of the balloon.

Then the misty curtain parted before her eyes, showing her a dreadful sight. Like shadows in some ghastly pantomime, she saw two men in the basket locked in a desperate struggle—a bearded burly ruffian in rags and the elegant Lord Cleary.

"No!" cried Felicia hoarsely out of a dry throat.

Now the man lifted something and brought it to bear with great force upon the head of the earl. Lord Cleary slumped over the edge of the basket.

Reacting instinctively without any conscious thought, Felicia hurtled herself toward the basket and grabbed at a rope hanging there to haul herself in. In her excitement she forgot the rope ladder which the balloonist had provided for the spectators. She hardly knew how she contrived to pull herself up. She had lost her cloak, and her green sprigged muslin gown tore as she clawed at the side of the basket and, holding on to the rope, tried to reach that murderous hand about to descend on the unconscious earl again. The thought that Lord Cleary might be killed was unbearable. In that instant, in a blinding flash she realized that she cared for him more than she cared for Darcy. Was it love? She was too confused, too distraught, to analyze her thoughts. She could only *feel*.

The ruffian must have seen or heard her, for when she looked up, he was lunging at her. Something glistened in the man's hand. A large heavy-handled knife swung at Felicia, missing her by inches.

Felicia screamed.

Abruptly she felt a sudden jerk and a swaying sensation. What had occurred? She heard a loud oath, and looking up again, she saw the earl move groggily and the man trying to push him over the side of the basket. She looked down—and froze in horror. The ground was receding at a fast rate. The balloon was rising swiftly upward. They were airborne. And the man was trying to throw Lord Cleary over the side to his death.

Felicia screamed again and tried to haul herself hand over hand up the rope, swinging and banging against the side of the basket.

Now the man's wicked-looking knife swiped at the rope. A shudder of horror went through Felicia. The man was going to cut the rope. He wished *her* to fall to her death too. The earl, blood pouring from his head, was hanging over the edge of the basket.

Suddenly he moved again, lashing out feebly at the killer. The man turned his knife on him. The uneven struggle continued.

Felicia, her senses reeling, but gritting her teeth, utilized this moment to clamber all the way up and grasp the edge of the basket.

The next moment she was inside and attacking the man, drawing him away from the earl. He lunged at her with his knife. Was he that escaped convict, it occurred to her, and was he taking this way to escape London? But what was Lord Cleary doing here, fighting with this villain?

The balloon was soaring high above the trees, high above the City of London, bathed in the golden rays of the rising sun. But Felicia had no time or inclination to enjoy the splendid view of the metropolis far below. Straining with all her might, she attempted to deflect the man's arm, to prevent the knife from being plunged into her body.

Suddenly the villain's arm was jerked backward, a split second before that death-dealing knife would have buried itself in her body, and the fist of a first-rate sportsman connected, felling the man. The earl, blood flowing from his wound, swayed on his feet groggily, then collapsed unconscious on top of the villain.

For a moment Felicia remained frozen with shock. But the red flow spurred her to action. She must stanch the bleeding—fast.

Her muslin gown was torn in shreds as it was, so off

went a wide flounce to be wrapped tightly about the earl's bleeding head. She hoped it would do it, and felt grateful her constitution did not cause her to swoon at the sight of blood.

Having bound the earl's wound as tightly as she could, Felicia dragged the unconscious ruffian to one side, then pulled off her stockings and used them to tie his hands and feet. Then, seeing a couple of blankets and pillows in a heap, she fashioned a rough bed for Lord Cleary, dragged him onto it, and wrapped him well in the blankets. It was a trifle difficult, for the basket was not large and Lord Cleary was tall, but she arranged him as best as she could.

While she was thus occupied, she suddenly noticed a lady's slipper caught on the edge of the basket, which puzzled her, for it certainly was not hers. But she did not waste much time wondering about it. Only now she became aware of the intense cold cutting through to her very marrow. And she was surprised by the silence and smoothness of the ride. They seemed to be hardly moving at all. Yet they were moving, and at a fast rate. A strong wind was pushing the balloon steadily eastward.

Recalling the balloonist's lecture, Felicia concluded that at this rate they would soon reach the coastline. And the full import of her predicament now struck her. She, dressed in flimsy attire, with a bleeding man and a criminal at her side, was being swiftly carried out to sea. . . .

# Twelve

A fit of hysterical laughter seized Felicia. But she cut it short, biting her lip till she drew blood. This was no time to lose her head. She must think. And she must get warm. Rubbing her arms and moving about, she tried to improve her circulation. Should she remove one blanket from the unconscious Lord Cleary? No, she dared not. But she must think, and the cold made her numb, made her mind numb. She must warm up.

She glanced at the ruffian. He was not moving, but she had no pity to spare for him. She looked at the earl, and her heart contracted. Oh, if only the blood loss was not too severe. He moaned and stirred, still unconscious.

Felicia took a deep breath. Improper or not, who was here to tell of it? And the earl *was* unconscious. She crawled in under the blankets covering Lord Cleary, pressing her cold body to his warm, strong, but insensible one.

A curious sensation flowed over her, thus being pressed to his lordship. A delicious warmth, yet something else too. He smelled of some pleasant face water. His powerful body was now helpless. Oh, God, make him recover, she prayed. She did not at the moment think of his insults and his hatred of her. All she could think of was how he had come to her aid—twice. She would do all she could to save him—to save them.

She took another deep breath, snuggling closer to his comforting warmth, trying to still the hammering of her heart, the pounding of her pulses.

A sudden chuckle escaped her at the thought of Lady Palmer's face had she caught a glimpse of her now. Her ladyship would have fallen into strong hysterics—no doubt about that.

She sobered up. Something had to be done to bring the balloon down before it floated all the way out to sea.

The balloonist would rise a hue and cry, but as he and his helper would not be aware that somebody was in the basket they would perhaps not set about recovering it with as much speed as if they knew what had really occurred. And it might be some time before that drunken man by the enclosure roused himself or the balloonist arrived to give his lecture. No, it was up to her, Felicia, to do something.

She screwed up her eyes, trying to think back on the lecture. The sandbags were there to make the balloon go higher. One pulled on the string to release some of the sand, to lighten the load. To make the balloon descend, one opened a tricky valve by pulling on another string, to let out some of the hydrogen with which the balloon was filled.

But that cord must be operated very carefully. If the valve got stuck and could not be closed again, the gas would escape at a very rapid rate and the balloon would plummet to the ground, killing its occupants. She shuddered. She thought she remembered where the valve cord was, but could she operate it delicately enough to bring the balloon down safely?

Then there was the hazard of descending in a strong wind, the balloonist had said. Oh yes, and one must descend over open ground, not over a populated area. Very difficult, that. Felicia poked her nose out from under the blanket. Brrr. But she had to crawl out to assess the situation.

She did so, shivering with cold, but being careful to cover the earl well with the blankets. The villain was coming to, moaning, and Felicia, not wishing to hear his vituperations, stuffed a handkerchief in his mouth and bound it with strips torn off her dress. No danger from him anymore, thank God. She came to the edge of the basket and looked down.

And felt suddenly dizzy.

They must be about half a mile up, she thought with a sinking heart. She looked out. Blue sky, sunshine. She wished the sun could warm her up. She looked down again, forcing herself not to feel dizzy. Houses like toys, far far below. And trees and bushes. If only she knew exactly where they were. She must watch for a meadow and—no, she should allow the gas to escape gradually to reduce the height, so that when a meadow opened up she would be able to make the descent before the balloon overshot the place.

She approached the valve and very slowly pulled on the string. Instantly she heard a hissing sound, and not knowing how long to hold it open, she shut the valve at once. She must do it slower still, she thought.

Eyes on the ground below, hands on the string, Felicia opened and released the valve twice more. At the third time, she found her numb fingers refused to function smoothly, and the cord slipped through her hands. And then when she grasped it again and pulled, she pulled too sharply and held the valve open too long. With a hissing sound, the balloon plumeted down.

Felicia tried to close the valve, but it seemed to be stuck. Or perhaps her numb hands could not operate the valve properly. She tried again, drenched in cold sweat and trembling violently. The valve was still stuck. Again she made the attempt. This time the valve closed and the dizzying fall halted.

She looked down. Rows of houses down below. She shuddered. If she had not been able to close the valve . . . Severe chills shook her body. She must warm up.

She crawled under the blanket beside the earl. His body was now burning hot to the touch. She placed her hand on his brow. Fever! Oh dear God, no. But that was to be expected. Shock and the wound and the cold.

Abruptly he moved. His arm shot out to go around her waist. Felicia stiffened, then jerked herself upright, throwing back the blankets.

The earl's eyes, burning with fever, were staring at her with a singularly insistent expression. "Come down here," he said. His voice sounded slurred. But his arm was strong as he pulled her down to him and pressed her close to his body.

Well, of all things! thought Felicia with outrage. The man is out of his senses and yet he—was he—

"Come down—I wish to make love to you. You are Felicia, aren't you? Or are you a dream?"

Felicia's cheeks were burning with shame and indignation. But he was delirious. He didn't know what he was doing. "Lie still, my lord. You are ill. But you shall b-be b-b-better d-directly," she said.

"I wish to kiss you," he mumbled.

I must humor him, thought Felicia. "Not now, my lord, later."

"I wish to kiss you *now*."

And with surprising strength he pulled her roughly to him, and his hot lips sought hers, hungrily, imperiously.

I must humor him, thought Felicia, or he will become violent. What does it matter? I can allow him to kiss me. Who is here to tell? That half-conscious brute? Not likely. And not likely someone would listen to his tale. She ceased struggling and relaxed, allowing the earl his will.

And suddenly, and without her volition, she found herself responding to his kiss. She found herself alive and burning with a passion which surprised and frightened her. Darcy's kisses, highly satisfying as they were, were chaste pecks compared to Lord Cleary's.

Blood rushed to her cheeks in shame, and the pulses in her temples pounded. She tore herself away, panting and gasping for air. No, no, what was she about? She was Darcy's fiancée, she was *not* in love with the earl.

She could not be. Oh, she cared for him, but she would have cared for anyone whose life was in danger. And it was but natural to care for someone who had saved her life twice. How was it then that his kiss could have such a strong effect upon her?

Abruptly she realized that her head was aching abominably, and relief flooded over her. It must be the atmosphere affecting her senses, she reasoned. She remembered the balloonist saying that high altitude often brought on a headache. No doubt it brought on other sensations, but one could hardly expect the balloonist to expound on the effects of kissing at high altitudes. Relaxed now, she turned to Lord Cleary, smiling up at him.

He had lifted himself up on one elbow and was regarding her strangely. "I must be dreaming," he said in disbelief.

"Yes, my lord. To be sure. It's the altitude," Felicia soothed him. "It gives one hallucinations. Pray close your eyes and lie still."

He sighed and complied wearily, and she covered him tenderly with the blankets. I trust he won't remember any of it afterward, she thought.

She went to the edge of the basket and looked down again. They were passing over a forest, but in the distance Felicia could see a large meadow, open ground. Now was her chance. Heart pounding, fingers numb again, she grasped at the cord of the valve and pulled. A loud hiss, and the balloon began to descend. In a moment she closed the valve again, judging the distance. The trees were rushing toward her. She mustn't allow the balloon to descend too quickly.

Some animals were grazing on the meadow. She must not land on *them.*

She pulled the cord again. Again the gas escaped, and the balloon sank lower. Was she doing the right thing, with this constant opening and closing? Was that how it was supposed to be done? She recalled that her attention had wandered a few times during the lecture, because of something Darcy had said. She tried to close the valve. The trees were getting larger, the ground closer. She must clear the trees.

The gas was still escaping. The valve did not close.

Felicia tried again. The valve was stuck. And this time it was stuck for good. It wouldn't budge. And the balloon was plummeting down toward the ground even faster, and the earth rose to meet it in its deadly embrace.

"No!" screamed Felicia. "No!"

Faster and faster, with a rush and a hiss, the balloon fell like a stone falling through the water, or so it seemed to Felicia's terrified senses. Hanging on to the side of the basket, she prayed that some miracle would save them, that they would not dash on the ground below. But they would land in the trees, she abruptly realized. Perhaps they stood a chance after all.

Her head was spinning. Then a loud crash, a bone-shattering jerk, the breath was knocked out of her body—and all was still.

Felicia dared to open her eyes. The balloon was stuck high up in a tree, its silken bag and the ropes quite entangled in the branches, which had broken its fall. Thank God, Felicia sent up a silent prayer. They were safe. But were they all safe? The earl? The basket was sitting in the tree at an angle. The ruffian, tumbled out of it, seemed stuck in a tree branch, but he was alive, for he was moaning. And the earl had slid to one corner of the basket and was motionless.

Felicia dropped to her knees beside him. He was still breathing. He was alive. Alive! Relief flooded over her. Now she felt and flexed her own limbs. Bruises and scratches, but that was about all, she concluded. And the basket seemed to be firmly stuck in the tree. Grasping a tree branch, she clambered out gingerly, then parted the foliage and looked out toward the meadow.

Two men in shirtsleeves, perhaps those tending the flock of cows and sheep, were rushing toward her. "Over here, over here," cried Felicia. "We're up here.

Up in the tree." Abruptly she felt her senses reel. With a last effort of will, she wedged herself firmly in a fork of the tree, and then her limbs relaxed and she collapsed in a deep swoon.

# Thirteen

Felicia blinked open her eyes to stare with relief at the ceiling of her bedchamber in Berkeley Square. She was drenched through with perspiration, and her heart was pounding so hard it threatened to jump out of her chest. She had just experienced again her terrible ordeal in the balloon, and the nightmare left her quite shaken. Still, she had had two nights without dreaming of the balloon ride, so perhaps the doctor was right and she would in time stop having those nightmares.

She sneezed and propped herself up on her pillows to stare at the sundrenched world outside her window. She had caught a cold in the balloon, which was not to be wondered at, but she had almost recovered. She had been able to accompany Lady Palmer to the modiste, and she would be able to attend the great fête the Prince Regent was giving in honor of Wellington. The great soldier, now a duke, had returned to London one day after the departure of the royal guests, and the metropolis was humming with excitement again. And Darcy had promised to teach her to waltz.

Lady Palmer had been quite vexed with Felicia for going off unattended for an early stroll in the park, and said it had served her right that she—with Lord

Cleary—had been taken prisoner by a demented criminal bent on escape.

Felicia did not correct her misapprehension, deeming this version of her accident least improper. But even so, her ladyship had tried to persuade her husband not to take Felicia to Carlton House again, as punishment for her lark. Lord Palmer overbore her protests. Felicia was going to the fête. Moreover, she was going in yet another new gown. Which decree revolted her so much, it almost brought on an attack of the spasms.

Since, however, Lord Palmer did not wish for a scandal for Felicia, Lady Palmer gave out, on his advice, that Felicia had gone out *with* her maid to the park, and the maid had fainted when attacked by the convict. That ruffian, who had had his arm broken during the perilous descent, was recaptured and no doubt had received his just deserts. Of the three of them riding in the balloon, Lord Cleary seemed to have suffered most unjustly, for it hadn't been *his* notion to go to the balloon site.

Who had lured him there remained a riddle to Felicia, for it couldn't have been that convict, and the earl did not tell Jerome or Lester who the obviously fake message was purported to be from. He was still laid up, recovering from his wound, though he was expected to be up and about soon.

The near tragic event with the balloon had one good result. Darcy, not realizing what had occurred, had started out on the race at the agreed time, without waiting for the earl, thinking Lord Cleary would no doubt catch up with him. And as he had reached Barnet with only one minor mishap, he had won the wager, a large sum of money, which he proceeded at once to gamble away—much to Felicia's disgust.

Would Lord Cleary make another attempt at revenging himself on Darcy? wondered Felicia. She must discover the whereabouts of that witness, and that meant going to Barnet again. But both Jerome and Lester tried to convince her that no urgency existed, with the earl laid up. Time enough for her to go later, after the fête.

Perhaps the earl would *not* attempt to destroy Darcy—out of consideration for her?

With a rush of blood to her cheeks, she recalled Lord Cleary's hungry passionate kiss, and her response, the feeling of his strong body so close to her own. Was she in love with him? she asked herself again.

She recalled her horror and despair on thinking he might be killed. She cared for him, certainly. But she *couldn't* be in love with him, for she was in love with Darcy. Or was she? Of course she was.

Felicia pressed her hands distractedly to her temples. She was so confused. Darcy was her betrothed. She couldn't be in love with *another*. She could not betray Darcy thus.

Yet her feelings for Lord Cleary could not be denied. They could not be true, not lasting. Her nerves were still overset from her harrowing experience, and she could not think clearly. Perhaps she was still suffering from the effects of high altitude on her senses and could not distinguish reality from fancy.

Would the earl recall his hallucinations? Would he allude to their kiss when they met next? It would be extremely embarrassing if he did.

But when she saw him at Carlton House, Lord Cleary's cool impersonal greeting did not give any indication that he entertained passion toward her. In fact, Felicia was surprised to see him, not thinking he was well enough yet to venture abroad. Still, there he was, just slightly ahead of Lord Palmer's party, resplendent in yet another velvet coat, claret this time, and cream-colored breeches. If Darcy looked elegant in his russet coat and drab breeches, the earl in his attire looked magnificent.

Felicia viewed his striking figure with mixed emotions. A strange excitement had gripped her upon seeing him, and her pulses and her breathing quickened. Yet she was also gripped with apprehension, for his being there meant that Darcy should be on his guard again, and also that the evening would not be now one of peaceful enjoyment as she had hoped.

Would he attempt to speak to her, perhaps to thank her for rescuing him?

She felt Darcy stiffen suddenly and realized that he must also have seen the earl. "I hope that fellow won't make himself a nuisance," he muttered darkly. "It's amazing how he always contrives to be thrown together with you."

Felicia experienced a slight irritation upon these words. "He won't have much chance of being thrown together with me *here*. Not with two thousand guests invited."

"It's a pity Jerome could not get an invitation," said Darcy. "He would help me to keep an eye on you, for I can hardly rely on Winwood."

"But you will be with me all the time."

"No, I shan't. Engaged or not, I can't sit in a girl's pocket all evening. I must do my duty to other damsels. Lord Palmer particularly told me to practice diplomacy and circulate. It's a shame—all I wish is to have every dance with you—but it cannot be."

Strange, thought Felicia, she did not feel very keenly disappointed at the thought of not being able to stand up for every dance with Darcy.

As they were conducted by an equerry through the house and the Gothic Conservatory to the polygonal brick pavilion built by Nash in the garden of Carlton House especially for the fête, Darcy commented again in an undertone, "Sometimes I think Lord Palmer is trying to throw a rub in my way, giving you a chance to meet other eligible men."

But Felicia would not hear of it. "No, no. You cannot ascribe anything underhanded to Lord Palmer. He has been my great help and protector since my aunt passed away. He has only my welfare at heart." She glanced lovingly at the kind, silver-haired man with the sharp intelligent eyes and strong angular features. She owed him so much. Of course, he was doing it because of her aunt. Had they been in love at one time, as Bertha romantically fancied? It was too bad they hadn't married, if such indeed had been the case.

Her glance fell on Lady Palmer in her stylish clinging yellow silk gown and headdress trimmed with a veritable forest of ostrich plumes. How *could* they have made a match of it? she wondered.

She viewed with satisfaction her own magnificent gown. This time Lady Palmer had not gotten her way in anything. Felicia's gown was of a soft cerulean-blue silk, enveloped in a cloud of paler-blue gauze, embroidered with silver bells, which shimmered with her every move. And it was even lower-cut over the bosom than her new green gown. Lady Palmer did not approve of the cut, but the modiste had overcome her objections, saying a dress less than in the first stare of fashion would reflect poorly on her ladyship. As for the low cut, the diaphanous folds of the silver-spangled gauze scarf could be so draped as to cover somewhat the low décolletage. Everyone had adopted the French fashions now, pointed out the modiste.

Jerome having revealed to Lady Palmer that Uncle Edward's necklace was paste, she no longer insisted on Felicia's wearing it, but instead reluctantly lent Felicia a strand of her own pearls. A blue velvet ribbon spangled with silver decorated Felicia's soft auburn curls, long white gloves covered her arms, and there were matching blue satin slippers on her feet. Her painted ivory stick fan on a blue ribbon was a recent present from Darcy. She knew her appearance was satisfactory, and the admiring glances cast her way only confirmed it. But though Darcy complimented her on her looks, he scowled each time he intercepted an admiring glance from another. Of course, he was jealous, and it was very flattering, but also becoming tedious, she had to own to herself.

"The Regent outdid himself again," Lord Palmer said as they entered the huge tentlike pavilion. As big as Westminster Hall, it was illuminated with twelve sparkling chandeliers. Its umbrellalike ceiling was painted to resemble gathered muslin and decorated with gilt cords. The walls were draped with white muslin and hung with mirrors. In the center a temple formed from huge banks of artificial flowers concealed two orchestras to provide entertainment and dance music.

Covered walks led from this chamber to various supper tents and a Corinthian temple, displaying a bust of the duke. The walls of all the chambers were lavishly studded with "W" monograms in honor of the conquering hero. Felicia learned subsequently Wellington was quite embarrassed by this display of homage.

The Regent himself in his field marshal's uniform decorated with his various foreign orders beamed upon his guests and welcomed them jovially. Felicia was granted the great honor of being presented to Wellington, whom Lord Palmer knew well. She was quite awed by him, finding him at first forbidding, though quite a striking man, with his long crooked nose and high-arched intelligent eyes. But when he unbent a trifle, Felicia could perceive how unaffected and modest he was and what a keen mind he possessed. And, to her surprise, he had an appreciation of feminine beauty.

With Lord Palmer, Darcy, and Lester by her side, Felicia felt reasonably comfortable in this glittering crowd. The dancing commenced, and she danced her first waltz with Darcy. It was all very agreeable, and she enjoyed the sensuous dance, once considered scandalous, but now made quite fashionable by the tsar at Almack's.

And then she espied Lord Cleary on the dance floor, and from that moment on, she fancied hard gray eyes following her constantly. Somewhere always in her line of vision was his tall imposing figure. When Darcy finally was obliged to dance with somebody else, the earl approached her and bowed gravely. "May I be permitted the honor of this dance?" he asked in a voice which betrayed suppressed emotion.

Felicia's heart leaped to her throat, and her breathing quickened. Again the picture of them both in the balloon flashed before her memory's eyes. She glanced at Lady Palmer. Her ladyship, busily talking away with a friend, nodded her assent.

Taking Felicia's arm, the earl led her onto the dance floor. "You quite take my breath away, Miss Mannering. Never have I seen anyone equal to you in beauty. Vellacort is lucky indeed to be betrothed to you." He was smiling, but it was an odd cold smile, and it did not reach his eyes. And while the words were complimentary, there was an undercurrent of savage anger in the carefully controlled voice. And a slight alcoholic aroma informed her that the earl must have been recruiting his strength with the Prince Regent's favorite beverage.

Excited, bewildered, and angered, Felicia allowed him to take her into his arms. And as the sensuous strains of the waltz enveloped them both in their magic, she forgot to be angry, or to be worried over Darcy's safety. All ceased to exist, save the two of them carried away on the music. Her lips parted, her chest rose and fell heavily. The music acted on her senses almost like the high altitude in the balloon, making her feel deliciously strange. But why didn't she feel that way when dancing with Darcy or Lester?

Abruptly the earl stopped opposite the walk to the Corinthian temple. "I wish to talk to you," he said.

He led her past the twirling and conversing couples to the promenade and the temple. There, by the bust of Wellington, they were for the moment alone. The earl released her arm and stood looking at her in a strange way. There was hunger and sadness and rage in that expression. Suddenly Felicia became frightened. She remembered his hatred of Darcy, his desire for revenge, and his insults.

He stood there, his massive chest heaving, staring at her and not saying anything for so long that at last she was compelled to speak up. "You wish to talk to me, my lord? We shouldn't be alone here."

He gave a short bitter laugh. "You did not think much of propriety when you ventured out alone to Hyde Park. My God!" he suddenly burst out with violence. "How far will you go to protect that worthless

fiancé of yours? You would not even stop at murder."
He lifted his hands and took a step toward her, murderous rage in his eyes. "I could strangle that beautiful
neck of yours," he said through his teeth.

# Fourteen

Shocked and completely dumbfounded, Felicia shrank back from the earl's outburst of wrath.

"What are you talking about? What am I supposed to have done *now*?" she added bitterly, as comprehension dawned that he was accusing her of something again.

"*You* are asking *me* that? *You*?" She could fancy seeing him foam at the mouth. "You lured me to that tryst, you made me believe you were in that balloon and in trouble, so that I should get in, and then you intended to cut the ropes and let me drift away. All to prevent that damned curricle race, to save Vellacort's neck."

"What? *I* sent you that message? You must have quite lost your senses, my lord," she cried, much outraged, her green eyes flashing angrily. The sheer absurdity and magnitude of that accusation acted bracingly on her spirit. "I did *not* write you a note, and I don't know who did. I came *after* you to the balloon site, for I wished to plead with you to abandon the race. But you were already struggling with that villain."

"A likely story," he said with a sneer. "What of the friendly female who had drugged the balloonist's helper, who was standing guard? What of the lady's slipper seemingly caught on the edge of the basket? On seeing it, what else could I think but that you had met with disaster? But instead of seeing you insensible in the basket as I thought, I met up with the convict. And I, fool that I was, wouldn't have gone to that tryst at all, but for the fact that I was worried you had gone there alone—with the town teeming with all kinds of people and that escaped ruffian on the loose."

"Surely you cannot believe that that criminal was my accomplice," Felicia cried, her cheeks burning, her voice quivering with indignation.

"No, no," he said sardonically, "I acquit you of *that* crime. I'll wager you didn't bargain on getting caught in your own trap."

Felicia's eyes burned with unshed tears as she glared at him. Here she had saved his life, she had almost lost her own life in the attempt, and instead of gratitude— this. No, this was not to be borne. "And where do you suppose I was hiding when you jumped into the basket to save me?" she asked with heavy sarcasm.

He appeared nonplussed for a moment. Then he shrugged. "You were hiding in the bushes, no doubt, to see how your trap worked. Perhaps you had regretted it and came forward, or perhaps you had betrayed yourself and the convict saw you and kidnapped you."

"Surely you cannot believe that."

"I can believe anything of someone who could hold me up on Hampstead Heath," he said, baring his teeth.

There it was again. Felicia stamped her foot in rage. "Oh, you are impossible. I don't know why you always think the worst of me."

"Don't you? Don't you? But for you my brother would still be alive."

"Now we come to that again. I've told you again and again that I hardly knew your brother."

"Then why was the duel fought over you? Answer me that, if you can," he said with bitter savage triumph.

Felicia stared at him, quite astonished.

"My lord, you must be foxed, or that wound has addled your brain. The duel fought over me? Where did you get this notion? It was over a game of cards. One accused the other of cheating, and, both being inebriated, they decided to settle the dispute with pistols. Not an uncommon occurrence in our enlightened times," she added with scorn.

"I wish I could believe that, but I know the circumstances were different. And I will not rest until I see justice done. Provoked or not, it *was* murder. And Vellacort shan't escape his just fate." But she was guilty too, he thought. Marcus would never have made up to another man's betrothed unless she had cast out lures to him first. Yet here she was, green eyes flashing, showing righteous indignation, and denying any guilt. How magnificent, how desirable she looked.

The urge to take her in his arms warred with the hatred he held for her now. She was ready to kill him to protect Vellacort and Vellacort had killed his brother. Here they both were, enjoying life, and Marcus was dead. Very soon Vellacort would go abroad and slip through his fingers. No, he must see retribution done. He must.

Abruptly a gleam sprang to his eye. Yes, why not? That would only be fitting. He had lost his brother because of Vellacort, so why not let Vellacort suffer the loss of his betrothed and punish her at the same time? But it wouldn't be easy to bring about. He took a deep breath and forced himself to an expressionless voice.

"I shan't dispute with you something which I know to be true. My brother was murdered. And the fight was over you. The maid at the inn in Barnet overheard what the quarrel was about. And she revealed it to my groom. As for the balloon fiasco, you had written that note—"

"But I didn't, I didn't. Just show it to me—"

"Unfortunately, I threw it away."

"But you don't know my hand. How can you tell if *I* wrote it?"

The earl was silent, nonplussed for a moment. "True. But if I recollect right, it was printed," he finally said.

"That just proves that I did not write it. Somebody wished to implicate me."

He passed his hand wearily across his face. "It is all to no purpose discussing that now."

"But you don't know, you don't know what occurred there at Hyde Park and during that ride. You were unconscious most of the time."

"Yes, I was unconscious." And dreaming. His lips pressed shut. Would that he could erase from his memory that sweet delicious dream. "I knew we both were taken prisoners by that convict who wished to escape in the balloon. And the balloon crashed."

"You don't know anything at all. You—" Her pride came to her aid. Obviously he did not remember. And she would not justify herself before him. If he was capable of believing the worst of her, so be it. She wouldn't disabuse him of his notion. She hated him for it, and held him in contempt. Let him think the worst of her. She didn't care, she told herself firmly.

But she did care, she did. A silent cry went up within her. And Darcy, her fiancé? She bit her lip. It was a melancholy truth, but in that moment she knew with a certainty that she no longer loved Darcy. Oh, she still cared for him, but somehow her feelings for him had undergone a change. As for the earl—she couldn't be in love with *him*. She couldn't. He despised her. Then why did his cruel words hurt so much? She pressed a hand to her brow. "Pray excuse me, my lord. I have the headache. Pray take me back. We mustn't start the tongues wagging."

"Ah yes—always thinking of scandal, scandal threatening your precious Darcy."

"No, just now I was thinking of Lord Palmer. He does not deserve to be embroiled in our differences."

The earl's countenance sobered. "You are right. Lord Palmer is my friend." He bit his lip. He had not thought of *him* when he conceived just now his plan of revenge. It would be a pity. But, he shrugged, it could not be helped.

What should he say to her, how could he start? No, they were both too overheated with emotion. It wouldn't work now. And in any case it would be difficult in these surroundings. He needed a less crowded place, and time to think up a strategy, a definite plan.

He took her arm. "I shall restore you to Lady Palmer," he said coldly.

She nodded, not trusting herself to speak, feeling tears welling up in her eyes. She was so miserable, and her thoughts were in such a chaotic whirl. Only one thought stood out clear. She *must* know the truth about that duel. She must know if it was fought over her. Jerome had said it was over a game of cards. Had Jerome been lying? And if he had been, would he tell her the truth now? Lester must go with her to Barnet—tomorrow. Oh, if only that night would end soon.

She did not dare to glance at the earl's handsome forbidding countenance as he was leading her back to Lady Palmer. She felt if she but once more looked at him, she would burst into tears. Oh, the injustice of that man. How could he accuse her of setting that trap? But he had the evidence of her actions on Hampstead Heath, and if the duel *was* over her, what else could he do but jump to conclusions? Yet who hated her enough to put her name to that message luring the earl to the balloon site? And why lure the earl at all? She could not find answers to these perplexing questions.

Felicia hardly knew how she endured the rest of that night until they returned to Berkeley Square early in the morning. And then, in a fever of impatience, she did not go to bed at all, but put on her sprigged muslin gown and chip-straw hat and was ready to go to Barnet as soon as she could get hold of Lester. She wished also to speak to Jerome, to ask him about the duel, but he was from home. She could wait to talk to him, but she could *not* wait a moment longer than absolutely necessary to secure the direction of Sam Stoddart.

# Fifteen

It was close on noon when a timid knock on the door of Felicia's bedchamber heralded that Lester had heeded her urgent message. Felicia, sitting by the window, called out, "Come in," and saw Lester's fearful countenance in the doorway.

Throwing a furtive glance over his shoulder, he slipped in and hastily shut the door. "Mustn't make a habit of it, Felicia," he said worriedly. "You ain't laid up now. Could have talked to me in the saloon."

"I don't wish to be interrupted. Pray sit down."

He cocked his head. "Going somewhere?" he remarked, noticing the straw hat on her head.

"Yes, with you—to Barnet."

Lester's eyes started from their sockets. He threw up his hands. "Dash it, Felicia—"

"Now don't you dash me. You don't know what Lord Cleary said last night."

"Was bosky. Most of the men were."

"Drunk or sober, he thinks *I* sent that message luring him to the balloon. That *I* wished to lure him into the basket, cut the ropes, and let him drift away, so that Darcy could win the race and the wager. Can you imagine anything more absurd?"

Lester, in the process of carefully lowering his primrose pantaloons onto the chair by the bed, was arrested. He straightened up, tugging pensively at his earlobe. "Don't know about it. It worked, didn't it?" he said, ruminating.

"Yes, it did, but who could have done it? *I* didn't write that note. But somebody signed my name to it. Who could it have been?"

"Fancy I know who," Lester said abruptly, and reddened.

"Who, who? Oh, Lester, pray tell me."

But Lester was suddenly tongue-tied. "Shouldn't have said it. Forgot whom I was speaking to," he mumbled unhappily. "Head is still heavy. Don't think I shall visit Carlton House again soon."

It took many promptings and threats from Felicia for him to finally reveal that it must have been Vellacort's onetime lady friend, who, wishing to save Darcy from the race, had written the note. But he also assured her that Vellacort wished nothing more to do with the woman now.

Felicia was shocked, but not as shocked as she would have been once. The little country innocent was fast learning the town ways, she reflected with a wry grimace. The thought of Darcy's having an affair with another woman would once have been inconceivable to her, and would have wounded her deeply. Today she could view this possibility dispassionately. In her brief introduction to town life she had learned enough to see that fidelity was not always something one took for granted. Well, it made no odds to her who had sent that note, but . . .

"Lord Cleary shouldn't think that *I* would play him such a dangerous trick," she said with indignation. "He thinks I wished to kill him, just as Darcy killed his brother."

Lester made a distressing clacking sound. "He's *still* got that notion. Should think he would have thought better by now."

"Well, he doesn't. So I wish to go to Barnet to discover the whereabouts of that witness."

"But Felicia—"

"Wait, you don't know the whole," she said bitterly. "Lord Cleary thinks the duel was over *me*."

"What?" Lester gaped at her and almost dropped his snuffbox, which he had produced from his pocket. "That settles it. The fellow's mad as Bedlam and ought to be locked up."

"You mean it isn't true?"

"Of course it isn't true."

"How do you know?"

"How do I—no, Felicia."

"You weren't there—you don't know of your own knowledge," reasoned Felicia. "Only Jerome knows the truth. It was he who told you about the duel. Right?"

"Yes, but dash it, how can anyone think the duel was over you? You hardly knew Cleary's brother. Oh, he *was* quite taken with you, but there wasn't anything in it for Vellacort to take exception to."

"Well, I have been sitting here racking my brains. They were both drunk and—oh, I don't know. I must know the truth. For if it was so, then I can hardly blame Lord Cleary for thinking me fast and guilty of casting out lures to his brother. But how could they have come to fight over me?"

"Don't make sense. Forget it."

"I cannot forget it. I've sent word to Jerome to come here as soon as he can. Meanwhile we must go to Barnet. And we must go today, for Lord Palmer has gone out and Lady Palmer will be resting until late, and I have told Bertha to say if someone asks for me that I am still recovering from the fête. Lady Palmer won't wonder at that. We shan't have a chance tomorrow, for we are to go to Lady Symonds's rout party, so we must go today."

"That rascally innkeeper. Just wait till I give him a piece of my mind, for sending me—us—on a wild goose chase to that tavern."

"Then you will go. Oh, Lester, I could kiss you." Felicia jumped up from her seat and made as if to throw her arms around Lester. He backed away in horror, casting a panicky glance at the door to the corridor.

Felicia dropped her arms with a chuckle. "No need to worry. I shan't. And your mama is still sound asleep."

"Lucky for us she is. You must take care, Felicia."

"Yes, yes. Now, about Barnet. How shall we arrange it? Perhaps Bertha and I can pretend we are going to Hookham's library—if somebody sees us going out, which I hope no one will. You wait for us there in your curricle and take me up."

Lester pulled at his earlobe, took a pinch of snuff, and restored the snuffbox to his pocket. "Yes, that is a good notion. But we must watch lest some acquaintance see me taking you up." He paused. "Trouble is, I have just promised to see Harry at his lodgings. He lives just on the other side of the square—I collect you wish to go now?—and I have other errands to do. Daresay I can arrange it somehow—get someone to do one errand for me, while I call on Harry. Don't think I can do it in less than two hours, though. Perhaps longer. Now, how shall we contrive to return unobserved?"

"It will be dark by then, or—or Bertha can wait for me at Hookham's. Oh, what does it signify? The main thing is to get out."

A tread was heard in the corridor, but it was only Bertha. "Sir Edward and Mr. Banister wish to see you, miss," she said. "They are in the Red Saloon."

Lester left the chamber, and a moment later in the Red Saloon, Felicia greeted Sir Edward and Jerome Banister warmly and begged them to resume their seats. "Did you receive my letter, Jerome?" she asked.

He nodded. "But we are here on another matter altogether."

Noticing his somber mien and the unhappy expression on Uncle Edward's ruddy countenance, Felicia was for a moment diverted from her problem. "What has occurred?"

Sir Edward heaved a deep sigh. "I don't know how to say it, child, and I'm not sure I should." He broke off, twisting and untwisting his hands.

"Sir Edward is quite distressed to be obliged to tell you this, but he thinks that you should know," interposed Jerome smoothly.

"Know what? Pray don't keep me in suspense, Uncle."

Sir Edward cast up his troubled hazel eyes at her. "Oh, child, I fear this will hurt you dreadfully, but—"

"It's about the necklace," supplied Jerome.

"But—" Felicia felt irritated and dismayed. "I've told you, Jerome, I don't wish—"

"No, no, you have been entirely mistaken. We know who took the necklace and replaced it with one of paste."

Relieved that it wasn't Sir Edward himself, Felicia turned to him. "Who did it, Uncle?"

"We have come to the one inescapable conclusion. It could have been only one person, and we taxed him with the theft this morning. I collect he was not quite himself, for he made a mull of it, trying to deny he was the guilty party. In short, we know."

"Well, who is it?" asked Felicia indifferently. After all, what was the theft of the necklace compared to the problem she was facing now?

Uncle Edward opened his mouth, swallowed, then shut it again.

Jerome came to his aid. "It's Vellacort," he said evenly.

## Sixteen

Felicia stared at them, a glazed incredulous look in her eyes. "But—but how—when—why—"

"To pay his debts," said Jerome. "As to when, on an occasion when you wore it and he offered to return it to Sir Edward. Well, he did return it, but much later."

Felicia was quite appalled. "But how could he steal?"

"I collect his reasoning was that the necklace would belong to you one day, so it would be his also. And he could reimburse Sir Edward for its loss when he came into some money, he explained," said Jerome dryly.

"How could he? How could he?" A common thief. How could she have been so mistaken in Darcy? "What will you do?" she asked Uncle Edward.

"I don't wish any scandal. And it is true, the necklace would have been yours, but . . ."

"You mustn't have him arrested, uncle," Felicia said with a rush. "It won't solve anything. I beg you, let things remain as they are. I shall have a talk with Darcy. I know exactly how much that necklace is worth, and I shall see to it that every penny is returned to you. But pray don't call in the law."

"But my dear," began Jerome, "you cannot protect—"

"No." Felicia turned on him fiercely. "If there is

something I don't wish for now, it is another complication. I shall give Darcy a scold—"

"Is that all you will do? You won't break off your engagement with him?" asked Uncle Edward.

Felicia debated for a moment. It hadn't occurred to her to do so, but now that she thought of it, it would give her a good excuse. On the other hand, she couldn't jeopardize Darcy's future—she must honor the love she had once had for him. So the whole would have to be arranged with great delicacy. And before she did anything, she must clear Darcy in the eyes of the earl. That at least she would do for him, as part of the recompense for crying off from the engagement. And she would show Cleary she did *not* lie.

"I don't know, Uncle Edward, what I shall do. I shall have to think over the whole thing very carefully, and I shan't act in haste."

Uncle Edward nodded gravely, heaving a sigh of relief. "I declare, your taking it all so calmly surprises me. I would have expected quite a different reaction."

"I have grown up in those last few months, Uncle," said Felicia. "And I hope I am a trifle wiser. I am very sorry and I beg your pardon for what he has done, but pray don't do anything to endanger his career."

"You must love him very much," said Uncle Edward, shaking his head.

"I wonder . . ." observed Jerome, gazing at her with a thoughtful look.

"But now that that is settled, I have something of great importance to talk to Jerome about." Felicia hesitated.

"You wish me to leave," said Uncle Edward. "No, no, don't apologize," he added as she wished to protest. "I'm glad you took the whole in such good spirit, and it's a load off my mind. Myself, I don't care about that necklace. I don't know how I almost came to sell it once, but I'm glad I didn't. And if I feel sorry for its loss, it's because it is *your* loss."

"Oh, dearest Uncle," exclaimed Felicia, throwing her arms around his neck and kissing him. "Oh, Uncle, I am ever so grateful to you. Kindest, dearest Uncle. I shall make it up to you someday. I shall see to it that you live in comfort with no worry whether you can pay for your lodgings or your clothes." But how and when would she be able to accomplish that if she did not intend to marry Darcy? She would just be obliged to seek some suitable employment, in spite of everybody's objections.

Uncle Edward kissed her roundly on both cheeks, patted her on the shoulder, and departed. And as soon as the door was shut behind him, Felicia began without preamble, "Jerome, what did Marcus and Darcy fight over? What was the reason for the duel?"

Jerome stared at her, astonished. "What a question to ask now! I have told you that—"

"Yes, yes, but—pray, Jerome, don't be offended, but I have reason to believe that they fought over me."

"What? Who could have told you that?"

"Well, if you must know, Lord Cleary, yesterday. Jerome, I beg you, pray tell me the truth. You could have told me otherwise to spare me, I understand that perfectly. But . . ."

Jerome shook his head, gazing at her with deep reproach. "You wound my feelings deeply, Felicia. You know I had always only your welfare at heart."

"I know, I know, and I feel just dreadful, but I wish to know—was the duel over me?"

"And what if it was? I am not saying it was, but if it was, what of it? They were both drunk."

"But how could that be? I have never given Marcus the slightest encouragement," protested Felicia.

"Women as beautiful as you don't need to encourage men to fall in love with them."

"Well, Marcus was *not* in love with me. To be sure, Lester said he was quite taken with me. But there was nothing to it, I'm sure. *I* hadn't noticed anything."

"How could you. You were fresh mourning your aunt."

"Is it true then?"

"I am not saying," Jerome repeated stubbornly. "Why

is it so important to you to know now, after all this time?"

"Don't you see? If the duel was over me, then Lord Cleary has every reason to think I had cast lures to his brother, even if it was not so. And I couldn't blame him then for thinking me a dreadful flirt and not believing anything I say."

Jerome's eyes narrowed to two slits. He released his breath on a low hiss. "I see," he said slowly. "Indeed, it *does* make a *great* deal of difference."

"There, you see?" cried Felicia eagerly. "It would explain why he is so angry with me. And on top of that, he thinks *I* lured him to the balloon. And of course he doesn't believe my denials. I am going to Barnet again today with Lester to find the right direction of that tapster. I am going to set Lord Cleary straight about that duel once and for all. And perhaps I shall discover from that man too what was the cause of that fight. Oh, Jerome, was it over me? Don't try to spare my feelings. If I provoked that duel and—"

"I would spare you any grief if I could," he suddenly burst out in such a vehement voice that Felicia was quite startled. Abruptly he dropped to his knees beside her, gazing at her in entreaty. "You *are* a most beautiful creature, and you *are* my cousin. Felicia, I begged you for your hand once before, and I'm now repeating my offer. Forget Cleary and the duel, forget Vellacort. He is not worthy of your love. I'm sure when you think things over you will come to that same conclusion. Tie your fate with mine and we both shall be the better for it."

Such was his fervent earnestness, almost despair, that Felicia was deeply moved—but also dismayed. "Jerome, pray do not—I beg you. You know what my sentiments toward you are. You are my dearest friend, and my cousin, but I cannot contemplate marriage with you. I—I do not love you in *that* way. I realize that—that Darcy is not the admirable man I once thought, and I daresay I shan't marry him after all. He is in no great haste to marry *me*," she added with a slight bitterness.

"Perhaps I shan't marry at all, but—pray, I am very distressed to be obliged to refuse you." Tears stung her eyes.

Jerome's face became expressionless. He rose to his feet. "So be it," he said in an even voice, with a curious ring of finality.

"But Jerome, you haven't told me what I wished to know!"

The door opened, interrupting them. Bertha, her countenance expressing fear, said urgently, "Her ladyship has woken up very cross, and it's my belief she intends to give you one of her scolds, miss. And even if you're her favorite, Mr. Banister, I don't think it's wise her catching you here with miss, alone."

"You are right. I am leaving. Your servant, Felicia. It was good of you to warn us, Bertha. Much obliged."

"Oh, and Mr. Winwood asked if you could spare him a moment. He is in the hall."

"I shall go to him directly." He paused. "I might wish to ask of him a small favor. Goodbye, Felicia, and . . ."

He hesitated and would have said something else, but Bertha cried, "Pray make haste. I can hear her ladyship's voice."

And he turned on his heel and departed, leaving Felicia with oppressively lowered spirits. If she had not her plan to think of, she would have burst then and there into tears.

Jerome had been so strange, so unlike himself. Had she hurt his feelings so deeply by implying he had lied to her? But there was no time to puzzle about Jerome now. Yet she was obliged to waste time, listening to Lady Palmer's tirade. At least her ladyship did not forbid Felicia to go to Hookham's, merely requesting her to pick up a book for her there. And as soon as she took herself off, Felicia and Bertha left Berkeley Square. It seemed to Felicia she had waited forever in front of the library when Lester's curricle drove up to her. He sprang down, helped her up, and dismissed the groom, and they set off for Barnet.

The streets were still crowded with people. "And

they shall be even more crowded," prophesied Lester. "Prinny has decided to give a fête for the people. He combined the last act of the Peace Celebration with the celebration of the Jubilee—the centenary of the House of Hanover. There will be pagodas and entertainment in the parks. St. James's Park will be open to the public, there will be fireworks and balloon ascents—"

"Don't mention *that*." Felicia shuddered. "I don't wish to see a balloon ever again."

He glanced at her with sympathy. "Must have been dashed uncomfortable for you, not to say frightening. Best forget it. Sorry I mentioned the word." He was turning off into a side road.

"Are we taking a different route to Barnet?" asked Felicia.

"No. Going to Sir Bellamy's first. With a package of snuff. Won't take us long. Thing is, the road to his place is in very bad shape. Hope you won't mind a few bumps."

"Of course not, as long as that side trip doesn't take up too much time."

"No, no. Not above half or three quarters of an hour, I daresay. Shan't stay there, just give him the snuff."

Felicia said she had no objections to a few bumps, but the first sharp jolt of the curricle almost changed her mind. The road was full of mudholes and water-filled ruts.

"Told you it was a very bad road," Lester apologized. "It ain't far though, just down—" He broke off and gave a distressed cry. A curricle dashing past them at top speed ran over a deep puddle, and splashes of mud spattered their vehicle and feet. "My Hessians," Lester lamented. "Dash it, Felicia. Every time I go somewhere with you, I end up ruining my togs."

"But Lester, it wasn't *my* notion to take this road," protested Felicia.

Lester muttered something under his breath about being obliged to return a favor, and they continued on their way.

The vehicle bumped and jolted over stones and puddles, sending fountains of muddy water high up in the air. Passing vehicles too sent up muddy showers. Mud splattered again over Lester's impeccable Hessians and primrose pantaloons, eliciting from him further cries of distress and anger. Those were not just mud puddles they were traveling through, they were mud pools.

"Where exactly is Sir Bellamy's place? How far is it from here?" asked Felicia.

They had come to the crest of a hill, and Lester brought the curricle to a standstill. "Just down there." He pointed. "See the gatehouse down there?"

Felicia looked, and gasped in dismay. The road sloped downward, gently at first, then to what almost seemed a vertical drop. Deep ditches, now filled with rainwater and mud, and unkempt bushes lined both sides of the road. But Lester was right. It was not very far.

The curricle started downward. The horses on their own increased their pace, splashing along this impossible road. They were coming to the sharp downward turn when Lester abruptly halted the horses. "No, I'll be dashed if I'll have my toggery ruined again," he cried. "You won't mind walking the short distance, Felicia? We can pick our way between the puddles or we can walk along the edge of the ditch."

"Will you walk the horses then?"

Lester, turning around, said, "Think I'll leave the curricle at that cottage back there. You can wait for me here at the side of the road, if you wish. No sense for you to walk here more than necessary. I'd leave you waiting for me at the cottage, but as I recall, ain't a female there on the premises. And Sir Bellamy's groom can drive us *up* the hill in a closed carriage."

"Now *that's* a good notion," approved Felicia. "I'll climb down and sit on that boulder by the road, while you get rid of the curricle."

Lester cast her an anxious glance. "Should be safe here. Not likely a strange vehicle would pass on *this* stretch of the road."

"Of course I shall be safe here. And pray don't worry

about helping me down. Just mind the horses," she said, observing the fidgeting and snorting steppers.

Lester watched worriedly as Felicia climbed down, lifting up her skirts, picked her way to a large flat boulder, and, after wiping it with her handkerchief, seated herself. Then he began to turn the vehicle around.

He was going about it slowly, no doubt fearing to send up splashes of mud, and it was fortunate it was so, for abruptly Felicia, intently observing the maneuver, noticed that one of the wheels was beginning to wobble. "Lester, the wheel!" she cried in alarm.

Lester, startled, lost control of the horses for a moment, and they started downward. The wheel was coming off, and at the same moment the traces gave way.

The next few seconds were a confused blur. "Lester, jump!" cried Felicia as the curricle careened and began to turn over.

# Seventeen

Lester, with a great presence of mind, jumped. But owing to the unfortunate position of the vehicle, he jumped headlong into a large puddle of water, sprawling in it almost up to his neck.

The horses were dragging the now overturned vehicle down the steep incline. The next moment, however, they broke free of the traces completely and, leaving the vehicle in the ditch, galloped off.

Lester, his elegant attire dripping with mud, struggled to a sitting position. His face, where the mud did not cake it, was purple. Felicia was afraid he might get an apoplexy.

"This is the last time I am going with you—*anywhere*," he declared in a voice full of wrath.

"Oh, Lester." Felicia didn't know whether to cry or to laugh. The expression on his countenance was so ludicrous. "Are you hurt?" she cried anxiously, rushing up to him.

"Hurt? Hurt? *I* ain't hurt, my *clothes* are hurt—ruined," he moaned.

Felicia, disregarding her own gown, bent to help him up. "I am so dreadfully sorry."

He waved her away. "No sense in your getting muddied too." His curly-brimmed beaver had been blown away somewhere, and his elegant pomaded hair was in disarray and splashed with mud also. "This is worse than the last time, much worse." He groaned.

He stared at the overturned vehicle. "I can't understand it. Those traces were repaired two days ago. And the wheel—why should it come off?"

"It was a very bumpy road. The wheel must have become loosened."

Lester glanced worriedly down the road. "Hope they did not sustain a harm," he said, thinking of the horses. He sloshed to his feet. Mud and water streaked his green satin coat and the purple-and-yellow waistcoat. The pantaloons and Hessians were all the color of mud.

Lester started to reach for his handkerchief, then let his hands fall helplessly to his sides. He gritted his teeth. "Better start walking. I'll take a bath at Sir Bellamy's, and his servant will look after the horses and the curricle. But my toggery . . ." He groaned again. "I'll be obliged to borrow some clothes. Sir Bellamy's servants won't be able to do anything with this ruin. Nobody will."

And so, sloshing mud with every step, he started downward, with Felicia accompanying him. But at least he wasn't hurt, only bruises, pointed out Felicia.

"Dutch comfort that," grumbled Lester. "I begin to believe Vellacort when he says you attract trouble. Dashed singular thing to happen to one. Never in my life had I experienced the like."

After that he relapsed into silence. Felicia walked beside him without speaking, thinking there was nothing to say that would help.

And since the walk wasn't long, they were soon being received by a startled old gentleman in a tweed jacket and breeches.

The next hour or so was spent on getting rid of the mud and regaining their composure. Then, at last, Felicia and Lester, wearing borrowed clothes, were on their way to Barnet in Sir Bellamy's gig, as his closed carriage was in disrepair. Lester's horses—fortunately not having sustained any damage—and his curricle would be brought to Barnet by Sir Bellamy's groom.

Once they were on an even stretch of the road and Sir Bellamy's placid horses were plodding along safely, Lester turned to Felicia. "Don't know whether I should tell you this, don't wish to alarm you, but—has never been somebody yet that would wish to harm *me*. Think I ought to warn you."

"What do you mean?" cried Felicia, alarmed.

"The wheel and traces. Was no accident we had. It was deliberate. The traces were cut half through. Somebody tampered with my carriage, hoping, no doubt, we would get overturned. And we would have, too. It's a dashed good thing I decided *not* to drive down that road, on account of the mud. Come to think of it, it was a good thing you warned me about the wheel. Might not have jumped in time."

"Lester, you mean somebody wished to kill us—or me?" Felicia asked, her eyes round with shock.

"Looks that way," agreed Lester unhappily.

"You don't think it's that girl again, Darcy's girl?"

Lester sighed. "As I said, nobody could wish *me* harm. I ain't a threat or hindrance to anybody. Trouble is, we have no proof it was she. And she couldn't have done it herself. Don't think."

"Oh, Lester, this is dreadful. What shall we do?"

"Must have a talk with her. Trouble is, can't accuse her without proof. Think we should tell Vellacort. Once we get back to London, I'll seek him out. I can understand her wishing to stop the race. But this! She ought to be clapped in Bedlam. And I mean it literally. Now don't you worry. You stay home and don't go anywhere without m' mother or father. Don't think anyone would try something with them around."

Felicia was deeply disturbed by this discovery. That she herself could have been killed by a jealous woman was bad enough, but that Lester—quite innocent—could have been killed too was unforgivable. That girl must be insane, and quite ruthless.

In quite lowered spirits, she and Lester finally arrived in Barnet. Felicia was hardly in the mood to start on her investigation, but since all that trouble had occurred *because* of her wishing to come here, and Lord Cleary still believed the worst of Darcy and herself, she would continue with her search now that she was here.

While Lester went to see if the staff could do anything with his bundle of muddy clothes, Felicia, who was waiting for him in another chamber, sent for the maid, Nancy, to whom she had spoken before. Lester would talk to the innkeeper.

The maid, wiping her hands on her apron, eyed her uneasily. "You wished to speak to me, miss?"

Felicia nodded. "Yes. You must recall me. I've talked to you before. I'm trying to find Sam Stoddart, and at the address his father has given us, nobody has heard of him. Now I wish to know his address. I won't cause him any trouble, I promise. I just wish to ask him some questions. Pray tell me where I can find him."

"It's not for me to say, ma'am. It's got nothing to do with me."

"But you and he were good friends. Surely you must know where he is."

The girl repeated stubbornly, "It's not *my* concern where he has gone. Mr. Stoddart knows where his son is, I'm sure. It's to him you should be speaking, not to me."

Felicia felt a surge of irritation. The girl was much too pert. She took a deep breath. "Sam Stoddart won't get into trouble with the law or with Lord Cleary over his assisting in the duel—not through my contrivance.

"You may be sure I shan't tell the constable or the magistrate about him. As for Lord Cleary, I doubt if he would take his anger out on Sam. Sam didn't start the duel, nor could he have prevented it, if, as I collect, it started on the spur of the moment."

The girl nodded eagerly. "That's how it was. When they came to the inn, all they could think of was the race. Then they took to playing cards, and—"

"Was the duel—the fight—over cards?" asked Felicia quickly.

The girl clamped her mouth shut, and the guarded look was back in her eyes.

Felicia's heart began to thud. "Was the fight over me? Now, don't be afraid to own the truth. I wish to know it, and I shan't be overset. Nor will telling me this get *you* into trouble. Was the fight over me?"

The girl said reluctantly, "Yes, miss. But it really wasn't. I mean, I don't think there was a reason—"

She broke off as Felicia slumped back in her chair, closing her eyes. So Lord Cleary had good reason to think she had been casting lures to his brother and had caused his death. But that still didn't excuse him from jumping to the conclusion that she wished to bring about his own death in the balloon.

"Miss, miss, are you ill?" The girl's worried voice recalled Felicia. Her eyes flew open.

"No, I am perfectly well. But how could you know it was over me?"

"I like Mr. Vellacort. Him having his estate here, he comes here to dine often, and I serve him." She reddened.

"You eavesdropped," supplied Felicia. "I shan't scold you for it. Did you hear my name mentioned?"

The girl nodded. "I had forgotten it, but when you came here, asking questions, and told me your name, then I recalled."

"Very well. But how—" No. More important first was to discover the direction of that tapster. "So now that you know I shan't get Sam into trouble, you can tell me where he is."

"*You* won't, but you might tell others. And the gentleman said as how Sam might be clapped in Newgate or be killed by Lord Cleary."

"Now who could have told him that? What gentleman?"

Before Nancy could answer her, the door of the chamber burst open after just a perfunctory knock and the innkeeper's red face appeared in the doorway.

"Nancy, you are wanted in the kitchen," he barked.

He bowed to Felicia. "Beggin' your pardon, miss. I'll attend to anything you desire."

"I doubt it," said Felicia crossly. "And you needn't look at her that way. She hasn't yet told me your son's direction. And now she probably won't. You'd better go," she said in a kinder tone to the girl.

After the girl had gone, she rose from the chair and, looking the landlord squarely in the eyes, said, "Now let me hear without any roundaboutation where your son is really hiding out. And you needn't fear that I'll cause him trouble, for I shan't. But if you don't tell me, then I shall be obliged to set a Bow Street Runner on his trail."

"No, oh no, miss," cried the landlord with alarm. "Not *that*."

The threat worked. "Well then, tell me. I am all out of patience with you over your lies. And I don't think Mr. Winwood will thank you either, for lying to him. Once he tears his mind away from his clothes for a moment, he will tell you what he thinks of that wild goose chase you sent us on."

"I am sorry, miss. I didn't wish to cause trouble, but he's my only son. And when quality fall out, it's us poor folks as get the blame, more often than not. He went to my brother who has a tavern—in Gretna Green."

"Scotland?" cried Felicia, dismayed. "Oh no. That's at least a three-day ride. And what is the name of that tavern?"

"The Three . . . Three Lions, miss."

Felicia eyed him suspiciously. Had he hesitated over the last word? No matter. There wouldn't be that many taverns in Gretna Green. "I hope you're not lying again," she said severely.

"No, no. It's . . . that tavern actually is a piece before you get to Gretna."

"Well, for your sake I hope you're telling me the truth. Though I doubt Mr. Winwood will be pleased with *this* intelligence," she added more to herself than to him.

He wasn't.

"You can't expect me to go to Gretna Green with you," ejaculated Lester, aghast upon hearing the good news. "No, dash it, Felicia. *Gretna Green*. People would think we have *eloped*." And he looked so revolted by the notion that but for the seriousness of the situation, he would have sent her into whoops. "And *Mother*, now if she thought *that*." He shuddered and paled at the notion. "No, no, Felicia. You can't expect me to go jaunting with you to the border. Out of the question."

Felicia realized she couldn't persuade him at once. He must get accustomed to the notion first. Besides, he was overset because of his clothes and the accident. She sobered up. "Well, we must discover first if Darcy's . . . friend was responsible for the accident, and then we shall talk about Scotland."

Lester wiped his face with his handkerchief. He still looked a sorry sight, in old Sir Bellamy's breeches and tweed coat, but he informed her that perhaps his coat and waistcoat might be salvaged. And his Hessians were reasonably clean.

Very soon after, they left the inn, both in a subdued and thoughtful mood. Felicia extracted a promise from Lester to question Darcy's friend as soon as he could and let her know immediately what he had discovered.

After this further frightening experience Felicia was too overset to take part in balls and fêtes. She explained to Lady Palmer that she was still quite tired from the ball for Wellington and would prefer to rest at home for a few days. Lady Palmer, not at all anxious to take Felicia along, received this information with equanimity. Lord Palmer was a trifle worried, but as he had many state matters on his mind, he had not much time to spare on Felicia. Soon, to her regret, he would be leaving town again.

Two days after the outing to Barnet, Lord Cleary paid a call in Berkeley Square, desiring to see Felicia. Felicia denied herself to him. He had hurt her too much with his accusations. Even if he had now discovered the truth about the balloon ride, he still would not change his opinion of her, nor his conviction that she was responsible for his brother's death. Only when she presented him with Sam Stoddart's statement would she allow him to speak to her. And that did not seem to be possible in the very near future—no matter how she wished it. It would take strategy to turn Lester to her thinking.

Actually, Lester half offered to go alone to Gretna, but Felicia doubted if he would be able to persuade Sam to return with him to tell Lord Cleary the truth. No, she could entrust such a delicate maneuver to no one but herself, for if Sam would not agree to come with Lester, he might very likely disappear, and they would never be able to find him again.

And Felicia could not ask Uncle Edward to go with her. The journey would have been too hard on him. As for Jerome, she had had no occasion to see him since she had returned from Barnet, but she was more disinclined than ever to ask a favor of him. Not only because he had lied to her about the cause of the duel—no doubt he thought he was sparing her embarrassment—but because of his second proposal. How could she take advantage of his kindness when she had just rejected his suit again? Asking Jerome for anything was unthinkable now.

Another alternative would be for her to go only with Bertha, which she could not quite like. Not with a killer stalking her. Though she couldn't perceive how Darcy's girl could pursue her to Gretna.

Darcy's girl couldn't, but she came to the grim and shocking conclusion on the day following the earl's call that a peer of the realm certainly could.

# *Eighteen*

Lester, looking more frightened and harried than ever, that afternoon stealthily entered Felicia's bedchamber. Begging Bertha to stand guard on the corridor and let him know if somebody was approaching in time for him to slip out, he plopped into a chair while Felicia perched on the bed.

"Well, what have you discovered?" She pounced on him eagerly, her heart pounding with apprehension. It was not a comfortable feeling to know oneself to be the target of a killer, and she hoped that perhaps Lester would tell her that his carriage hadn't been tampered with after all.

But the carriage *had* been tampered with. And to Felicia's great surprise and consternation, it hadn't been Darcy's lady friend who had done it. Nor, Lester assured her, had she ordered someone to do it. But she had been the one who had drugged the balloonist's assistant. She had secured a lady's slipper to the rim of the basket and heaped up pillows and blankets inside to resemble a covered body. Her intention was to cut all the ropes but one, and this one to cut almost through, then to hide herself and give a moan. Seeing the slipper and hearing the moan, the earl would climb inside the basket. She then would sever the remaining rope and the balloon would go up. But the escaped convict apparently saw her hacking away at the rope, knocked her out, and dragged her into some bushes. And the arriving earl was caught in the trap.

Lester thought they should go to Bow Street with their tale of the curricle accident, except that he did not wish his mother to discover he had gone to Barnet with Felicia. "If only we knew who could wish to do us in," he muttered unhappily.

Abruptly Felicia felt a cold hand clutch at her heart. "We know," she said in a hollow voice. "It has been staring us in the face all along."

"*We* know? Felicia—"

"It can't be anybody wishing to kill you, Lester. You said so yourself. And there is only one other person who would benefit from my death, or at least get a morbid satisfaction from it. Lord Cleary!"

"What?" Lester started in his chair. "Cleary try to kill you? First you suspect the fellow of trying to do away with Vellacort, and now yourself?"

"But Lester, it must be so," she persisted. "And it does make sense. You said yourself he is obsessed with his brother's death. I believe he intended to kill or ruin Darcy in that race. That didn't work, so he decided to deprive Darcy of the person he loves, just as Darcy deprived him of his brother. Don't you see?"

Lester's jaw dropped as he stared at her in consternation. Then he shook his head in a bewildered manner. "Put that way it makes a sort of queer sense," he conceded. "But he would have to be quite touched in his upper works to contemplate it, yet alone carry it out."

"Well, who else could it be? Who else has reason to hate me so? Besides, you don't know, I didn't tell you. The fight *was* over me. I discovered that in Barnet. So he holds me responsible for his brother's death too."

"But—" began Lester.

"The only thing is," she added, her brow creasing, "I don't see him callous enough to sacrifice *your* life in his thirst for revenge. Perhaps he thought only I would be thrown off the curricle and you could save yourself.

Oh, what's the odds? Lester, it is most imperative that we start at once for Gretna Green."

"What?" Lester's eyes started from his head in horror.

"Lester, it's a matter of life and death for me now. Perhaps the earl has indeed run mad. Only the truth about the duel could save me now. Don't you see how urgent it is, how imperative? We would prevent him from committing murder. We must do that. And your mother needn't know at all that you're going with me. Tell her that you wish to visit your friend in the country. Pack your portmanteau, drive your curricle to the posting inn, hire a chaise, and wait for me there. You can leave the curricle at the inn. Bertha will carry my portmanteau to the inn, then come back to fetch me. I shall again pretend I'm going to Hookham's or shopping, and then disappear."

"Couldn't Bertha go along too—for propriety? That is, if I ever do go—which I don't at all think I shall agree to."

Felicia was greatly relieved. Lester was already thinking of the impossible. "We must leave Bertha behind to fob off Lady Palmer and the rest, to prevent a hue and cry before we have had a chance to get away from London. As for your notion of going to Bow Street, you don't wish the scandal of having Lord Cleary visited by a Bow Street Runner and being obliged to repeat your accusations to his face."

Lester shuddered. But his sense of propriety was still offended. "Don't like your going with me without a female accompanying you. Not all the way to Scotland. Not the thing." He tugged at his earlobe. "I don't like it. Jaunting to Barnet was one thing, but several days on the road . . ."

"Who's to know that we are together?"

"Yes, and that's another thing I daresay you haven't thought of—all impatience to leave. Dash it, Felicia, what will everybody think when you disappear? What will Mother say?"

"As far as she's concerned I'm beneath reproach already. I don't think it will take her too long to persuade Lord Palmer to her thinking after all that has occurred. At all events, I—"

"But what will you do *then*?"

"Well, the most important thing for me is to stay alive. Time to think what to do next after we have removed the threat of danger."

"Always assuming that it's Cleary who did it. Dash it, Felicia, I can't believe it. I—"

"But you will go with me to Gretna?"

"I—we must be careful about it. Lull everybody's suspicions—if we do go. I'll have to see to my toggery and cancel my engagements. And—and I'll—dash it, I can't believe it of Cleary. I'll try talking to him, draw him out. And we'll go after the Jubilee."

"Oh no, Lester!" Procrastination could have been his other name.

"Not long to wait. And nobody will suspect anything if we sneak out the morning after the Jubilee celebration. Everybody will sleep late the next day, and m' mother won't wonder if you don't come down to dinner or even supper. Vellacort has promised to take you to the park?"

"Yes, to all three parks in turn. A seven-story Chinese pagoda is being built in St. James's Park, and there will be a reenactment of a naval battle on the Serpentine. And the fireworks at night. I had expected to enjoy it all so much."

"Daresay you will. Daresay I shall be able to reassure you it's not Cleary."

"If it's not Cleary, then who? Who is the hidden enemy?"

Lester remained silent, baffled.

"There you are—you have no answer. So you have everything ready, and I'll have my portmanteau packed. And, you must contrive to talk to me before then, so we can settle on the exact time I am to meet you at the inn."

Lester glanced at her worriedly. "Be very careful until then. Daresay you will be safe with Vellacort. This time he won't leave you alone, not after I tell him about somebody trying—no, on second thought, he would think right away it's Cleary and challenge him to a duel."

"Oh no," cried Felicia, horrified.

"Yes. It's a dashed good thing I persuaded you to keep quiet about that attempt until I checked with Tessy."

"I think Lord Palmer should be told," pondered Felicia.

Lester nodded. "Only thing—shan't be able to sneak off to Gretna Green then. He'll be watching over you. You know, that's a dashed good notion to tell m' father now. Can beg him not to tell Mother and—"

"No, we shall tell him, but after Gretna. I promised the innkeeper to keep the law away from him. But Lord Palmer, kind as he is, would send someone in official capacity to investigate the matter. Everything would come out in the open then, before I have had a chance to speak to Sam Stoddart. And what's most important, I'll wager he wouldn't allow me to go to Gretna. And everything might go awry then."

Lester heaved a deep sigh. "Oh, how I wish that was a plain accident and not a tampering with the carriage. I wouldn't even mind having *two* of my suits ruined."

Felicia was deeply touched. "Oh, Lester," she said, her large green eyes shining with gratitude, "you *are* such a good friend to me. I shall make it up to you somehow. Oh, how I wish it was the day of the Jubilee already," she cried impatiently.

"Won't have long to wait."

Which was all very well for Lester to say, but for her impatient heart to wait until after the fête was quite another matter.

And the waiting wasn't made any easier for her by Lord Cleary's repeated calls on her. Did he know the truth now about the balloon incident, and, regretting his insults, did he want to apologize to her? She refused to see him even though in her heart she wished to. Her reason and her fear fought against this wish and prevailed. But oh, if only she could be sure he was *not* the killer. But if not he, then who?

Perhaps Lester would somehow discover who the real culprit was, thought Felicia. Discover that it was *not* Lord Cleary after all. The thought that *he* could be doing it to her was not to be borne.

Hurt and angered at the earl, she yet knew in her heart of hearts that were the incident with the balloon repeated, she would run just as headlong to save him—again. Surely she could not be in love with him now. More confused than ever, Felicia impatiently waited for the day of the Jubilee, wishing that something would occur to at least help her to know her own mind.

# *Nineteen*

Felicia greeted the day of the Jubilee with a sigh of relief, not thinking of the celebrations, wishing only for this day to end soon. Yet in the evening she was obliged to appear unconcerned when in the company of Darcy and Jerome she departed for Hyde Park. Jerome procured chairs for them, for to ride or drive would have been impossible—it seemed all the people of the kingdom had congregated in the streets of London. (Subsequently she learned that half a million people had thronged the streets and parks that day.) But the crowds were friendly and cheerful, and everyone was in good spirits. Everyone except Felicia.

She had debated with herself whether to tell Jerome about the accident with the curricle, and had decided against it. Jerome was her good friend, and upon hearing such news he would at once constitute himself her guardian, and apart from not wishing to stand any more in his debt, she was sure he would hamper her in her plans. And to go with Jerome to Gretna was unthinkable. Nor did she ask Jerome about the cause of the fight. She knew now, so there was no point; and she did not wish to embarrass him by letting him know she was aware that he had lied to her about it.

Would Jerome have been able to cast a light on the accident with the carriage? She doubted it. What could have been worse, perhaps he would have come to the same conclusion she had.

She would have continued brooding over this whole matter, had not Darcy remarked upon her being in a brown study, and she forced herself to concentrate on her surroundings.

Although this last phase of the celebrations was intended for the masses, Darcy thought it would be fun to mix with ordinary people for a change and watch the spectacles. Lady Palmer did not approve of the notion, but again Jerome brought her around to his thinking; and since he was to be there to watch over Felicia, she gave her consent. She also grudgingly ordered a new hat for Felicia for this occasion, a fetching high-crowned satin poke bonnet with velvet ribbons.

Felicia found Hyde Park changed beyond recognition. Sand covered much of the grass. Pagodas, Chinese temples, bridges, and towers were erected everywhere, and what space was left was covered by merchants' and entertainers' booths and tents. Food and drink could be had to everyone's taste. The odor of beer and liquor mingled with that of flowers and of victuals.

Gaming booths were set up here also. But as soon as Felicia noticed them, she begged to remove to Green Park, where a curious castle with a round tower and ramparts had been erected. It was called the Castle of Discord, with "Napoleon's soldiers" manning the battlements. Darcy revealed to her that it would go up in smoke during the fireworks finale, as a symbol of the end of the war with all its horrors.

Here, as in Hyde Park, many people picnicked under the trees in the fresh evening air and merry laughter and chatter reverberated through the park.

But it was the Grand Finale that they had come to see here, and having selected a vantage spot under a tree, Jerome spread a blanket and Darcy opened the picnic hamper, which held cheeses, cold meats, fruit, and champagne, and they sat down to consume the meal.

In spite of her heartache, Felicia could not help taking pleasure in this simple diversion, for it reminded her of picnics with her aunt in the country.

They had just finished their repast when Lord Cleary appeared.

"You here *again*," exclaimed Darcy, jumping to his feet.

Disregarding him, the earl turned to Felicia. "Miss Mannering, you denied yourself to me each time I attempted to see you. But I *must* see you. I must apologize." His voice and his countenance betrayed his agitation.

"She doesn't want your apologies. Apologize for *what*?" Darcy abruptly asked, his eyes narrowing in suspicion.

The earl paid him no heed. "I must and shall have word with you. How was I to know that it wasn't you who played that trick on me? I knew you would do anything for Vellacort. But when I discovered from my butler—" He broke off.

Suddenly breathless, heart thudding, Felicia gazed at the earl. How splendid he looked in his maroon coat and buff breeches. So ruggedly handsome. And he sounded sincere in his regret. It seemed inconceivable that he could have planned that accident with the curricle, planned to murder her and Lester.

"Yes, Felicia would do anything for me," cried Darcy. "And she is capable of doing bird-witted things, but only an imbecile would think she could be capable of planning murder."

The earl flushed. "I ought to call you out for that, but unfortunately you *are* speaking the truth. Miss Mannering, I must speak with you in private for a few moments."

"No, you shan't," cried Darcy hotly. "You have apologized and owned your mistake—now take yourself off."

The earl took a step toward him, throwing the dark cloak he was carrying over his shoulder. "I won't tolerate that from you, Vellacort," he said threateningly, raising his fists.

Jerome's cool, smooth voice cut in on this heated interchange. "Pray recollect where you are. It would not do to create a vulgar brawl here for the entertainment of these cits."

Lord Cleary's fists fell. He stepped back a pace, glancing at the interested faces of some strolling citizens.

"You are right, Banister. But I shall see you soon, Vellacort. Pray accept my most humble apologies, Miss Mannering." He bowed, turned on his heel, and strode off.

"I believe he was foxed," said Darcy. "He was reeking of brandy. I hope we have seen the last of him."

"I sincerely hope so," echoed Jerome fervently. "And you are right—he wouldn't have come here attempting to speak to Felicia, with the two of us present, were he not in his cups."

Felicia was quite disturbed by this encounter. Her uncertain peace was all cut up. But she could not help feeling glad that Cleary wished to apologize, that he owned to his mistake. Would that he had apologized about thinking that she had flirted with his brother. "Oh, it's impossible," she suddenly exclaimed, highly vexed. She didn't wish him to be guilty of trying to kill her. But perhaps he was not.

She became conscious of her fiancé and her cousin staring at her and recollected herself. "That man is impossible," she added lamely. "I wish he would forget all about you and me, Darcy. But I still think he means to take revenge on you."

"He'd better watch that *I* don't take revenge on *him*, if he tries to make up to my betrothed," said Darcy, pushing out his chest.

But the sad truth was, thought Felicia dispassionately, that Darcy would do precisely nothing.

She glanced at the handsome face of her betrothed. He appeared just as handsome as before, but his handsomeness was somehow not as appealing to her now. Now she could observe the lines of weakness in his countenance and none of the ruggedness and strength of the earl.

How could she have been in love with him? Oh, he *was* charming, and an agreeable companion when he wished to put himself out, but . . .

She sighed. Was she in love with the earl? She could not help searching her soul again. She thrilled at his touch, her heart leaped on seeing him. Yet she was angry at Cleary because he thought ill of her—with some good reason, as she knew now. And it seemed he had been trying to kill her. "Oh, I wish he hadn't come here," she exclaimed.

Jerome threw her a keen glance. "Don't let his appearance overset you and spoil the picnic and your enjoyment of the Grand Finale. Yes, the Grand Finale," he repeated, and stared into space.

The Grand Finale came at midnight. With a great explosion, the Castle of Discord went up in smoke. And when the smoke cleared, a revolving Temple of Peace stood before the startled eyes of the spectators. Foot guards on the roof held aloft the royal standard and cheered, water flowed from the jaws of lions into golden basins, and the whole exhibit was illuminated by colored lights. Thus Peace triumphed over War, the display proclaimed. And then another deafening sound as the fireworks exploded in the sky.

Golden and multicolored stars, Roman candles and girandoles, stars in clusters and in all shapes, streaked the heavens and showered on earth in brilliant fountains and cascades. The dazzling sight was overwhelming, and the acrid smoke from the explosions tickled Felicia's nostrils.

Abruptly Felicia felt—rather than heard—something whistle close by, and she whirled round, thinking a fragment of one of the fireworks had somehow come close to her. For a moment as her head was turned, she saw in the crowd the face of Lord Cleary. Then Darcy grabbed her arm. "Look, look," he cried as another golden star exploded in the sky.

Felicia turned back to stare at the display and again felt something whiz by very close. And above the noise of the fireworks she heard a familiar voice cry out, "Damnation!"

Darcy must have heard it too. "No, that is the outside of enough! That settles it. I'm taking you home, Felicia. We have seen the fireworks—we can go. Can't turn around without coming across him. And he is quite drunk; he is reeling.

"Jerome, where are you? Jerome, we are leaving." Jerome materialized at their side.

"We are going home," said Darcy angrily.

It was easier said than done, for the crush was tremendous, but they made it somehow to the less populated streets and were just turning a corner when Felicia, glancing back, saw Lord Cleary, wrapped in his cloak, staring after them. "He's been following us all the way," she exclaimed with mixed feelings.

"I know—I've seen him," said Jerome grimly through shut teeth.

"That fellow is an infernal nuisance," exclaimed Darcy, pulling Felicia along.

Some time later, having said goodnight to Darcy and Jerome, Felicia was removing her hat in front of the mirror of her dressing room. Suddenly her eyes dilated in horror. In the crown of her hat was a round hole—a hole that could only have been made by a bullet, and it flashed through her terror-stricken mind that she had noticed something whistling past her ear.

She felt cold and sick at heart. Lord Cleary had struck again. And it was only by a stroke of luck that she had escaped death.

# Twenty

It would have been hard for Felicia to describe her feelings upon that terrible discovery. Horror and hurt and shock, certainly, and a dreadful sense of loss, such loss as she had felt upon the death of her aunt, but this was even worse. Was it the sense of trust betrayed that gave her that feeling? For here was confirmation of her worst suspicions. Yet he had stood her good friend in the matter of the necklace and at Vauxhall. She recalled his gentleness and his strength upon both occasions. It seemed inconceivable that he now would be trying to extinguish a life he had saved.

She gave a strangled sob and pounded with her fist on her dressing table. No, no, no! Now that she had proof, irrefutable proof of his guilt, now at last she realized fully that she loved him. And the irony of it was that she had fallen in love with a madman. For that was the best possible explanation of his actions. His mind had become completely deranged by his grief and his hatred for Darcy.

A great sadness overcame her next, and despair of ever being able to penetrate his obsessed mind with the truth. But she must try, at all costs. Her own life was at stake now, not only Darcy's or Darcy's career. And the matter was most urgent, for the earl might try again soon and succeed. She would be dead and he ruined and locked up in Bedlam. Perhaps the certain knowledge, the conviction, that his brother was *not* murdered would sooth his hurt and restore his reason. She must do her best to accomplish that.

She shuddered at the prospect of that magnificent figure imprisoned in that hell for the insane. But she was *not* going to be killed. She would find that witness and somehow convince the earl that Darcy had not murdered his brother. Therefore he had no need to revenge himself upon Darcy.

She sighed. That took care of Darcy. But what of herself? How could she explain to him the fact that the duel was over her? How could that have come about? She had no way of explaining it. She would have to ask Jerome to tell her how it had happened—much as she disliked the notion.

But perhaps the tapster would know how it happened, how the quarrel arose, and would be able to explain it to the earl's satisfaction. After all, both Marcus and Darcy were in their cups, and anything was possible between two hotheaded men in an inebriated state. She should have asked the maid at the inn about it. She would have asked her had the landlord not come in and chased her away. She would see her again, but after finding Sam Stoddart. That was most important of all.

Felicia hardly slept at all that night, checking and rechecking the contents of her portmanteau, and wishing she could wake up to discover the whole terrible occurrence a nightmare.

Alas, it was not a dream. And her patience and her nerves had quite worn thin by the time Bertha came to fetch her. Having already carried Felicia's portmanteau and bandbox to the inn, Bertha informed her that Mr. Winwood, though thoroughly unhappy, had arranged everything satisfactorily and was even now waiting for her in the chaise.

Once more Bertha begged Felicia to take her along. But Felicia was adamant. "You must keep my disappearance undiscovered for as long as you can. We must get a good head start—on no account must we be turned back. And Lady Palmer is quite capable of doing that, once she knows I have gone, so she mustn't have time to do so."

Bertha, with a long face, and shaking her head, accompanied her mistress for a "stroll."

In the event, no one observed their departure except an underfootman and an upstairs maid. And the sight of Felicia, attired in her apple-green walking dress, going out in the company of her maid was nothing out of the ordinary.

Once they had left the square, Felicia increased her pace. Soon they were at the posting inn and Felicia was being handed into the waiting post chaise. As a tearful Bertha bade them farewell, Felicia slammed the carriage door and settled back against the squabs beside Lester. The coachman set the horses in motion and they were on their way.

Lester looked thoroughly unhappy, but as usual his attire was impeccable—blue riding coat, yellow leather breeches, and dazzlingly polished top boots. "Waited for you here," he mumbled. "Thought 'twould be better if I didn't show my face too much."

Felicia patted his hand. "Poor Lester. I am putting you in a dreadful fix. But I hope your mama won't tumble to the truth." At that moment she chanced to glance out the window, and she froze. There in the middle of the yard stood one of Lady Palmer's footmen, gaping at the chaise.

Felicia quickly pulled back from the window, averting her face, but she was afraid he must have seen her. At least she hoped he had not seen Lester. "You did tell Lady Palmer you were going to spend a week with your friend in the country?" she asked.

He nodded. "Mother took it in good part. Said I needed to go on a repairing lease."

"So I'll wager she won't associate *my* disappearance with your departure."

Lester refused to be comforted. "I hope not," he said glumly. "But what happens after we return?"

"We shall think about that later," cried Felicia impatiently. Then, lowering her voice, although she didn't think the coachman or the postboy could hear her, she said, "Lord Cleary tried to kill me last night."

Lester's eyes started from their sockets. "Impossible," he cried. "You are bamming me."

"No, I'm not. I am wearing the same hat I wore last night. There's a hole in the crown, and it could have been done only by a bullet, I am sure of it. And I heard or felt something whoosh by, but there was so much noise from the fireworks I thought it was a piece of a Roman candle or something flying over my head. And Lord Cleary was there. Darcy saw him, and Jerome."

"No, no," groaned Lester. "He couldn't have done it. He knows the truth about the balloon now."

"Oh yes, he knows—and he tried to pretend he wished to apologize to me, to pull the wool over my eyes and lull me into trusting him. When *that* didn't work, he shot at me outright."

"But he wouldn't. He couldn't have. I've told him about the accident and our suspicions."

"You have what?" Felicia rounded on him in wrath. "Lester Winwood—"

"Dash it, Felicia," protested Lester, "he couldn't have done it. He isn't queer in his attic yet. And if he did, he wouldn't have tried anything now, knowing we are on our guard."

"Well, he did try it. Yes, and you said I should go to the park so as not to make anybody suspicious. You said I should be safe with Darcy and Jerome."

"You should have been. Should have told you, though, to get home *before* the fireworks. Should have thought of *that*. As for telling Cleary, I met him at White's, and he was so—so—dash it, he didn't sound like a man who would wish to kill you. On the contrary. So I told him."

"Well, I just hope you didn't tell him about our going off to Scotland together," she said with asperity.

"No, no, couldn't do that. Nobody must know." He

kept shaking his head. "He's not the man to do it, Felicia. I can't believe it of him."

"You can't believe it?" she said bitterly. "You think I find it easy to believe? I am still numb with shock, and I don't think I shall ever be myself again. Don't you think I wish with all my heart that it were anybody else but the earl?" She heaved a deep sigh. "At all events, we shall find that tapster and persuade him to come with us to London. Perhaps what he can tell us will make Lord Cleary give up his notions of revenge."

The rest of that first stage was spent in gloomy silence. They changed horses at Barnet, but did not alight for refreshments. Only when they reached Welwyn did they halt for a repast and rest and a change of horses again. The horses were not the best one could get, so frequent changes were necessary to ensure their proceeding at a fast pace.

"Daresay you didn't think of it when you persuaded me to go to Gretna with you," grumbled Lester as he was pulling out his purse, "that this ride will burn quite a hole in my pocket. I was obliged to take the blunt I was going to pay my tailor with."

Felicia was immediately contrite. "Oh, Lester, I did forget completely. It must be quite a shocking expense—and how and when shall I ever repay you?"

"Don't worry over that. Thing is Mother thought she gave me enough to last me for a while. She'll think I've lost it gaming when I approach her for more."

"Oh dear. Oh, Lester, I am exceedingly sorry to have caused you so much trouble. I shall somehow contrive to pay you back the money. And we must return separately to Berkeley Square, just as we have left. That way nobody will know we have been together."

"Just hope nobody has seen us get into the same chaise and tattles to mother," said Lester.

Felicia, not daring to tell him of the footman, hoped so too.

"And if she made inquiries," he continued, "and discovered we were bound for Gretna, she would be bound to conclude we were eloping." He moaned and shuddered.

In spite of her distress, Felicia chuckled with amusement at the picture conjured up in her mind: Lady Palmer thinking her son was eloping with Felicia to the border, with marriage at the anvil in mind. She would have a spasm without a doubt. "I should like to see her face when she hits upon *that* notion. Not that she will hit upon it," she added hastily. "She won't discover it, for nobody saw us going off together."

But there she was mistaken. Somebody had seen them. And at the very moment that Felicia and Lester were entering Welwyn, Lady Palmer was treating her domestics to such a display of spasms and rage as they had never seen her fall into before, while urgent messages were being sent to Miss Mannering's betrothed, her cousin, and her uncle. Sir Edward was from home, but Felicia's cousin and betrothed heeded that urgent call, almost colliding on the stoop of Berkeley Square.

"You received a note too?" cried Vellacort.

Jerome Banister nodded. "What has occurred?" he asked as he plied the knocker.

Darcy shrugged. "Some lark of Felicia's, no doubt. I had a note from her today."

Jerome's eyes narrowed. "What did she say?"

Darcy grimaced. "The same as always. Warning me to be on my guard against Cleary. Only this time she says she has the proof that he intends to do me great harm. She implores me to take the greatest care for the next few days, but assures me she will make sure that the threat is removed once and for all."

More he could not say, for the door was opened to them by a grave-faced Siddon. Both men pounced on the butler. As he ushered them in, he addressed himself to Jerome. "Thank God you were at home, Mr. Banister," he said with relief, his usually starchy impassive face betraying his agitation. "I do hope you will contrive to relieve her ladyship's distress and restore her calm."

"But what has occurred?" interrupted Darcy irritably. "Why should she be so agitated?"

The butler's lips pressed shut in a strongly disapproving line. Then he said acidly, "Mr. Winwood has eloped with Miss Mannering to the border."

"What?" both men cried as of one accord. And Darcy gave an irritated laugh. "Don't be absurd. The notion is preposterous."

Siddon, preceding them up the stairs to her ladyship's dressing room, turned around, saying mournfully, "Alas, it is only too true, even if Miss Mannering's maid denies any knowledge of it. And if only her ladyship had been apprised of certain facts in time, we might have been able to avert the disaster."

Darcy was losing his patience. "What facts? Tell us the whole, immediately."

"Yes, pray do, Siddon," agreed Jerome. "If Lady Palmer is prostrated, as I collect she is, then we shan't be able to get a coherent story from her."

The butler obliged. "I noticed Miss Mannering's maid stealing out of the house with Miss Mannering's portmanteau, and feeling it my duty, I informed Toller, her ladyship's dresser. If only she had not been afraid to disturb Lady Palmer's sleep—her ladyship had taken laudanum for her headache. But Toller begged me to set a footman to watch Miss Mannering's maid, and I did so."

Now he was conducting them along the corridor to a door farther down, from behind which distressing sounds could be heard. "Bell, the footman, kept an unobtrusive eye on Bertha, and he followed her and Miss Mannering when they left, ostensibly to go to Hookham's. Instead they went to a coaching inn. And Bell saw with his own eyes Miss Mannering climbing in and Mr. Winwood leaning out to assist her. And furthermore, he has ascertained that they are traveling to Scotland."

Jerome and Darcy exchanged baffled glances as Siddon threw open the door and announced their arrival.

The next few moments were a scene of confusion, disjointed speech, and tears, which ended with Lady

Palmer imploring Jerome to accompany her, in the absence of Lord Palmer, in her pursuit of the elopers.

Jerome tried to convince her that she could trust him to bring the fugitives back to her, but she was adamant, and he was obliged to agree to her request. Felicia's betrothed also assured her he would go after his wayward bride, and both men hastily left the chamber.

"Do you think she has really eloped with Winwood?" asked Jerome, after they were let out the front door.

Darcy shook his head. "Not she. I fancy I know where the little ninnyhammer has gone to—to search for Sam Stoddart. She thinks she will present Cleary with the proof of my innocence and he will cease to hate me. The little fool," he added with a mirthless laugh. "Of course, I have to stop her. The last thing on earth I wish is to have Sam tell his tale to Cleary."

"Exactly," echoed Jerome. "We must prevent that at all costs."

"We shall," said Darcy grimly. "You may be sure of that. I value my career too much to have that pea-goose spoil everything now."

A short time later, Darcy Vellacort was back at his lodgings, where he was obliged to reveal his problem to a blond girl with a yellow rose in her hair. He ended up the tale with what was vexing him most. "And the little fool thinks she is doing me a favor by trying to find that tapster from Barnet. I must stop her. Banister will try too, but I daresay I shall catch up with her first, for with Lady Palmer he won't be able to travel fast."

The blond girl blinked and frowned. Something that Zemelda had once let slip came to her mind now. "But Darcy," she began, "what if Miss Mannering is right? What if . . ."

He stared at her incredulously. "Have you taken leave of your senses, Tess? Go. I have no time for you now. I must make haste."

"But Darcy—"

He glared at her and gave her a push. "Take yourself off. At once. You know I won't tolerate your disobedience and interference with my plans."

Tessy nodded, realizing she wouldn't be able to talk to him now, yet alone persuade him to the notion which had suddenly taken hold of her mind. She was not clever, like Zemelda, but she had some perception and could put two and two together. She would see Zemelda and make her tell her if that startling notion could possibly be true, and if so . . .

Her heart leaped in fear. And she prayed she was mistaken in her fancies.

Some time later, she had her worst fears confirmed by a disgruntled, dissatisfied Zemelda, who said she was washing her hands of the whole affair and its perpetrator, but wouldn't lift a finger to rectify matters. It was up to her, Tessy, to attempt it, and she dispatched her maid with a note to Lord Cleary while she herself rushed to Darcy. But Darcy did not answer her knock, as she had expected. He had gone. And Lord Cleary was not at his town house either. Although Tessy did not know it, he had gone to pay a call in Berkeley Square. But he arrived after Lady Palmer had departed, and on being informed by Siddon what had occurred, he returned home with some haste. An hour later he was on his way, taking the Great North Road to Scotland.

And not much later, Tessy, her yellow rose still in place, was riding in a hired post chaise toward that same destination.

# Twenty-One

"I'll be dashed if I sleep in such a hostelry again," complained Lester, as he entered what went for the private parlor of the ramshackle inn where they had put up. "I've been scratching myself all night. This place ought to be shut for sanitary reasons."

He sounded and looked so comically outraged and disgusted that Felicia, sitting by the rickety table laid out for breakfast, bit her lip to suppress a smile. Poor Lester. This journey was a severe trial to him. She heaved a sigh, sobering up. If it weren't for her desperate cause, she would feel dreadfully guilty about subjecting him to such discomfort. But what meant one uncomfortable night as a price for preventing murder? She herself had hardly slept at all either.

"What a fleabag," grumbled Lester, sitting down carefully after inspecting the chair seat with deep suspicion. "Wouldn't be surprised if this thing collapsed under me. And my boots—the fellow who cleaned them must have spat on them and polished them with a dustrag." He shuddered. "If only we could put up at some of my friends or acquaintances. Many of them have their estates off both sides of the road, but for one, it would add extra hours to our jaunt, and for another, I don't wish to present myself to them with you. Dashed awkward to explain, and they would tattle."

"I am dreadfully sorry for the inconvenience," said Felicia, "but it won't be for long. And perhaps we shall sleep in a better place tonight." They had been traveling by day, hardly leaving the chaise for refreshments, stopping over just long enough to change horses, and putting up at a posting house late at night, to avoid being recognized. They went under the name of Mr. Smith and sister, and they left early in the morning before the other guests would be up and about. The journey was taking them longer than anticipated, but Felicia hoped that they might make it to the border with just two more overnight halts.

Lester, inspecting the kidney pie before him with even greater suspicion, then lifting it to his nose and sniffing at it, shook his head with disgust. "Hardly looks digestible. But we shall be putting up at a better place tonight, I've made certain of that. The coachman's cousin is an innkeeper, and the man assures me the place is most superior—good food and clean sheets. Only thing against it is it's off the main road. We will be obliged to take a side road through the woods. It will take us a trifle out of our way, but I fancy it will be worth it just to get a good uninterrupted night's sleep." He glanced anxiously at Felicia. "It will add only an hour or so to our journey, I daresay. Are you agreeable?"

"Of course I am agreeable, Lester. I could do with a good night's sleep myself."

But it hadn't been only the poor conditions of the bedchamber that had robbed her of sleep. Troublesome thoughts and vexing painful emotions had kept her tossing and turning all night. She was quite worn out, and as soon as they mounted into the carriage and deposited themselves as comfortably as they could against the squabs, she dozed off, and so did Lester. She woke a few times, mostly when the postboy blew up for the tolls, then dozed off again.

The last time Felicia was startled out of her doze, by a jolt of the carriage, it was late evening and they were traveling through the woods. Lester took out his watch again and, lifting it to the window, squinted at the dial.

"It can't be," he exclaimed. "Dash it, Felicia, that inn was supposed to be only an hour or so down a side lane, but we have been traveling much longer than that since we turned off the main road."

He poked his head out the window and ordered the coachman to stop. Clambering out stiffly, stretching his legs, he engaged in a spirited argument with the coachman. After some moments he climbed back inside, plopping into his seat, and as the chaise jerked into motion, he said disgustedly, "Dashed fellow has been lying to us. That inn of his cousin's ain't close to the main road at all. It will take us even longer to reach the border than we thought."

Felicia was vexed, but there was nothing they could do about it now. "As long as they don't catch up with us before we reach the border, it won't matter much," she said, thinking of Lady Palmer's footman. "I collect it wouldn't serve the purpose to turn back now?"

Lester shook his head. "Almost there. Just hope the place lives up to expectations."

It did. The hostelry was spotlessly clean, the sheets aired, the food and wine excellent. But Lester, still annoyed at the time lost in reaching it, ordered the coachman to be ready to start around five or six in the morning, so that they could make up for lost time.

Thick mist shrouded the inn, which stood close to an intersection of three roads, the crossroads and the woods when Felicia and Lester, heavy with sleep, mounted into the carriage very early the next morning, Felicia rubbing her eyes.

Lester covered his yawn with his hand. They had slept well, but could have slept twice as long.

Lester, his foot on the chaise step, eyed the coachman with misgivings. That worthy man was bleary-eyed and holding his head in his hands, and the postboy was in no better shape.

"Hope he won't overturn the chaise," Lester muttered with disapprobation as he climbed in. "Seems he and the cousin made quite a night of it. *That's* why he wished us to go all the way here. He fancied a visit with his cousin."

"But it is a good inn," said Felicia. "And we should make up the time."

"If we don't overturn," said Lester gloomily, settling in and smothering another yawn.

The chaise lurched into life and rattled off into the thick mist toward the crossroads. Felicia shut her eyes, trying to shut out her worrisome painful thoughts, which hardly left her while awake. But the need for sleep reasserted itself, and soon she was dozing off. As the previous day, whenever she woke up, she saw Lester nodding in his seat; and through the window she caught glimpses of steep brown rock walls, and later, when they seemed to be traveling through a wooded valley, she saw rolling hills with wooded slopes and steep outcroppings of cliffs and rock spires here and there. Some boulders were strewn about also. And the road seemed to be going upward. Felicia recognized no landscape, but fancied she must have been dozing when they had passed these cliffs before. But was it her imagination, or was the ride much more bumpy now? Perhaps she had been so tired before that she did not even wake up with each jolting of the chaise.

The last time Felicia woke up, she unfastened the window and, holding onto the hand strap, leaned out to survey the terrain. A tangy sweet fragrance hit her nostrils. The scent recalled to her the time when she had traveled with her aunt to the—

Moors? Here?

She tugged at Lester's arm. "Lester, Lester, wake up. I don't think we are traveling the right road," she cried.

"Huh? What?" Lester rubbed his eyes. "What did you say?"

"I think we are going in the wrong direction," said Felicia with sharp alarm.

Lester sat bolt upright in his seat. He stared out the

window for a moment, his brow darkening. "That damned—beg pardon—dashed drunken clodpole. We *are* heading in the wrong direction. My God, I know this place," he suddenly cried. "We are in the Peak."

"What? What's that?"

"The Peak District in the Pennines, Derbyshire. And we are not even heading north. Stop, stop," he shouted to the coachman. The chaise, now rolling downward, rumbled to a standstill.

"Where are you going?" Lester cried. "We have gone completely off course, you dolt." He opened the carriage door, jumped down, and began to give the coachman a thoroughly deserved trimming.

The upshot of it was that the chaise turned around, the coachman springing his horses to make up for lost time. Felicia had to hang on to the hand strap as the coach swayed from side to side and jolted over potholes and stones. She had not paid much attention to the coachman's excuses, but Lester, fuming with anger, his amiable countenance reddened and cross, explained to her the situation. "That sodden addlepated fellow took the wrong fork when we started out. It was misty and his head was still heavy from imbibing all night. So was the postboy's, I daresay. He was riding on the box, fast asleep."

"Of all the stupid luck," exclaimed Felicia. "I can understand his taking the wrong road, with everything shrouded in mist and with both of them in such an inebriated state, but later, when the mist cleared, didn't he realize what he was doing?"

"He fancied he would come to another road at the next turn, which would cut across to the main coaching highway. That's what *he* says. To my mind, he's still as drunk as a wheelbarrow. Must have drunk his breakfast, not eaten it. He and the postboy."

A sudden sharp jolt elicited from him a low curse—shocking in such a mild-tempered man as Lester.

"I wish he would go at a slower pace. He might overturn us," Felicia said worriedly. "*That* would not advance our cause at all."

Hardly she had said that when the post chaise, taking a corner at great speed, careened sharply to one side and with a bone-jarring jolt and cracking sound came to a standstill in the ditch.

# Twenty-Two

Felicia was thrown against Lester, almost landing on top of him. But the chaise did not overturn, just rested in the ditch at a drunken angle.

As soon as all motion had stopped, Lester disentangled himself and, helping Felicia to an upright position, scrambled outside to bawl at the hapless coachman. "You were going too fast around the bend," he shouted.

"It's the rabbit that did it," cried the coachman. "The rabbit startled the horses, and all of a sudden we were in the ditch."

" 'Twas so, milor," corroborated the post boy. 'Tall happened sudden-like. It *was* the rabbit."

"It was your all-night libations," said Lester severely. "You were still half sprung this morning. Now what's to be done? What's the damage?"

Felicia, climbing out of the chaise, joined the group on the ground. The damage happened to be a broken axle. And no town or habitation was in sight.

"There is only one thing to be done," said Lester with a fatalistic shrug. "We must seek refuge with Lord Ransom."

"Lord Ransom? Who's he, one of your friends?"

"More an acquaintance. Stayed at his manor once or twice. That's why I recognized the road. Banister knows him much better. There is another chap I know well, has his country home in these parts, but his wife is an inveterate gossip. Don't dare to show our faces there. This other chap, Ransom, is a bachelor. Bit taciturn, but can be trusted to keep his mouth shut. Let the postboy ride over to his place with a note from me. That would be best."

"How soon can the chaise be mended?" asked Felicia.

The coachman spread his hands and shrugged.

"Daresay Ransom can help us in that quarter," soothed Lester. "We shall be obliged to stay with him today and tonight. Perhaps by tomorrow morning I'll contrive to procure another vehicle, if the chaise cannot be mended."

"Another day lost," cried Felicia. "They will catch up with us by then."

"No, they won't. Even if they have discovered we have gone to Scotland, they'll never tumble to it that you are here in a place so far removed from the main coaching highway."

But in this he was mistaken. Jerome Banister, traveling with Lady Palmer and not stinting money for good fresh horses at every stop, had contrived to keep track of Felicia and Lester up until their last stop on the main road. Then, when he discovered on arriving at the next posting inn that the fugitives had not been there, Lady Palmer became very agitated. And as she was unwell from eating something that had disagreed with her, Jerome had his hands full to soothe and calm her and bring her to a more optimistic frame of mind. He told her he would ride over to all the inns in the neighbourhood, particularly all the better inns, to inquire after Felicia and her son, while she remained where she was.

Lady Palmer, quite ill from overset nerves and bilious stomach, was glad to remain in bed, while Jerome, after a hasty meal, rode out on his quest. It took him some time, but at last he met with success and was able to report to her ladyship that he had picked up her son's trail.

"They had stopped at a very good but rather remote inn—I almost did not go there—and then apparently they had an accident." Lady Palmer moaned in distress.

"They were not hurt," Jerome was quick to reassure her. "The innkeeper at that inn is a cousin of the coachman who drove them. He, the coachman, sent word to the innkeeper that they took a wrong turn and later their carriage landed in a ditch with a broken axle. Winwood decided to seek help at Ransom Hall. It's a country seat of the Earl of Ransom. I know him very well."

"We must go there immediately," said Lady Palmer, lifting herself weakly on one elbow and falling back again with a groan.

"No, no, ma'am. You cannot go. You will remain here. I shall fetch a doctor for you and see that you have the best of care. Then I shall ride out alone. Believe me, it's best this way. Never fear that I shan't contrive to persuade them to return to you, for I shall. You may be sure that I shall clear this matter once and for all," he said with strong emphasis.

Lady Palmer gave him a weak smile. "Dear boy—it's so comforting to know that you have everything in your capable hands," she murmured, closing her eyes in exhausted relief.

Meanwhile, Felicia and Lester, in blissful ignorance of what had occurred, were taking their meal with Lord Ransom. This tall, thin gentleman with side-whiskers and a shock of gray hair was a misogynist and regarded Felicia with great disfavor, hardly uttering a word to her. But as long as he kept quiet about this escapade, that was all that mattered to Felicia. He agreed not only to do that, but to put them up for as long as they wished, and he placed his carriages and his grooms at their disposal. He also proved an invaluable friend to them in another way.

The meal ended, Felicia repaired to the drawing room, leaving Lester and their host to their port. Lester joined her later, looking very pleased with himself, but also a trifle angry. "Just wait till I get my hands on old Stoddart. I shall wring his neck," he cried. "That old rascal has been hoaxing us again. Well, not entirely—"

Felicia jumped to her feet. "Why? What have you discovered?"

"I told Ransom that we were looking for Sam Stoddart, and dashed if he didn't say that he knows of an inn-keeper near Doncaster whose name is Ben Stoddart."

"Oh, Lester," cried Felicia with shining eyes. "Could it be Sam's uncle?"

"Could be. And hear this—the inn's name is the Three Bears, and that rascal told us Three Lions, but he did say it was on the north road, *before* Gretna Green. Well, Doncaster is on the north road, and it is before Gretna Green, quite a good distance before."

"Oh, Lester, let us go there immediately."

"Whoa, whoa! Not you. The chaise isn't repaired yet, and it's of no use your going, in case it isn't our man. I shall go in Ransom's curricle. It's better for you not to show your face abroad, if you can help it. If Sam Stoddart is there, I shall fetch him to you here. I might not be able to persuade him to return to London with me, but I fancy Sam would not object to coming here just to talk to a lady."

"But Lester—"

"Now, Felicia, trust me to know what is best to be done in these circumstances. This is the best way to go about it."

Felicia fretted and demurred, but was obliged to concede that here in the privacy of Ransom Hall she would have a much better chance of persuading Sam to return with her to London. And if not—well, she was prepared to force him to go with her, to kidnap him if need be. And here it would be much easier than at the inn.

So she allowed Lester to go, while Lord Ransom lent her a horse and a moth-eaten green riding dress unearthed in the attic, and told her to explore the countryside for her amusement while she waited for Lester to return. He was not going to put himself out to entertain a female, even a winsome one like Miss Mannering.

Lord Ransom's spacious Palladian manor was situated on a wooded slope of a hill, above a lush valley which was rimmed on both sides by hills, interspersed with limestone cliffs and rocks. High up was a gently rolling plateau, where his tenants had their cottages and farms. Beyond this cultivated land stretched the vast wasteland of the moors. This region apparently was honeycombed with caves gouged out of limestone. Lord Ransome particularly warned her not to enter one if she happened to come across its entrance, because of the danger of getting lost. Winwood could take her later to one of the well-known caves a little farther down, where guided tours were provided for visitors.

Freed at last from being obliged to skulk about in fear of being recognized, Felicia roamed about the countryside, exploring the different aspects of the region. What an exhilarating sense of freedom it gave her to gallop across the fields after a whole year of confinement at Berkeley Square. She could not help reveling in this freedom in spite of the constant ache in her heart and her impatience to watch Sam Stoddart tell his story to Lord Cleary. Which should be sooner then she had expected, for of a surety this Ben Stoddart was Sam Stoddart's uncle, and the Three Bears inn had to be the Three Lions old Stoddart had told them about, so she and Lester would not be obliged to travel any farther.

Perhaps, she began to hope, everything would turn out well, with Lord Cleary restored to reason, once he heard Sam Stoddart's tale.

But even if he was restored to reason, her common sense told her sadly, it was of no use hoping her sentiments toward him would be reciprocated. The best she dared hope for would be for him to cease his quest for revenge on Darcy and herself. Darcy would be safe and free to pursue his diplomatic career. And she—she would contrive somehow, she told herself firmly, the fresh air and freedom lifting her spirits in spite of her unenviable situation.

She fretted a little at Lester's tarrying, but knowing that an accident to his breeches or his coat could very well hold him up for hours, she did not worry overmuch. Also she had no clear notion how long it would take him to reach Doncaster, and if the roads leading there were in good condition. And with Doncaster much closer than Gretna Green, she really had no reason to fret, and continued to spend most of her time on horseback.

But though she had roamed quite far afield, she hadn't come upon a cave yet. Perhaps they were not as plentiful as she had been led to believe, or their entrances were well hidden by the thick bushes growing on the slopes of the hills.

Oh, if only that dreadful suspicion—nay, a certainty—were not tugging at her heart, if only the earl's apologies had been sincere and he had not attempted to kill her, how happy she would have felt roaming here. But the thought of him was never far away, and she often wondered what his thoughts had been on hearing of her disappearance. What would he do?

She would have been surprised and frightened had she known that Lord Cleary was even now drawing near to the inn where Lady Palmer was staying.

Lady Palmer, although glad to see the earl, was surprised, for it was Darcy Vellacort she had expected.

"I daresay he will be here anon," said the earl grimly.

Lady Palmer eyed the bruise on his cheek with suspicion. "I trust you did not have a vulgar brawl with him?"

"I did," he answered curtly. "I went to see him on a matter of importance, but he wouldn't listen to me and became abusive. One thing led to another, and we exchanged blows."

"But—but he said he was leaving right away. How is it that you contrived to catch up with him?"

Lord Cleary, wincing, as his shoulder was still throbbing painfully, strode to the window and looked out.

"The only reason I was able to catch up with him is that he did not leave right away, having been drugged. And as I had hurt my shoulder before, the only reason I was able to knock him down is that he was still suffering from the effects of laudanum."

"Laudanum? Now who could have drugged him, and why?" asked Lady Palmer, much astonished.

But Lord Cleary did not enlighten her, instead asking her if they had any word of Felicia. And when she told him that Felicia was probably at Ransom Hall and Jerome Banister had gone in search of her there, he rather abruptly departed, leaving her moaning and complaining about the cruelty shown to her by everyone on this wretched journey.

Meanwhile the earl, exhausted as he was, set off in his curricle on the road to the Pennines.

# Twenty-Three

Felicia and Jerome were standing on the edge of a cliff,
looking down at the valley and Ransom Manor to the
right. The lovely view and the fresh air exerted a calm-
ing affect upon her again, and she felt her vexation
subside. After all, Jerome had behaved with the greatest propriety and consideration, and she couldn't blame
him for rushing after her to save her, as he thought,
from a marriage at the anvil. Of course, Felicia was
obliged to tell him the truth, which he received with his
usual calm and good sense. He also advised that nothing should be done until Lester returned from Doncaster.
Meanwhile he would accompany her on her rides and
walks. Perhaps they might even come upon a cave, and
he would explore it with her. Eager for the experience,
Felicia had provided herself with a tinderbox and candles, although Jerome said a lantern was what was
really needed in such places.

They had just come up to the edge of the cliff, the
better to look down, and Jerome was pointing out to
her the limestone cliffs to the right, at the bend of the
river. Felicia, quite close to the edge, stumbled suddenly, and Jerome caught her arm. "Be careful—it's a
long drop," he admonished.

Felicia looked down, and felt dizzy. Farther to the

right the slope of the hill was somewhat gentler and thick underbrush reached almost to the top, but here the steep side of the hill was almost perpendicular, bare limestone rock till about halfway down, where the cover of vegetation began. And it was a long drop.

She shivered, gratefully feeling Jerome's protecting arm on her shoulder. A cold wind was blowing and whistling about their heads, a herald of an approaching storm.

"We should be going back," she cried to make herself heard above the wind that had suddenly picked up.

Abruptly in a momentary lull the sound of running feet could be heard, and the next moment a shape hurtled itself on Jerome, felling him, while her own arm was seized roughly and pulled.

Startled and shocked, Felicia stared into the wild-eyed countenance of the Earl of Cleary.

Oh my God, he is insane, she thought, horrified. He has tracked me down to kill me.

Bitter pain shot through her heart, but fear was the uppermost emotion. She gave a mighty wrench and tug and tore herself free from his grip. Meanwhile, Jerome was picking himself up and going for Cleary.

The wind tore away Jerome's words, but Felicia could hear the almost deranged cry of the earl—"Felicia, Miss Mannering, wait"—as she turned around and fled, her heart pounding in panic and anguish.

His feet and his words pursued her. Felicia's breath came and went painfully, and the whistling wind made the breathing even more difficult. He was almost upon her. "No, no," she screamed, as, glancing back, she saw his blue-coated, buckskinned figure gaining on her. She rushed on to the right, close to the edge of the cliff.

He was hard at her heels, cutting off her escape. Her only way out was down, it flashed through her disordered mind. And she scrambled down the slope, grabbing at bushes and undergrowth, tearing the old riding dress and scratching her hands. Stumbling and grabbing a branch for support, slipping and sliding—down and down. And already he was coming down after her.

But Jerome was coming to her rescue. Jerome was rushing after him, engaging his attention. Felicia saw the earl hesitate, saw Jerome clamber down also; then, without looking back anymore, she continued her descent, gasping, heart hammering, pulses pounding, throat dry. It was a nightmare and she would wake up, she thought.

A grunt, a cry, the sound of a fall—had Jerome felled the earl, or the other way around? She had no time to look back. Down and down she scrambled and slid, fell and picked herself up, bruised and torn and dirtied. The earl's strident voice pursued her. "Wait, wait, Miss Mannering, don't—"

She must hide. She could not run anymore; she could not escape him on foot. She fancied she must be about halfway down the slope by now. The bushes, trees, and underbrush were a tangled mass of vegetation, affording good cover—so she hoped. But he would follow her and find her, she despaired. He would know she was here. She pushed her way through the undergrowth, aware that her strength was almost spent, that she must rest. Her movements slowed. Almost mechanically she kept parting the bushes and pressing herself into the thicket, to escape.

Abruptly she stumbled over a boulder and fell into a thick clump of bushes. The momentum carried her forward, and she came crashing through the undergrowth to fall and skin her knees on some stones. When she picked herself up, she was in almost total darkness. She blinked and scrambled to her feet, abruptly realizing that she was in a dark recess in the slope of the hill.

Recess? A cave!

She had stumbled into the entrance of a cave. She groped and stumbled forward, trying to make as little noise as possible, until she touched a damp cold wall. Then, gasping, she leaned against it and caught her breath.

"Miss Mannering, Miss Mannering!" She could hear the earl's voice coming closer, ever closer. Then the crash of branches quite close—and receding. Thank God! He did not realize she was here, in the cave. But she dared not rush out, for she had no strength to run as yet. She felt for her reticule. It was still hanging there at her waist. With trembling fingers, she extracted the tinderbox and the candle and lit the candle, shading the light with her cupped hand.

Heart in her throat, she waited a moment, but the earl's voice and movement did not grow closer, and she dared to take a few steps forward, shining the candle here and there. It was a small chamber with craggy rough walls, and there was nowhere to hide in it.

The earl's voice came suddenly very close, freezing Felicia into brief immobility. She must escape. There must be a hiding place here somewhere. Mindful of Lord Ransom's admonitions not to venture inside a cave, she yet went hesitatingly forward. After all, in front was uncertainty, but behind was certain death.

A dark narrow cavity yawned in front of her—a tunnel. Shivering and thinking of bats, Felicia entered it cautiously. The tunnel sloped downward at a steep angle, with the ground strewn with rubble and boulders as the passage widened. She almost fell, stumbling over a large stone, but caught herself at the damp rough cold wall. A chilling dampness permeated the atmosphere, and the ground was damp underfoot.

Felicia groped her way on, her tongue clinging to her dry palate, her throat bone-dry, the pounding of her heart choking her. Abruptly she heard a clatter and a loud cry and oath somewhere behind her. The earl had found the entrance to the cave.

Felicia increased her pace, trying to shield the light of the candle with her body. Presently the roof of the tunnel became very low, obliging Felicia to walk almost bent double. She thought with satisfaction that the earl might find it quite difficult, if not impossible, to venture here.

The flickering candle threw only a small pool of light in front of her, and all around her was total darkness.

Suddenly Felicia became aware that the roof was no longer hemming her in and she could straighten out. She lifted the candle high, and though its illumination was weak, she realized she had come to a chamber—a large chamber.

Fine strawlike spikes littered the floor—broken stalactites. A large stalactite dangled above her head, and the roof was lost somewhere in the darkness. Groping along the jagged wall to the right, she soon perceived that it was a very large chamber indeed. And it was even colder here.

A cry behind her caused her to stumble and drop the candle. The flame went out. Now Felicia was in total darkness—and the earl was coming closer.

"Miss Mannering, Miss Mannering!" She could hear his voice clearly now.

And from far away, another voice: "Felicia—where are you?"

Jerome! Warmth and hope rushed into Felicia's heart. Jerome would save her. All she had to do was to keep quiet and to hide until Jerome caught up with them.

She groped in the darkness for a recess in the wall, but found none. Not daring to leave the protecting safety of the wall and cross the floor, she kept groping her way around its perimeter for some time. The circumference of the dark silent cave was enormous. And still she hadn't found a recess, a hiding place.

Abruptly a loud clatter of feet over stones and the flickering light of a candle told her that the earl was advancing. So he had come prepared for any eventuality, she thought. He was calling her name, saying something. In her terror she could not grasp his words. All she could think of was escape. All of a sudden her groping hand struck air. A break in the wall, an opening—another tunnel. Felicia glided in and waited with bated breath.

She heard the earl stumble, and looking out, she saw the flickering candle move. She heard Jerome's cries coming closer, and prayed Jerome would hasten to her aid. The earl's candle moved off in the opposite direction. Then it disappeared, and darkness once more engulfed all space. He had entered another tunnel, thought Felicia.

"Felicia, Felicia, where are you?" Jerome's voice. He had entered the large chamber.

"Here! I am here, Jerome! Help!" cried Felicia, and heard Cleary's loud oath reverberate in the chamber. He had come out of the tunnel, and Jerome, with a candle in his hand too, was groping toward her. So was Cleary.

Felicia, frozen, unable to move, watched the two flickering lights and shadowy figures converge in the middle of the inky blackness.

Then the figures grappled, the lights went out, grunts and cries followed, and there was the noise of fighting bodies.

A fresh wave of panic seized Felicia, unlocking her frozen limbs. She rushed forward, groping along the wall, not heeding in which direction she was going. A gaping hole—another tunnel—invited her. She slipped in. She would have gone to help Jerome, but in the total darkness it would have been useless.

Abruptly she went sliding and fell with a hard bump. She painfully picked herself up, her hand encountering wet slimy cold walls. And there was wetness under her feet, she realized. Then she became aware of a sound of rushing water. Rushing water? Of course—an underground river. Felicia's teeth began to chatter, with both panic and cold. The old riding dress was hardly a protection against the intense cold pervading the cave. And the tunnel sloped even more steeply down. Dared she go forward or should she turn back?

The sound of feet behind, and the earl's voice calling, decided her. The earl must have knocked Jerome down again. Oh, if only Jerome was unhurt.

She carried on, sliding and slipping in the dark. Now the rush of water was getting quite strong. Perhaps it would drown out the sound of her footsteps, she hoped.

But it also made it more difficult to hear Cleary's. She kept glancing back, but no flickering light showed yet. Perhaps he had not found his candle and would not be able to find her in the dark.

Felicia had just reached the underground river—as evidenced by the very loud noise of rushing water and more intense cold—when, glancing back, she saw in the inky darkness a glimmer, a faint flickering light. Her heart leaped to her throat, and her body turned to ice with panic. Her teeth chattered uncontrollably.

She took a few more hasty steps, and abruptly her foot encountered—nothing. She screamed as she swayed and threw herself backward, clawing at the wall for support. Somehow she regained her balance and realized with a sinking feeling that she had almost tumbled into the river. Apparently the passage had become a narrow ledge alongside the stream.

As she stood there pressed against the wall, panting and fighting off nausea and shock, the earl's cry—"Miss Mannering! Felicia!"—added to her horror and fear.

She wished to flee, to rush headlong on, but she knew she must proceed with caution. The slippery uneven ledge, strewn with gravel and loose stones, was extremely difficult going.

Making her way forward along that wet treacherous ledge, she was pursued by the earl's repeated calls. And then her head was touching the roof again and the ledge grew even narrower. Felicia was afraid to go forward, but the flickering light of the earl's candle showed her that he was drawing near. How could she escape him by stumbling along this narrow shelf?

Yet she felt her way on, pressing herself against the rock wall, until a few moments later her hand encountered a break. Another passage?

She groped carefully forward. Yes—it was a passage, branching off to the right. A narrow passage. But perhaps she could hide herself there. Above the rush of water, she could hear Lord Cleary's call—quite close. She tried to move noiselessly up this other passage, which was difficult, as it was also strewn with rubble. And, numb from the cold, she was tiring fast.

A recess in the wall gave her a notion—a desperate thought. Bending down, she felt on the ground for a handy stone, picked it up, and, pressing herself into the recess, held her breath. The earl was now quite close. The candle flickered as his figure loomed into view. He had taken the turn and was even now coming forward. Felicia raised the stone in her hand and tensed herself. She did not wish to hurt him, but he was a madman. She had to fight for her life.

# Twenty-Four

Lady Palmer, in a lilac negligee, reclining on her bed in the inn's bedchamber, stared querulously at the handsome but irritated countenance of Darcy Vellacort. "I understand perfectly your wishing to catch up with your wayward fiancée, but it would be far better for you to wait for Banister's return. He will, I'm sure, fetch them both here. He has promised."

"Well, I shan't allow Cleary to stick his nose into my affairs again. Felicia's eloping with Winwood" —Lady Palmer gave a shudder and a moan, closing her eyes—"is none of his concern. Besides, there is this intelligence that Tessy has brought me to consider."

Lady Palmer shook her head. "I don't believe it at all. He couldn't be guilty of such gross impropriety, yet alone a criminal act. No, no. And that is another thing against you, Vellacort—even if she had been your . . . fancy piece"—Lady Palmer choked on the word she finally settled on—"it is the height of impropriety and an insult to drag her here."

Darcy Vellacort gave an impatient exclamation. "How many times must I repeat, ma'am, that I *did not* drag her here? *She* has been pursuing *me*."

"Then send her packing."

"I can't forbid her to put up at the inn," Darcy said sullenly.

"Well, get rid of her. I won't be housed under the same roof with a demi-rep. What's more, I think this tale of hers is trumped up for the express purpose of getting your attention."

"I own I find it hard to believe her, but I shall make sure just to be on the safe side. I shall ride over to Ransom manor and discover all I can."

"Well, you shan't be going alone," declared Lady Palmer stoutly.

"But—" Darcy opened his mouth to protest.

Lady Palmer did not allow him to speak. "I am going with you."

All remonstrations availed him nothing. Lady Palmer insisted that Darcy Vellacort accompany her to Ransom manor.

With poor grace, Darcy submitted to her demand, riding with her in her chaise—which progress seemed much too slow for him—and thoroughly vexed with all women. First Felicia played this trick on him. Now Lady Palmer insisted he ride with her, and to top it all he couldn't persuade Tessy not to follow him to the Pennines.

They would make a fine procession arriving at Lord Ransom's, he thought with a curling lip. And what would Felicia think when she clapped her eyes on Tessy? In a way the two were alike—both sought to protect him, which ought to have flattered him and made him feel grateful. Instead it only made him feel dissatisfied and cross. As for that tale of Tessy's—no, no. He shook his head. It didn't make any sense at all.

"But it don't make any sense at all," complained Lester Winwood, sitting at the table in the private parlor of Ben Stoddart's inn and trying to follow Sam Stoddart's involved tale. "If Vellacort didn't act dishonorably in this affair, why does he think he did?"

"I'll wager it's because he doesn't remember what

occurred, that's why," said the round rosy-cheeked man before him. "He was badly foxed."

Lester nodded sapiently. "Might have done it, being in that condition. But *you* could have told him."

"Aye. But I didn't know Mr. Vellacort fancied he fired before the signal was given, making it murder and not an honorable affair. I had no notion what was going on. After being told to make myself scarce, for I might be clapped in Newgate or get shot by Lord Cleary, I fled Barnet. I didn't know the tale was going around that the quarrel between the two was over a Cyprian, nor of the rumors that Mr. Vellacort had murdered the earl's brother. It was *him,* it had to be him, who spread the tale—couldn't be anybody else. And he probably made Mr. Vellacort believe in it too."

Lester shook his head in strong disbelief and absently took out his snuffbox and helped himself to a pinch of snuff. "It still don't make sense," he muttered. "I can understand his wishing to cause mischief for Vellacort because of Felicia. But I never would have thought his affections were so deeply engaged as to make him act in such a dastardly way. No, no—I fancy you must have misunderstood the matter. Vellacort should be much relieved to know that the duel *was* a fair fight, and so should Miss Mannering. As for the rest—I shall try to discover the truth when we return to London."

He pushed away his plate of cold meat and rose from the chair. "Time we were on our way." He glanced anxiously at his buff breeches. "I do hope Cassel can remove this spot," he said worriedly.

"It is hardly noticeable, sir," Sam assured him. "I did my best, Mr. Winwood."

"I know you did. Well, we must hope for the best. I am only glad we were not obliged to travel to the border to find you. I shall give old Stoddart a piece of my mind, and no mistake about it. Gretna Green indeed. If it weren't for Lord Ransom, we dashed well *would* have gone there—and all for naught."

\*　　\*　　\*

The earl was approaching the small recess where Felicia was hiding. As yet the feeble light from his candle had not touched her. Fortunately for her, a moment earlier he had stumbled, emitting a soft oath, and now he was throwing the light of the candle on the rubble-strewn floor of the passage. He was negotiating his way past a larger stone when Felicia, gripping her dry lip between her teeth, decided. The next moment the flickering light would betray her presence to him. It was now or never. Her life against his aching head.

He was turning toward her slowly, sweeping the tunnel with the candlelight. Just before he became aware of her, however, Felicia sprang forward and dealt his lordship what she hoped was a not too severe blow to the head.

With a surprised cry of pain, he crumpled up. Instinctively Felicia stretched out her arms to break his fall, almost going down with him. As he slipped unconscious to the floor, the candle fell from his nerveless fingers. The flame was extinguished, and total darkness enveloped them both.

Felicia's breath came and went on painful sobs. Tears were stinging her eyelids. That she had been obliged to hurt *him!* She knelt beside him on the ground and groped for his pulse. He was alive, thank God. Already he was stirring and moaning. She must escape.

Felicia became galvanized into action. Forgetting she had a second candle in her reticule at her waist, she searched on the ground for the fallen candle, found it, took out her tinderbox, and lit the candle. Then, with a last anxious look at the earl, she fled the passage, not heeding now if she made noise, intent only on escape.

She hardly knew how she negotiated the narrow ledge alongside the river, her ears straining for the footsteps of the earl. But there were none, or at least she couldn't hear them for the rush of the water.

On she scrambled and fell and picked herself up, until she entered the steeply sloping tunnel. Then at last she paused to catch her breath, and saw ahead of her a flickering candle held by a shadowy figure.

Jerome?

"Felicia!" His call confirmed her guess.

A great wave of relief washed over Felicia. Jerome was alive and moving under his own power. Cleary had not killed him or even hurt him badly.

"Jerome, Jerome," she cried and stumbled forward toward him as fast as she could.

"Felicia!"

A few more moments, and he held her in his arms, or rather one arm, the other being outstretched with the candle.

"Jerome, Jerome," sobbed Felicia, almost singeing her hair with her candle. "You are alive and well."

"I am perfectly well," said Jerome, a trifle out of breath. "And you?"

"Just bruises and cuts—but oh, Jerome, I'm afraid I have hurt Lord Cleary badly. I have knocked him senseless with a stone. I was obliged to. He has run completely mad."

"Indeed. The poor man needs to be clapped in Bedlam."

"Ah no, no. If only Sam can tell him his story, I have high hopes he will be restored to reason. Jerome, do go and make sure he is not dreadfully hurt. Perhaps he needs to be helped. Oh, pray make sure. You—you can take care; I do not think he will have the strength to hurt you. I've left him in a passage to the right, the first tunnel one encounters when walking along the river."

Felicia could not distinguish his features, but there was a long moment before Jerome said evenly, "Certainly I shall go and make sure. But you stay here. Don't go anywhere, mind. Wait for me. I do not wish to lose sight of you again. You have caused me no end of trouble, Felicia."

"Oh, Jerome, Jerome, I am so dreadfully sorry. That you, my dear friend, were subjected to this long journey and to being attacked by the earl—all because of me. How shall I ever repay your kindness and concern?" She bit her lip.

"You know how—but I shan't speak to you on that

head again. I am perfectly aware it is useless, and it won't serve to ask you now. Pray stay here and don't move while I make certain of Cleary."

It seemed to the trembling Felicia that Jerome took an inordinate amount of time to return, and he returned alone.

She was relieved to see him unharmed, but she asked anxiously, her heart skipping a beat, "Lord Cleary—is he—is he—?"

Jerome nodded. "Perfectly stout. Well, not precisely. His head hurts, but it is his ankle that makes it difficult for him to walk. He twisted it when he fell. And he is still in a murderous rage at both of us, so we had better make haste to leave the cave."

Relief that the earl was not seriously hurt mingled with sadness. "But—" she began.

"You need not be concerned," Jerome said, quick to reassure her. "He will hobble out presently, and in the meantime we shall make ourselves scarce."

"But how can he find his way back in the dark? He might be lost."

"I had a spare candle with me. I lit it and left it there for him to pick up. Indeed, there is no need to worry. We shall return to the manor, and Lord Ransom will send his servants to rescue Cleary."

Felicia relaxed somewhat. Jerome's words made sense.

"Then let us go," she said, as she now became fully conscious how chilled she was. Her teeth were chattering with cold. Her feet and hands were numb. Before, in her feverish attempt to escape the earl, she had not paid much attention to the intense cold freezing her body. Jerome, seeing her shiver, took off his coat, first extracting something from the pocket, and slipped it around her shoulders. "Let us go forward," he urged.

Grateful for the warmth of his coat and his supporting arm, Felicia stumbled and scrambled up the slippery treacherous slope until she emerged into the large main chamber. She was still holding the earl's candle, which, however, was almost gutted.

They traversed the chamber in silence. Felicia, shaken

and sick at heart from her encounter with the earl, was grateful to Jerome for refraining from talking. How could the earl have so far forgotten himself as to attack her and Jerome openly? Bedlam indeed seemed the only place for him.

Sunk in such depressing thoughts, she suddenly became aware that Jerome had stopped. He had affixed his candle to a large boulder and stepped back a little from her side.

"Are we waiting for Lord Cleary after all?" asked Felicia, her heart leaping with apprehension. The earl wouldn't take too kindly to being knocked unconscious by her.

"No, we are not," Jerome said in a strange voice. "But I think I shall make you join Cleary now. It is a great pity, but it must be done."

Abruptly and to her horror his hands shot up, his long fingers curled themselves around her neck, and he began to squeeze the breath out of her body.

# Twenty-Five

Lester Winwood, seated in the Blue Drawing Room of Ransom Hall, stared at the blond girl with the yellow rose in her hair with undisguised horror.

"But this is monstrous, appalling," he muttered, his eyes round and glassy with shock. "Her own cousin! I cannot believe it."

The fair Cyprian took a turn about the chamber, her green silk dress swishing with her every move. "Oh, you men. Darcy does not wish to believe it either." She stopped in front of him, tapping her palm with her finger. "One—he wishes to marry Miss Mannering."

"All the world knows that," complained Lester, mechanically smoothing a tiny crease on his elegant russet coat. "That don't make him wish to kill her." His jaw dropped. "No, no. That's a Cheltenham tragedy—'If I can't have you, nobody shall.'"

"That's as it may be. But it is not love that is causing him to do these things. He is in love with Zemelda. He is Zemelda's mysterious benefactor, who supports her in that elegant establishment of hers."

Lester's jaw remained sagging open. His eyes fairly bulged. "Not the Incomparable Zemelda, the Fashionable Impure, one of *your* set? Banister? No, really." He shook his head, blinked, and pulled at his earlobe.

The girl tossed her blond head. "What is so singular about Mr. Banister's falling in love with someone like myself? Scores of men have, and do."

"Yes, but Jerome—so—so respectable—"

"So respectable that he made Zemelda engage a man to kidnap Miss Mannering at Vauxhall Gardens and keep her hidden in one of the summer houses until a hue and cry went out for her—to give himself the chance to rescue her or to create a scandal for Miss Mannering and make her part company with Darcy. Either way, she would have been obliged to feel very grateful to Mr. Banister, and Darcy would have been placed in a poor light, perhaps even lost his chance with Lord Palmer. *I* had no notion when I agreed to draw Darcy away from her sight that any such thing was intended. Mr. Banister wished to be alone with Miss Mannering in a romantic place—that was all *I* was told. Only Lord Cleary spoiled it for him by rescuing Miss Mannering. Yes, and it was Mr. Banister who provoked the curricle race, which I prevented by luring the earl into the balloon. When I discovered that, I knew Mr. Banister meant only mischief for Darcy. But I still did not think then he would stoop to murder."

Lester Winwood swallowed hard. "Must make Sam Stoddart my apologies. He told me Banister provoked the duel by hinting that Marcus was making up to Miss Mannering. He would know that Cleary's brother, quite taken with her beauty, could not resist in his state to hoax Vellacort a little and boast of his success. That's what he did, and Vellacort, not sober enough to realize Marcus was only funning, took umbrage and called him out. And Banister, instead of scotching the quarrel, insidiously fanned it, no doubt thinking either Marcus would kill Vellacort, or Vellacort would kill Marcus and be obliged to flee the country, leaving Felicia to be consoled by himself." He swallowed again. "Must hand it to him—he *is* clever. But what a villain."

"Oh, his villainy knows no bounds. I knew he spread tales about Darcy—he spread the rumor that the fight was over one of our set, thinking Miss Mannering would hear of it and cry off from the betrothal."

"But he told Miss Mannering the duel was over a game of cards," Lester objected.

"He pretended to be her friend. A friend wouldn't tell her something that would hurt her feelings. Oh no. He wished her to hear the tale—but not from him. And telling her the duel was over her would not have given her a disgust of Darcy. Where was I? Oh yes—I knew he spread tales about Darcy, but I *didn't* know that he also spread the tale that Darcy murdered Marcus. *That* was intended to cause Cleary to take revenge on Darcy, even perhaps call him out. Only Lord Cleary, while he talked of revenge, was too slow to act. So then—and I had no notion of it, either—he induced Darcy to join the Hellgate set, thinking Darcy would get into such a scrape Miss Mannering would be obliged to terminate their engagement. Oh, he tried all kinds of ways to part Miss Mannering from Darcy. That I did not object to. But those ways also included discrediting Darcy. He even wished Darcy to be accused of being a thief. Something about stealing a necklace. But I don't know much about *that*."

Lester blinked. Banister had revealed to him that Darcy had stolen Sir Edward's necklace and substituted a fake in its place, but that's one thing he, Lester, wouldn't blab about abroad. And now he recalled that it was Banister who had mentioned to Cleary the existence of the necklace. He wished Cleary to buy it from Sir Edward, discover it fake, and create a scandal. Vellacort's theft of it then would have come out in the open. Now *that* would have effectively removed Vellacort from Felicia's side. Yet there was something here that did not fit.

"But the shot—the shot during the fête at Green Park," he pointed out. "It was Cleary who shot at Felicia, not Banister. She said so."

"Did she *see*, actually *see*, Cleary shoot her? No. And let me tell you—Lord Cleary was wounded that night. Perhaps he took a bullet intended for Miss Mannering

—if, as you say, he persisted in following her. The tampering with the curricle did not work, so Mr. Banister tried shooting her. That's why Zemelda is finished with him. Kidnapping, provoking a duel or a race, spreading tales—those she could tolerate, but not murder."

Lester took out his scented handkerchief and mopped his perspiring face. "Miss Mannering will be deeply shocked. But why did you come with this tale to me, not to her?"

"I knew you would listen to me. She might not. It was providential that our vehicles arrived at the manor almost at the same time."

"And providential that you warned me that Lady Palmer is coming here." He shuddered. "I must endeavor to keep out of her way."

"Oh, she will keep to her bed for a space, no doubt. The ride here was none too gentle, and already she was obliged to stop at the inn to recruit her strength. That's why I arrived here first. Darcy wouldn't give me directions, but I found out anyway. I have to protect him. Mr. Banister is here—and who knows what mischief he is brewing now?"

Lester, who had slumped in his seat, sat bolt upright, his eyes starting from their sockets anew. "Here? Banister?"

"Well, that's where he was heading. Darcy said Lady Palmer had told him to fetch you and Miss Mannering home. He came with Lady Palmer, you see."

"But—but—but dash it, where is he? And come to think of it, where is Felicia?" He tugged irritably at a bell pull.

It was some moments before a footman entered the room.

"Shocking bad help here too," commented Lester. And to the man, "I desired Miss Mannering to join me here. I had sent a maid to fetch her. Why hasn't she come?"

"Possibly because her being the only maid in an all-male establishment, her assistance was urgently needed.

Unexpected visitors arriving," he added with relish, enjoying the dramatic interruption of a somnolent country existence. "Lady Palmer, quite unwell—"

Lester shot up from his chair. "Mother—already. I must hide. Felicia! Must have a word with *her*. Fetch Miss Mannering to me yourself," he said to the footman.

"I regret to say that Miss Mannering is not in her chamber. She left some time ago with Mr. Banister, to explore the countryside. And Lord Cleary went after them," he added, hoping for an effect.

And he was not disappointed. "What? Cleary here too? Well, if that don't beat the Dutch," said Lester. "The whole dashed family congregated in the place. Don't think Ransom'll like it above half."

"He detests it," said the footman with even greater relish. "Shut himself up in his chamber and won't come out. Three females—one of them hysterical—under his roof at the same time. And a bunch of gentlemen, some of whom he never clapped eyes on."

Abruptly Lester seemed to grasp the import of this new intelligence. "Banister went with Felicia," he cried. "He might—might—" He choked on the words.

"Might kill her," supplied Tessy. "Very likely. But if Lord Cleary has gone after them, he'll prevent it."

"Must go after them. You fetch Lord Ransom this instant," he said to the gaping footman. "And where is Mr. Vellacort? Or do you know?"

"Fortifying himself with brandy in Lord Ransom's library."

"Fetch him here too. And have horses saddled and ready for us. And pistols," he commanded.

Such was his concern about Felicia that he did not even perceive the large smudge on his highly polished top boots.

# Twenty-Six

"Jerome!" gasped out Felicia, her eyes starting from her head, disbelief and shock on her countenance. Terror paralyzed her body. "No, Jerome! Why?" she croaked before the words were choked off at her throat.

"Why? You know why," said Jerome, his hold on her neck tightening. "You wouldn't marry me, that's why. You preferred that spoiled cub Vellacort, and now Cleary. Oh, don't look so surprised. I saw it coming at Vauxhall." His mouth pressed into a thin hard line. "That infernal meddler—he *would* throw a rub in my way every time. Vauxhall, Green Park, and even now. Well, he *shan't* rescue you this time. I've made sure of that!" He squeezed her throat harder, as Felicia now began to struggle.

Blood pounded in Felicia's temples, and her lungs were gasping for air. Her senses were failing her, and darkness was clouding her eyes. But the words "I've made sure of that" struck even greater terror to her heart. What had he done to Cleary? Had he killed him? No, oh no. Rage and grief and a fierce desire to save the man she loved sent a surge of strength to her body. She clawed desperately at Jerome's hands and contrived to pry them loose for one moment to take in a gasping choking breath, before the vise clamped itself on her neck again. But that one breath cleared the mist from her eyes.

In a flash she realized she was doomed without a weapon to use against him. Her desperate eye fell on the candle on the boulder beside which they were struggling. Before the haze clouded her senses again, she twisted her body, snatched the candle, and pressed the flame to Jerome's arm.

He howled with pain and relaxed his hold. Felicia tore herself free. But the candle went out, and they were in total darkness.

Felicia, reeling back, gasping and choking and stumbling, heard Jerome stumbling too as he groped after her.

Desperation and the thought of Cleary sharpened Felicia's wits. She dropped to the ground and tried to crawl away, meanwhile feeling among the rubble on the damp rock floor for a handy stone. She found one just as he was about to grab her, and struck him on the shin—she thought—with all her might.

He screamed with pain, and she could sense him stumble backward.

"You little devil," he swore. "You have broken my leg."

Good, thought Felicia, rubbing her sore neck. But she needed light to leave this chamber in the right direction. This time she recollected the candle in her reticule, and she lighted it.

The flickering flame showed her Jerome on the floor holding his leg, his countenance twisted in rage and pain.

For a moment she hesitated, the desire to succor him stirring within her. But he had tried to kill her—and worse, he had perhaps already killed Cleary. "Very likely it's only bruised," she said coolly, and, turning around, she made her way as quickly as she could toward the slippery, steeply sloping passage.

Heart pounding, breath coming in quick short gasps, she negotiated the wet and slimy walk, impatiently fretting that she could not run to the earl's side. In her acute concern for him she was hardly conscious of the biting cold of the cave. It seemed to take her forever to reach the passage and the place where she had left him. Now a deadly fear gripped her heart as she perceived that he was no longer there. And she had not met him anywhere along the way. Where was the earl? What had Jerome done with him?

"Lord Cleary, Lord Cleary!" she called out in despair. "Where are you? Lord Cleary, pray answer me."

But would he hear her, and she him, above the rushing sound of the river?

Where to look for him? Which way to go? If only she had a clue which way he had gone or been dragged by Jerome. She shone the candle on the ground, and her eye fell on what seemed a droplet of blood on the rock floor. Her heart contracted. Was it the blood from the wound *she* had dealt him, or ...? Sick at heart, she swept the light in a circle across the floor and now noticed another red spot, and another, leading back toward the river. The earl did not seem to have been bleeding profusely, but steadily.

With quickened breath, Felicia stumbled along this trail of blood, toward the river.

Soon she found herself on the ledge beside the rushing stream. And no sign of the earl. She threw the light of the candle on the floor. Two red spots leaped to her eyes. She *was* on the right track. But where was he?

"Lord Cleary, Lord Cleary!" she called out. Only the sound of rushing water answered her.

Abruptly she froze. The river. Had Jerome ... drowned him? She felt nigh to swooning. But the droplets of blood still showed her the way, and she struggled on.

The rushing noise increased and the ledge grew even narrower. Felicia realized that she must be nearing a waterfall.

And then her heart turned over in her breast and she caught her breath. She saw him. She rushed forward, stumbled and almost fell, but somehow contrived to keep her balance. More cautiously, she went forward until a moment later she was on her knees beside the inanimate form of the earl. He was lying half in and half out of water, his arm crooked around a jutting boulder. He was quite wet through and icy cold. It appeared that he had fallen or been pushed into the river and then somehow contrived to pull himself partly out before he collapsed.

Even as she thought that, the earl's arm slipped from around the rock and he began to slide deeper into the water.

Glancing about, wild-eyed with panic, Felicia wedged the candle in a crack in the rock and grabbed the earl by the arms. She pulled and heaved, and with great difficulty she managed to pull him out of the icy water. Her hands were numb, and he was wet through. Now she must rub his limbs, she must restore circulation, she must bring him around, or he would die of exposure, and her heart would die with him.

She was facing away from the direction of the main chamber, and the noise of rushing water muffled all other sounds, so she was not aware that Jerome Banister, hugging the wall, a candle in one hand, was painfully hobbling ever closer to her and the earl.

## Twenty-Seven

Felicia, having rubbed her own numb fingers, was now chafing the earl's icy-cold hands and rubbing his arms. "Lord Cleary, Lord Cleary, oh, speak to me," she kept repeating over and over. Then she observed blood seeping through his coat. His shoulder was bleeding. Had he been shot? She must stanch the bleeding.

Quickly she set about binding up his shoulder, using his neckcloth and her handkerchief for a pad. She was not missish, but as she worked by the light of the flickering candle with the river rushing in her ears, she was obliged to strive against swooning. The whole experience was too much for her senses.

Abruptly he stirred, and her own woes were forgotten. His eyes were open, and he was staring at her in disbelief, relief, and wonder.

"Felicia, Miss Mannering ... once more ... you are coming ... to my rescue," he whispered through stiff lips.

"Oh, thank God. Oh, Lord Cleary, I was worried to distraction. We must get out of here, or you will be dreadfully ill of an inflammation of the lungs. You are chilled through. How did you come to fall in the river?" she asked, but with sick certainty she knew what his answer would be.

"Banister tried to drown me. He knocked me senseless and threw me into the river, but the water revived me."

Felicia had finished binding up his wound. "It is my fault," she cried with remorse. "It was I who knocked you out—there in that side passage. Oh, I do beg your pardon for hurting you so dreadfully. But I had no notion—I thought—I thought you had run mad and were trying to kill me. How was I to know it was not so?"

"So it was you, not Banister."

"Oh, I do hope I haven't done you great damage."

"No, no. Hardly drew any blood. If I hadn't been in such a poor state to begin with, the blow wouldn't have rendered me senseless at all. But I was *not* trying to kill you. I was trying to save your life. When you were standing there, on that cliff, and I jumped on Banister, he was about to push you over the edge."

Felicia shuddered, horrified. "Oh no. Then you have saved my life. And I have repaid you so horribly. Can you ever forgive me?"

"It is I who need to seek your forgiveness, and humbly beg your pardon for all the insults I have heaped on your head, for thinking *you* wished to kill me. Instead you have been trying to save my life—and you have."

Felicia smiled at him through a sudden mist of tears. "It seems we both were working under a misapprehension."

The earl tried to raise himself on one elbow. In the dim light Felicia couldn't be certain, but she thought his gray eyes were gazing at her in a strange way. "But you no longer think I have lost my reason. And you believe my words. Why?"

"Jerome tried to kill me just now, up there in the main chamber of the cave."

"Thank God you have contrived to escape his clutches."

"Not quite, I'm afraid." The hoarse voice startled them, and the malevolent laughter that followed chilled them. "Not quite."

Jerome Banister, a candle in one hand, a pistol leveled at Felicia in the other, towered over them.

"J-Jerome!" stammered Felicia, her eyes wide with fright. "P-pray, Jerome, don't!"

Jerome aimed his gun at the earl. "Whom shall I have the pleasure of dispatching first? You or his lordship? On the whole, I think you. Cleary is in too sorry a state to put up much of a fight, but you—you are hard to kill, my dear cousin."

Once more his pistol was leveled at Felicia. He was about to fire it. Felicia formed a soundless no, as she stared at him, terrified with fear.

Abruptly Jerome was jerked off his feet, for Lord Cleary, somehow finding the strength to do it, had grabbed him by his legs.

The next moment they were struggling, rolling on the ground. Jerome was trying to put a bullet into the earl, and the earl, twisting Jerome's arm, was endeavoring to avoid being shot.

Jerome's candle, dropped, had gone out, and the scene was illuminated only by Felicia's candle. Felicia got to her feet, wishing to come to Cleary's aid, but in the dim light and with this writhing tangle of arms and legs, it was difficult for her to take action.

Suddenly a shot reverberated off the walls of the cave, and the writhing bodies became very still.

"Lord Cleary! Richard!" Felicia cried, and she stumbled toward the two.

They were both lying motionless, their bodies still intertwined, both deathly pale. She dropped to her knees.

"Lord Cleary," she wept.

"Not stuck . . . my spoon . . . yet," gasped out the earl, his eyelids fluttering open. Then the eyes closed, and his head lolled back.

Felicia grabbed his wrist, feeling for the pulse. Thank God, he had merely fainted. And no wonder. Her makeshift bandage had come off and his shoulder was bleeding again. Trying to pull him away from Jerome, she only now perceived blood welling up from Jerome's side. He had been shot with his own pistol. But he was still alive, for he moaned slightly.

Two men to bind up now, Felicia thought distractedly. But Lord Cleary had the priority. He looked so pale, so very pale.

And grabbing his pulse, she discovered that it was growing weaker. "Oh, Lord Cleary, Richard, my darling. Oh, pray don't die," she cried.

"I collect I know how I am to take this," a cold injured voice suddenly said. And only then she perceived that the scene was now much better illuminated. Darcy, Lord Ransom, and Lester, with lanterns and other men behind them, had arrived.

"Thank God," cried Felicia with great relief, disregarding Darcy's comments. "They are both bleeding. Oh, pray make haste. The earl—I'm afraid—" Her voice broke.

Lord Ransom was bending over Lord Cleary.

"I shall release you from our betrothal. It is the only right thing for me to do," said Darcy stiffly. "Since obviously you have transferred your affections from me to him."

"Oh, Darcy, this is not the time," exclaimed Felicia, crying and laughing hysterically. "Oh, very well. I would be only a hindrance to your political career. But I shall make sure Lord Palmer keeps you on. And I hope you will not be dreadfully hurt by this."

"I shall endeavor to hide my bruised heart," said Darcy, who, truth to tell, felt some relief along with his irritation and wounded self-esteem.

Lord Ransom was directing his grooms to bind up and carry out the injured men, a task made a trifle difficult by the width of the ledge, while Lester placed his arm around Felicia. "No need to be in a taking, now," he said kindly. "Fellow can't harm anybody now."

"Lord Cleary—his pulse is so weak." Felicia's lips trembled.

"Merely the loss of blood. He is a strong man," Lord Ransom reassured her. "Pray don't agitate yourself.

And for God's sake don't fall into a fit of the vapors," he cried in alarm as Felicia gave a loud sniff.

She took a deep breath. "I—I shan't become hysterical," she assured him, though her teeth chattered from cold and the strain of her ordeal.

Lester took a blanket from a groom and placed it around Felicia's shoulders. "Ransom thought you might wind up in one of the caves," he explained.

"But how did you know precisely where to find us?" asked Felicia.

"Signs of struggle, broken branches, tangled grass—and Ransom brought his dogs with him."

Abruptly he gave a horrified exclamation as he caught sight of a large smudge and water stain on his coat.

"Dash it if I didn't dirty my togs again," he complained. "Not your fault," he hastened to reassure Felicia. "Banister's. That's one more thing to chalk up to him."

In a haze, Felicia felt herself guided along the passages, up the slippery tunnel, through the great chamber, and at last, blinking against the sudden glaring daylight, into the open fresh rainswept air. The storm had passed, and a rainbow graced the blue sky.

Would that the storm had passed from her life, thought Felicia. In a way it had. Lord Cleary—her heart still leaped with apprehension, but also with hope—would be restored to health. And he was still in full possession of all his senses. Jerome was no longer a threat to them, and she had freed herself from Darcy. But what would be her fate? And what exactly were the earl's sentiments toward her? Dared she hope that perhaps . . .

She shook her head resolutely. She must not assume anything. That way lay only disappointment.

℘

# Twenty-Eight

Felicia, her apple-green walking dress freshly washed and ironed, was sitting on a damask sofa in the Blue Drawing Room of Ransom Hall close to a crackling fire to warm her limbs, and beside her sat Lester. Opposite her in a blue velvet chair reclined Lord Cleary, still very pale and with his arm in a sling, but quite elegant in an olive-green coat and bisque pantaloons; and in the chair next to him sat that distinguished silver-haired diplomat Lord Palmer. Darcy had already left for London—with the blond Cyprian.

Lord Palmer had just come from the bedside of Jerome, who, thinking he was dying, had confessed all to him. Felicia had had a talk with Lester, and he had revealed to her Jerome's part in the unfortunate duel.

"He wished to marry you in the worst possible way and tried his best to part you from Vellacort," Lord Palmer was saying to Felicia. "But Cleary here he deemed a more powerful rival"—Felicia colored and carefully avoided the earl's eyes—"and he decided that killing you would be much easier and quicker than attempting to gain your hand in marriage. Yes, he owned up to tampering with my son's carriage, which is a thing I shall find very hard to forgive—if he lives. Oh yes, he admitted giving laudanum to Vellacort, so as to have a head start in his search for Felicia. Vellacort would have hampered him in his attempt to kill Felicia."

"He ought to be shot," said Lord Cleary through shut teeth.

"Fellow ought to be clapped in Bedlam. Plain as pikestaff—mad," said Lester.

"Oh, perhaps not truly mad," countered Lord Palmer. "Just a very clever villain."

"Aye, clever and a villain too," agreed Lester. "It was he who frightened Sam Stoddart into hiding, for he didn't wish Sam to tell anyone the truth about that whole dashed affair. He must have suspected that Sam knew he had provoked the duel. Stands to reason he didn't wish Felicia and the rest of the world to hear of *that*."

"But Jerome must have known that Sam's father had given us a wrong direction," said Felicia. "We were going to Gretna, not Doncaster."

"Good chance we could have halted at Ben Stoddart's inn on our way to Gretna. He didn't want that. What has me in a puzzle is, why would Banister wish to kill Felicia? Didn't think he was the kind of chap who would go for this 'if I can't have you nobody shall' stuff. Besides, his affections are for Zemelda. Wishing to kill Felicia don't make sense."

"On the contrary, it makes very much sense," said Lord Palmer grimly. "What you all don't realize—though I fancy Cleary here has seen a glimmer of the truth—is that Banister had a much more potent motive and reason, both to wed and to kill Felicia, than unrequited love. Money."

"Money!" cried Lester and Felicia in unison, astounded.

"Yes, money. He was chronically short of funds."

"And that prime article Zemelda is shockingly expensive," supplied Lester. "Can understand him to be in need of the ready, but—"

"But I am penniless," Felicia finished for him.

Lord Cleary cocked an eyebrow at her. "But you, Miss Mannering, have expectations."

"Expectations? What in the world are you two talking about?" She blinked from the earl to Lord Palmer.

"You seem to forget that old relation of yours in Jamaica," said the earl. "Am I correct, sir?"

Lord Palmer nodded. "I did not wish to tell you of it, child, for fear of raising your hopes to no purpose, but I have made inquiries, and I wrote to Sir Wolsey. As a result I discovered that he is going to will his entire fortune to you."

Felicia gasped, and Lester's jaw sagged.

"Oh yes," continued Lord Palmer. "He is rich, and you will be an heiress."

"My felicitations," said the earl, inclining his head.

"Very happy for you," muttered Lester, overwhelmed with this intelligence.

"And I am delighted," said Lord Palmer. "To resume, you, Banister, and Sir Edward are his only living relations. Sir Edward is old and not well, so he doesn't count. And you are more closely related to him than Banister. And although Sir Wolsey wouldn't answer your aunt's letter, he had decided to make you his heir—if your conduct was impeccable."

Lester smote his knee and cried, "Vauxhall Gardens! Banister wished scandal for Felicia! Beg pardon, sir. Pray go on."

"Apparently Banister obtained Sir Wolsey's address—"

"Stole it, most likely," said the earl sardonically.

"—and he wrote to him," carried on Lord Palmer. "I don't know what he wrote, but I could hazard a guess. At first he intended to marry you, then to make sure you wouldn't become Sir Wolsey's heir, leaving himself as the only suitable relation. And the most permanent way of ensuring that would have been to kill you."

Felicia stared at Lord Palmer, her eyes round with wonder. She was not penniless anymore; she wouldn't need to worry about a roof over her head or be obliged to tolerate Lady Palmer's whims. And Jerome knew of it and had never let on.

She shook her head. "This is too much, coming on

top of everything else. My head is whirling. What will happen to Jerome if he survives?"

"I don't wish a scandal for you," said Lord Palmer. "I don't wish your relation to end on the gallows, however much he might deserve it. But he cannot remain in England."

"I know," cried Felicia. "Send him to Jamaica. I don't think he would try any tricks now—not when you can expose him to Sir Wolsey. With that over his head he would mind his conduct."

"No, that is the outside of enough," cried Lester. "Causing all this trouble for Felicia, not to mention the suits I have ruined, tramping all over with her, all on account of his misdeeds—and he should go free!"

"It goes against the grain with me too," agreed Lord Cleary, "but I don't wish a scandal for Fe—for Miss Mannering either."

"Well, we shan't need to worry about it for a while," said Lord Palmer, rising. "If he lives, he will be ill for quite some time. Come, Lester, I have something to say to you—something that you might like to hear. I have decided that you are to have full control of your money after all."

Lester's eyes lit up with pleasure and gratification, but he quizzed his father. "Afraid *I* might start dangling after an heiress?" His jaw dropped. "Good God. Surely you didn't think I was eloping with Felicia because of her inheritance?"

Lord Palmer nodded. "The thought did cross my mind fleetingly before I discarded it. At any rate, you won't need to take recourse to such drastic actions."

Lester beamed at Felicia. "Goodnight, Felicia, Cleary. All's well that ends well, what?"

He was following Lord Palmer when abruptly he stopped. "Felicia and Cleary alone—not the thing," he muttered.

Lord Palmer pulled him by the arm. "We can trust Felicia and Cleary to behave with propriety. I need to talk to you now. I am obliged to return to London immediately. And Lady Palmer is too indisposed to act as chaperon."

He bid them goodnight and fairly dragged Lester out of the chamber.

Silence fell upon their departure.

"Well, Miss Mannering," asked the earl, "do you agree all's well that ends well?" His gray eyes were burning with a singular light. Felicia's heart began to pound, and her breathing quickened.

"That depends, my lord, on the all," she said, peeping at him from under her lashes. "A fortune, though very welcome in my circumstances, is not all by any means."

"I agree entirely." He rose from his seat and negotiated the distance between them in a few shaky strides.

"Oh, you shouldn't be walking," cried Felicia in alarm. "You are still dreadfully pale. Pray—pray sit down here." And she patted the place on the sofa beside her.

He lowered himself onto it heavily and immediately possessed himself of her hands, wincing a trifle as the movement caused pain to his shoulder, while a pleasurable tingle coursed through Felicia's body at his touch.

"Miss Mannering, my recollection is a trifle hazy. I don't know precisely what I said to you in that cave, but I humbly beg your pardon for my crass stupidity. How could I have fancied you could be anything but honest, forthright, and kind? I should have known better than to suspect you of base conduct. In my heart I knew better, but I would not listen to my heart." He drew near, his face quite close to hers. "Pray accept my most profound thanks for saving my life, and pray forgive me. Say that you do." The speaking look on his countenance—a mixture of remorse, tenderness, and desire—set Felicia's pulses racing. She grew quite breathless.

"If you forgive *me*, for suspecting you of trying to kill me. But I thought you wished to strike at Darcy through me—to take your revenge on him by depriving him of me."

He released her hands, and his countenance grew

stern. "And you were not far wrong in your assumptions," he said in a self-accusing tone. "I did wish to take revenge on Vellacort, but I am no good at plotting schemes. And then I hit upon the notion of striking at him through you."

"Then I *was* right," cried Felicia, aghast and growing pale.

"Not in the way you had fancied," he was quick to point out to her. "I intended to take you away from him by making you fall in love with me, and then to punish you by rejecting you. God help me, I would have been punishing myself much worse. And it wasn't really the notion of revenge that prompted me to form *this* plan. It was the desire to have you fall in love with me."

Felicia's heart leaped with joy at these words. Her lips parted in expectation. And the earl was gazing at her with love shining in his hard gray eyes, and his own lips parted in hunger for her kiss.

"I love you, Felicia. I have been in love with you since you held me up on Hampstead Heath. Can you guess at my tortures—knowing you belonged to my enemy? Can you fancy the rage and jealousy that possessed me? All feelings which I tried to deny. And couldn't."

"Miss Mannering, Felicia," he said in a hoarse voice. "Your trying to save me gives me hope that you are not quite indifferent to me. Indeed, I fancy quite to the contrary. Up there in that balloon I even fancied that you kissed me."

"I did," said Felicia.

"You did? Then I didn't dream the whole. Miss Mannering, Felicia—would you give me great pleasure by repeating the performance?" His arms went about her shoulder, and this time he did not even feel the pain of his injury. Felicia warded him off.

"And what of Hermione Silverdale, my lord?" she asked.

He smiled at her tenderly. "If that isn't like a woman. Forget her. She was just a passing diversion."

"And I?" asked Felicia, catching her breath, her eyes shining with happiness in anticipation of his answer.

"You are my lasting passion. The most adorable female in the world, one whom it would make me deliriously happy to cherish all my life. Miss Mannering, Felicia, would you do me the great honor of bestowing upon me your hand in marriage? Both my rivals having been removed, I can ask you this now with a clear conscience. And I, being possessed of a reasonable fortune myself, cannot be thought to have designs on yours," he added, his eyes twinkling.

"Even if you were penniless, I know you would not do so," she parried. "You are quite a cut above Jerome."

"I should hope I am. Felicia, will you marry me?"

"Yes, oh yes," breathed an enraptured Felicia.

"Then what are we waiting for?" cried the earl, and he swept her into his arms. "I've wished to do this for a long time."

Upon which his lips fastened onto hers in a hungry passionate kiss.

Felicia's arms went about his neck, as, forgetting her modesty and decorum, she responded to his passion in a manner which would have made Tessy or even Zemelda proud.

*About the Author*

MIRANDA CAMERON was born in Europe. As a child, she and her parents moved to Canada, where she eventually graduated from the University of Toronto. A pharmacist, Ms. Cameron wrote as a hobby for many years before deciding to give up her career and become a professional writer. In her leisure, she enjoys painting, sculpting, reading, gardening, and traveling.

*Also new from Signet*

# MAGIC TO DO: PAUL'S STORY

*by Melinda McKenzie*

What disturbed Paul Sand most at Berkeley's Psychic Fair wasn't the phony fortune-tellers. It was his chance encounter with an elegant blue-eyed woman. When they met, Paul felt the instant magnetism that magically draws two people together across space and time. No other women had ever affected him so deeply before. The beautiful stranger, Dr. Kirsten Andersson, was, like Paul, a talented scientist. But Paul's controversial psychic ability had long ago forced him to abandon his scientific career. Now it could cost him Kirsten too. For her job was to expose all ESP as a hoax—and Paul as a fraud! Instead of his soulmate, Kirsten could become Paul's worst enemy . . . unless his love could change her doubting heart . . .

☐ 0451-13858-9 $2.50, U.S./$2.95, Canada

---

**Buy them at your local**

**bookstore or use coupon**

**on next page for ordering.**

## More Regency Romances from SIGNET

(0451)

- ☐ **AN INTIMATE DECEPTION** by Catherine Coulter. (122364—$2.25)*
- ☐ **LORD HARRY'S FOLLY** by Catherine Coulter. (115341—$2.25)
- ☐ **LORD DEVERILL'S HEIR** by Catherine Coulter. (113985—$2.25)
- ☐ **THE REBEL BRIDE** by Catherine Coulter. (138376—$2.50)*
- ☐ **THE AUTUMN COUNTESS** by Catherine Coulter. (114450—$2.25)
- ☐ **THE GENEROUS EARL** by Catherine Coulter. (114817—$2.25)
- ☐ **AN HONORABLE OFFER** by Catherine Coulter. (112091—$2.25)*
- ☐ **THE ENCHANTING STRANGER** by Barbara Hazard. (131959—$2.50)*
- ☐ **THE SINGULAR MISS CARRINGTON** by Barbara Hazard. (131061—$2.50)*
- ☐ **THE CALICO COUNTESS** by Barbara Hazard. (129164—$2.25)*
- ☐ **A SURFEIT OF SUITORS** by Barbara Hazard. (121317—$2.25)*
- ☐ **THE DISOBEDIENT DAUGHTER** by Barbara Hazard. (115570—$2.25)*
- ☐ **THE EMERALD DUCHESS** by Barbara Hazard. (133307—$2.50)*
- ☐ **THE MAD MASQUARADE** by Barbara Hazard. (135202—$2.50)*

\*Prices slightly higher in Canada